Earth's Blood

Hillary and Tinsel Spelunker

J. Todd McMillan

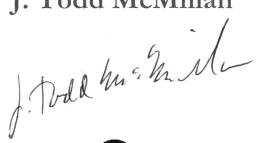

Copyright © 2022 by J. Todd McMillan

All rights reserved. No part of this publication may be reproduced, stored electronically or transmitted in any way by any means without prior permission of the publisher, except as provided by copyright law.

Published in the United States, by JTM Publishing

JTM and its cloud colophon are trademarks of JTM publishing house

Book cover design by J Todd McMillan, author, and Ayan Mansoori, illustrator

First edition, October 2022.

ISBN: 979-8-9871661-0-9

Look for other upcoming releases from J. Todd McMillan:

"The Ackwards Banimals" series

To my precious wife Naomi and my Lord

Acknowledgments

Kathy Herman, best-selling author of twenty-two inspirational suspense novels, whose advice and encouragement propelled me along.

Ursula Burback, whose countless hours of reading and editing vastly improved this work.

Rosi Bratz, who headed me in the right direction with her excellent critical feedback.

The third through fifth grade teachers and students at Woodburn Elementary, whose 'beta listening' and response to my readings provided the engine for greatly improving and revising. Special thanks to Arun Cameron and her 3rd grade class and Brittany Stephens and her 3rd grade class.

CHAPTER ONE - Skinned Shins

Hillary enters the room with smiles and confidence. She fills the room with light. To look on her face is to smile. She moves easily. Every step is placed exactly where she wants it. She finds her favorite spot on the couch and curls up with her favorite adventure book.

Tinsel has a different approach. She squats down and puts one leg through the doorway. Her palms on the ground before her, she is like a cat. You won't see her sneak in behind the couch. Sometimes you catch her green eyes slowly rise above it and peek at you. If you do see her at all, it's because she wants you to. She grins and squints and her eyes dart curiously around the room. Then she throws herself into the room, toppling over the couch, feet in Hillary's face, onto the cushions, rolling in laughter.

When Tinsel and Hillary were born, twin stars disappeared from a far unknown galaxy. Some believe all that energy was transformed to create them. Others say that one star must die so that another could live. They are twins just like the stars. One is only just so older and the other is only just so younger. But unlike the billions of years of stars, these young stars have burned for only 10 years.

Hillary and Tinsel. Tinsel and Hillary. One is a little smaller and one is a little bigger.

Bigger is better when you want a boom. Smaller is better when you need extra room.

2

Their home is a wonderful two-story house. The wonderful part is that Hillary and Tinsel's room is the only room on the top floor. It *is* the top floor. It is a fort. It is a tower. It is 'The Citadel'. It is bright and spacious with all four sides having windows, and a vaulted stairwell leading down to the main part of the house. From their loft in the sky, Tinsel and Hillary can see miles and miles. There is no hiding place they can't spy from their eye in the sky. Atop the rocky hill where their home is perched, the towering doug firs, the gnarled black spruce and exposed igneous rock covered with moss and lichen offered a kingdom of over and underground adventure.

Tinsel and Hillary love waking every morning to brilliant yellows and reds beaming into their world from all sides. They love weekends the most when they awake to one or the other playing some prank or surprise.

"Hillaaarrryyy!!!...," was the only thing poor Tinsel could get out of her mouth in time. Well, maybe not *poor* Tinsel. Maybe *careless* Tinsel? Maybe a *little on purpose* Tinsel?

On the way down, jumping and falling from her top bunkbed, Tinsel could only see a blur of blankets and pillows and stuffed animals as she hurled towards Hillary. If only Hillary had not looked up. If only Tinsel had not cried out her name. If only... if only Tinsel's knee had not landed squarely on Hillary's right eye.

That must be why they call it a shiner. The bruise pulls the skin tight like a shiny balloon. Starting out the new school year with a fat shiner of an eye was not Hillary's favorite idea of meeting her new best friends.

3

Because that's what they always were to her before she met them, best friends. Anyone Hillary didn't know was just one hello from being her best friend. Everyone was Hillary's best friend for different reasons and Hillary loved all people. Mama and Papa loved all people.

"Mama! Mama!" Tinsel cried loudly as she ran down the stairs, two and three treads at a time, from the twin loft bedroom. "Hillary is hurt and I don't know what happened!" As soon as the untrue words came out of her mouth Tinsel regretted them because they made her heart hurt. It felt like a black mark she had to carry with her and she couldn't make it go away. The worst part was that it was hidden so no one else could see it and she felt alone.

Tears and apologies are a hard way to start a Monday morning when you have to get up for your first day of school. It's hard on sisters and on Mama and on Papa. They hadn't really left time for something like this. So now it was all hurry. By the time Hillary's tears stopped, breakfast should have been done already. Half of the scrambled eggs were left cold and the Spelunkers never even got to the bacon, which now sat in the frying pan, the grease turning cold and white.

Tinsel was sad and sorrowful. She miserably thought to herself, *How many times have Mama and Papa asked me to be more careful with my swinging and climbing and jumping when others are around?* But soon she began to think that maybe it was possibly or even *probably* Hillary's fault. *If Hillary hadn't looked up, my knee would have harmlessly landed on the pillow beside her head. If only...*

Papa liked to ask a lot of questions. Sometimes his questions were fun. Sometimes they were smart and made you think hard. Sometimes they put a lump in your throat and made your heart hurt, not because they were wrong, but because they were right. Tinsel sat on the couch next to Papa.

"Tinsel... what are the three things Spelunkers do when we have hurt someone?" asked Papa gently.

"But Papa, I didn't hurt anyone. It wasn't my fault. I was just playing. I don't know what happened. Hillary shouldn't have been there. It was her fault," whispered Tinsel as she kept her eyes down at her shoes.

"Tinsel... what are the three things we do when we have hurt someone?" repeated Papa calmly.

Tinsel was quiet for a long time before she wanted to speak. Then slowly, "We say we're sorry," and now she felt her eyes starting to swell and water. "We make it better if we can," and now warm wet tears began to roll down her cheeks. "And we say we'll do our best not to do that again."

By now, poor little regretful Tinsel's body was shaking as she couldn't hold back the sobs and tears. Papa hugged her.

Papa's hugs wrapped you in a thick, warm blanket. You could cry and cry until you were all cried out, and there was no hurry. There were no words spoken. After the crying stopped, you didn't want to move and you sunk into Papa. And now that you weren't shaking you could feel and hear Papa's deep breathing and you breathed deeply too. With your eyes closed, you were just heavy in his arms and time stopped and the hurt drained from your heart. Then you felt your strength coming back. You could face things again. Tinsel snuggled there for a long time.

"So, what do you do now Tinsel?" asked Papa.

"I just can't Papa. I don't want to. I can't yet," protested Tinsel.

"There is time," said Papa. "We're not in a hurry. Think about it and let's see about it when you get home from school today."

At that moment, Tinsel wished she had just apologized then and there. Now she would think about it all day long. And she might worry about it. There was a cloud forming over this afternoon's adventure. Even still, a part of her felt a stirring hope...

For all the excitement promised later on that day, the excitement now was seeing the big yellow bus approaching. It seemed like it would never get here. Hillary and Tinsel could see it far off, stopping now and again to pick up new friends and schoolmates. The long winding road separating the houses in the country, rocky, hilly, forested neighborhood could be seen for miles as Hillary and Tinsel looked down through the valley. The bus seemed the size of an ant and crawling the speed of a snail when seen from so far away. *But doesn't it always go that way when you can't wait for a favorite thing?*

"I wonder if there will even be any room for us on the bus?" asked Hillary.

"Every day and every year you say the same thing," replied Tinsel. "You're probably just hoping the bus will be really full so you can sit right next to a new or already friend."

Hillary was never the type to be alone if there was any chance of being shoulder to shoulder. *How else could you bump elbows and laugh and share secrets?*

Hillary plopped down into the green vinyl overstuffed bench seat near the front of the bus. The first seat she found open. It was the right seat because her best of best friends Elka was there, so excited to see her for the first time in a week. Elka's smile really gave Hillary no other seat choice and she made it gladly.

Tinsel stood front and center of the bus taking in the many seating possibilities, then almost did a cartwheel down the center aisle. But only almost. Just as she had the wild excited idea and began to move her body to throw her hands at the ground, she remembered her knee crashing into Hillary's eye. Abruptly stopping herself from cartwheeling, she tripped and fell, banging her shin hard on the metal leg holding up the bus seat, and her leg began to bleed. Some kids laughed loudly at her. Hillary frowned and winced as she saw Tinsel grab her leg in pain.

Tinsel hopped to the nearest open seat, grasping her bleeding shin hard in her hand. In the seat in front of her, she saw two sets of eyes and noses peeking from behind the bus seat, staring hard back at her. It was the annoying brother and sister twins, Cassie and Kori, the only other twins at Mountain Star Elementary School.

Their rude stares infuriated her and she snapped at them, "How about I poke those eyes out for you?!" As she jabbed her two fingers towards each of their eyes.

Cassie and Kori stuck their tongues out at her, then snapped back forward in their seats and slunk down so Tinsel couldn't see them.

Tinsel, thought Hillary loudly at her, *Don't be rude!*

Leave me alone Hillary! I am too mad right now, thought Tinsel right back at her.

How many times have Mama and Papa asked me about being more careful? thought Tinsel, as she felt a lump grow in her throat. She heard a small, but loud, thought say to her, *You'll never learn. You'll always do stupid things like this.* With the bleeding pain in her shin, the hurtful laughing, the staring eyes, and the shaming thought in her head, Tinsel was crying for the second time and it wasn't even lunch. She didn't want to cry, but couldn't seem to stop the tears and she began to burn with shame. The tears came without asking her and made the other kids stare all the more. Eyes and seatback gripped fingers peered back at her. If the bus had not been a mile from her house, she would have broken the bus door off its hinges and ran for home. But just then another bigger, but quieter, thought said to her, *That's not true. You did just stop yourself. You can learn to be more careful. It will just take time.* It didn't stop all the hurt, but it began to dry the tears. It began working a wonder in Tinsel's brain. She began to think maybe she wasn't quite so bad. Then she knew she wasn't bad. No one else was being hard on her. Why should she be so hard on herself...

The bus lurching forward, jostling Hillary against the back of her seat, Elka leaned low towards her and looked Hillary in the eyes, "You've been crying."

Elka and Hillary were a perfect match because Elka easily asked the right questions and Hillary wasn't a girl that would be embarrassed or hide her feelings. *Is there anything better than someone who really knows you?*

"Yes, I have been crying. I knew you would notice. You always notice," smiled Hillary.

"Well, you don't seem very upset about whatever it was now?" smiled Elka with questions in her eyes.

"Oh, just a bump in the eye without an apology. But my eye doesn't hurt any more than it should, and my feelings are more worried about Tinsel," replied Hillary. "I'm not really worried much because with Tinsel it's only a matter of time until she does the right thing. I just hope we can make it better before school is out today so our afternoon isn't ruined."

"Depending on what color that bumped eye turns, you could have a nice matching color coordination," hinted Elka.

"What do you mean?"

"If your bruise turns black, it will nicely match your long, beautiful, straight hair. And if it turns blue it will match your sky colored eyes," said Elka trying to lighten the mood.

"You're hilarious Elk. Leave it to you to brighten my day."

"We need to get to Mrs. Caroline's classroom right away so we can get seats next to each other," said Elka excitedly.

"Oh I hope she lets us pick our own seats," said Hillary with bright eyes. "If she separates us, this will be the first time in three years that we haven't been room buddies."

"Remember when we met in first grade and had assigned seats next to each other with Mr. Adder?" asked Elka.

"And in second grade, Mrs. Simpson was so nice to let us move next to each other," reflected Hillary.

"Somehow I just think we have always been meant to be together," smiled Elka.

Tinsel was quite calm now as the brakes of the bus gave a grinding squeal and a final lurching stop. It became a swirling and bouncing sea of books and bags, jackets and jeans, and messy morning hair as all the kids tried to get off the bus at one time.

"Idiots!" winced Tinsel, yelling at the crowd, her injury starting to bleed again. "Who just kicked my shin?"

She was tough, but she never did like to bleed. It scared her like she was losing something. She wanted to go to the nurse's office to patch up her shin and her feelings. *They don't make bandages big enough to cover the pain in my brain!*

As Tinsel stepped off the bus, she found Hillary faithfully waiting with a sister's arm for comfort.

"Let's get you to the nurse's office and have that owie looked at," winked Hillary.

"Owie! What do you think I'm three years old?!" cried Tinsel. "It's not an owie. It's a boo boo!"

They hugged and laughed so hard neither of them could breathe as they headed into their day.

Hand in hand, step in step, a sister's blood thicker than water to protect.

After dropping Tinsel off at the nurses office, Hillary and Elka ran to their new classroom and found the perfect new seats just near the front and center of Mrs. Caroline's class. It was always in Hillary to be front and center.

Ava had seen Hillary on the bus. She had seen her get off the bus and wait. She had seen how Hillary protected and cared for Tinsel. As she walked into Mrs. Caroline's class for the first time, she stopped just inside the door and slowly looked around at the quickly filling seats. There was only one seat left open next to Hillary so she ran to get to it, knocking into several desks on the way causing kids to stare. Plopping into the prized seat and dropping her backpack under her chair, she glanced over to see if Hillary had noticed her. Hillary was already smiling at her.

"I saw you at the bus. What happened to your eye?" said Ava shyly.

"I'm Hillary and I want you to come to my party this Saturday night for a sleepover."

Ava's shyness melted into a big smile. Hillary had just found her first best friend of the day in Mrs. Caroline's class.

"Who was that you helped off the bus?" asked Ava.

"Oh, that's my troublemaking twin sis Tinsel," joked Hillary.

"Twin? I'm sorry…um… but you don't look much alike. Even if you aren't identical twins, isn't there usually a little bit of family resemblance?"

"Well, we do like to tease her that she was dropped off by a lost stork…"

Ava smiled at Hillary's teasing and said, "I wish I had a sister that cared about me that much. It makes me want to laugh and cry at the same time."

****

Always the last two off the school bus, far out in the hilly country, Tinsel and Hillary jumped from the stairwell of the bus onto the gravel road, landing at the bottom of the winding road up to their Lookout House. This was the last part of their school day and was always a good time to laugh and chat and share about their day. But this day, Tinsel didn't want to talk about school.

"Hillary… I'm sorry."

"What are you sorry about?"

"You know…"

"Yes, I know," smiled Hillary. "I forgive you."

Tinsel grabbed Hillary's hand and spun her face to face and grabbed her other hand. She gently kissed Hillary's swollen eye and said, "I don't want to do that again."

Hillary smiled such a forgiving smile.

"How is your shin doing Tins?" asked Hillary.

"Oh, I'm tired of this bandage and it must be fine after all these hours of itching," said Tinsel, ripping off the stuck-on bandage. It was so stuck that it ripped off the scab that was newly forming, causing the wound to bleed again. A drop of blood began to fall. Before it fell an inch, a small blue spark jumped from the ground to the drop. Within another inch a steady stream of blue white electric spark flowed. One more inch and a blue lightning electric storm was firing and making the drop of blood glow bright golden orange-red light. It looked like magma.

The glowing drop of blood wet the graveled dirt road. The wetted gravel began to glow. Then heat. Then hot. Then melt. A yellowish white-hot molten blob the size of a marble slowly began to melt the ground below it and sink down and down as Tinsel and Hillary watched. The twins felt dizzy and strange and wonderful. Hillary and Tinsel felt a small humming flood through their bodies. Something small and powerful went to and from and in and out of them. They felt a thousand years of wonder and forgiveness and Mama and Papa. Their vision became sharp, as vivid colors hardened and colored everything around them.

"It is finding the way home," said Hillary. "It will go all the way down."

"Yes, I know," replied Tinsel. "I have never seen it happen so strongly."

"It must be getting near our time," said Hillary. "What can we do? We can't do it alone. And it's our time to do something without Mama and Papa."

"But who will go with us to make us strong enough?"

"It's time to see which of our friends might have the Regeneration in them."

"Maybe we'll find out at the party," replied Tinsel.

In the distance, near the Willowlands, almost unnoticed by Tinsel and Hillary, a murder of large black Krows slowly circled and took turns diving at something helpless on the ground.

As they began the walk up the hill to their Lookout Home, the gravel crunched under their feet and they could feel the swirling molten core and the pull of gravity and the depth of the earth.

CHAPTER TWO - Beagles

Hillary and Tinsel would be home any time now. They had to be. The sun was already behind the house and was casting afternoon shadows into the front yard where his human heroes would be home soon. The day had been so long without them. Every day without them was filled with waiting and hope and wanting. Wanting to be outside with them. Wanting to run and jump and bark and chase. Papa gave up on trying to keep the door windows and behind the couch windows clean from a thousand adorable nose prints. The doggy nose prints were reminders that make you smile at how much love can patiently want and glow while you wait for your favorite thing coming.

Sparks was whining his good whine again. He loves the sun and the rain and the snow. Every season and different weather have flavors for him. He loves mud as much as he loves warm grass. His snow socked feet dancing off the floor as he marches in place waiting for the door to open. His whine reminds you of the good that is just outside the double door windowpane. His excited whimpers warm your insides as you wait with him.

Beagles are the best. At least that's what Tinsel and Hillary knew. Is any other dog as smart? Well, maybe so, but not beagle smart. Sparks' perfectly medium sized three year old colorful body is wrapped in milk chocolate and orange caramel and black coffee and snowy white. Some dogs are too heavy. You can't carry them or put them in a backpack if you need to. Some dogs are too light and you think they might just crumple or break into pieces. Sparks can fit into perfectly sized Sparks spaces. Tunnels and caverns and nooks and boulders. His four-paw power pushes him anywhere he decides to go. He would be able to climb a tree if only he could get the traction.

Sparks announced to the whole house that he could see Tinsel and Hillary's heads bouncing over the horizon of the hill sloping down and away from the house. His beagle bark was sharp and penetrating and rang like a bell hit by a bullet. The Spelunkers love his excitement, but sometimes it is almost too much. He just never can contain himself when his girls arrive home every day. Sometimes there are broken lamps and knocked over water glasses as the victims of his running and barking and bouncing! Once in a while he even backflips off the couch.

At least this time Sparks was not doing what Papa called *Sparks Barks*. When he spotted and fixated on something that demanded his attention, neither an elephant nor a germ could sneak onto the Spelunker property because of *Sparks Barks*. The site of a trespassing squirrel would set off the Sparks Barks machine gun, "bark bark bark bark bark bark bark bark bark bark bark bark bark," rapid fire gunning down every deer, wolf, bird, squirrel, possum, raccoon, groundhog or hedgehog within a mile. And neither treats nor shouts could distract or shut down the Sparks Barks until he was satisfied he had done his job properly.

When Mama finally opened the front door, it was like dropping the gate at the Kentucky Derby. At first Sparks didn't go anywhere as his paws spun on the polished wood floors. Slowly he moved forward until his feet hit the rough wood of the front porch. And if he had been a car, you would have wanted double seat belts on! Off the porch like lightning and skipping all four stairs he did a somersault, landing flat on his back as he tripped over his own body which was moving far too fast for his feet. But dogs don't mind that kind of thing and it never embarrasses them. In fact, he didn't even realize it happened.

"Brace for impact!" shouted Hillary.

"Here we go again!" laughed Tinsel.

There really is no stopping Sparks' excitement or energy. And every day it is the same, as if he is seeing them for the first time after a long trip. He never tires of greeting and admiring his heroes with the same jumping, spinning, licking, barking, dancing and wagging. He is a blur of fur and all his beautiful doggy colors.

Sparks led Hillary and Tinsel to make sure they safely made the last leg of their journey home, looking over his shoulders left and right all the way up the stairs and into the home.

Coming through the front door, Tinsel and Hillary dropped their unusual backpacks into their usual places.

"Welcome home my wonderful little muffins!" smiled Papa.

"Papa, you're so silly," said Tinsel, "but that's why we love you."

"Can we play in the Citadel before we go outside and then do homework later Papa?" asked Hillary.

"Do you have any planning to do before your sleepover this weekend?" asked Papa.

"We sure do," replied Tinsel. "That's why we want to take time upstairs now before we go spelunking today."

"I'll make you a deal," said Papa. "Do half your homework now and you can do the other half later so you have time outside before it gets dark."

His twins eagerly agreed. Papa's heart was full of pride because he knew he wouldn't have to ask Hillary and Tinsel to do their homework later. Tinsel and Hillary loved to learn.

Normally when Hillary and Tinsel went upstairs in such a good mood and full of ideas, you could hear them all over the house. Four feet running and pounding up the long stairs to the Citadel loft bedroom, double stairs at a time. And of course, the click clacking of Sparks' nails and paws could be heard right behind them and trying to beat them in a race to the top.

But this time, Tinsel's shoes and socks were off in a flash and she flew up the stairs and was gone before Hillary even got started.

Hillary suspected foul play. She crept as cautiously as an alarmed squirrel up the stairs.

As her view crested the top stair she found herself staring right into Tinsel's frozen wide open electric emerald green eyes. It was almost creepy.

"Why are you upside down Hillary?" asked Tinsel.

"Maybe because the house flipped over?" replied Hillary.

"If that's true, why aren't I falling to the ceiling?"

"Probably because your frizzy curls of red hair are holding you to the carpet like velcro."

"Oh, is my head on the carpet?"

"Either that or my feet are on the ceiling, which I don't think is very likely unless we have had a gravity failure," joked Hillary. "How long can you stand on your head like that before all the blood runs to your head and you faint?"

"Oh, I learned in gymnastics that I can do this for hours."

Hillary tried to squeeze by Tinsel who was now purposefully waving her tall stick legs around, trying hard to stick her feet in Hillary's face. One foot almost clubbed her in the face, so when the second foot came around Hillary was ready. She grabbed the skinny ankle and bit Tinsel just a little bit hard on her left big toe.

Violently jerking her foot away, she almost pulled Hillary's front teeth out along with her big toe.

Tinsel hollered, "Yowch! What did you do that for?!"

"Tinsel! Yuck! When's the last time you took a bath or changed your socks? Your big toe tastes like dog poop!"

Tinsel found this very funny and said, "How do you know what dog poop tastes like?" She began to laugh so hard she couldn't keep her balance and almost fell down the stairs.

"That's not what I meant. I meant your big toe tastes the way dog poop smells."

"But that's not what you said Hilly-Billy."

"Hillary eats dog poop. Hillary eats dog poop," was all Hillary heard Tinsel singing for the next hour as she tried to do her reading homework.

"Elka is coming to our sleep over for sure this weekend," said Hillary. "I asked her today at school. What about Luisa? Did you ask her?"

"Darn, Darn! I can never remember these things. Why didn't you remind me?!"

"Tinsel…"

"I'm sorry Hillary. I know it's not your fault. I just get so frustrated always forgetting things. Taking the time to do my homework, then leaving it at home. Leaving my jacket on the bus. Not meeting Luisa on the playground like I told her I would. Luisa must think I don't care about her."

"You know that's not true Tins. It would take a lot more than that for a good friend like Luisa to think bad about a wonderful friend like you. Keep trying, you'll do better in time."

"Thanks. I'll keep trying, but I don't feel like I can do any better sometimes."

"I met a new friend today at school. Her name is Ava. I would just love for her to come, but I don't know where she lives." said Hillary. "That's ok though. We have a few days and I'll invite her tomorrow at school."

"Time for Lookout!" shouted Tinsel. "You check the North and the South! I'll check the East and the West!"

"Gotcha Tins!" as Hillary bounded towards the North Lookout.

At the same time Tinsel leapt to the West where both of them tried to cross paths and just about knocked each other down in the excitement to get to their sentinel places. It wasn't the first time the girls had bumped heads! They grabbed each other in a hug to keep from falling, laughed at each other, grabbed hands and ran to the North and West Lookout corner.

They could always see better when they held hands.

Sometimes the best way to see is to not look too hard. Hillary and Tinsel stopped in the North and West corner of their lookout room. The wall-to-wall windows let them see wonderfully from anywhere in the room in all directions. North was always the girls favorite because that was where The Raven River poured from. Sometimes the Raven flowed above ground. Sometimes below. Sometimes rising and dropping through deep holes and passages no one knows of back into the deep.

But that is what normal eyes see.

21

Tinsel and Hillary held hands, closed their eyes, and took a deep breath. They breathed deeply until their hearts began to beat together and they could feel each other's hearts in their hands. When they knew the moment was right, each of them slowly opened their eyes, looking straight ahead and very still. So still that Sparks would notice and hold just as still, copying their frozen stance.

When Hillary and Tinsel held their gaze very still, focusing on one small branch or blade of grass, every tiny movement was big.

Hillary saw a snail with a grain of sand on its back gliding along a smooth, wet, mossy rock.

Tinsel saw a pine needle break and fall. It took what felt like forever to fall half way, then it slowed and stopped in mid-air as time seemed to stand still. Tinsel stared intensely at its long green rough textured form. Every curve and rough spot. Its sharp tip and its sappy root. It slowly started moving again until it finally came to rest after bouncing on the soft forest floor into a pile of needles.

Hillary saw the wind. It was bright today with breezes of sky blues and gusts of daisy whites. It was a cleaning wind. Today it was brushing and spreading the pollen from branches and needles.

Tinsel and Hillary held their gaze until their eyes and thoughts were full and had seen all they could see in the North and the West. Then they broke hands and their vision became dim like it had been before. But there was still the South and the East.

Bolting to the other corner of their loft fort, jumping over the small couch in the middle of the room and almost tipping it over, they stopped sharply, Hillary facing the South and Tinsel the East. Clasping hands and waiting, the scene changed for them.

Hillary saw sun rays shooting and reflecting everywhere. Bouncing and lighting and shadowing. The beams had no colors of clouds today as there was not a single puff in the sky. Only sharp blues, clear brilliant reds and piercing yellows. She loved days when the rays were crystal clean color like this.

Tinsel saw something quite different. She saw distressed color. She saw scare and worry. It was small and it looked dull gray. It was the color of an animal. A small animal. A scared animal. She couldn't see it well. She pulled at Hillary's hand. Hillary knew right away it meant Tinsel needed help. She quickly moved to Tinsel's window side and joined her gaze.

Racoons can be a maddening problem when they turn over your trash cans or try to break into your house. But if you see through better eyes, they are really only looking for food and trying to take care of their babies. If you slow down and watch them as Tinsel and Hillary always did, you see an amusing, entertaining band of little thieves. But good thieves.

As their eyes joined in the same gaze, the picture became clearer and clearer. Now it was a creature. It was a critter. It was a mama racoon and one babe all alone. Hillary and Tinsel had seen her many times before as they roamed their rocky over and underground kingdom. Her hair was gray and white and wirey, and they had nicknamed her Frizzely. Just last week they had seen her leading her little bandits. Cute little masked playful explorers that would take peanuts right out of their hand. Frizzely trusted Tinsel and Hillary. She trusted them with her babies. But now her little thieves were nowhere to be found. This might not be a good thing. In fact, this could be a terrible thing.

Frizzely was near the hidden mouth of the Eastern Lava Tube.

Sparks could always sense the excitement in the air that told him Hillary and Tinsel were about to embark on an adventure and he was not going to be left behind. By now he had already flown down the stairs and convinced Mama that he needed out into the front yard.

From their Citadel, the twins could see him doing Sparks Circles in the front yard, which is what he always did when there was excitement or danger in the air. His front feet would go crazy to the left and his hind feet would go frantic to the right, spinning him in dizzying circles. His feet cut paths in the grass and leaves, leaving what looked like donuts all over the ground. Lots of them. Like a giant had been playing checkers all over the front yard.

It was a problem that with Sparks Circles you couldn't tell if he was excited or if there was danger. It was one or the other and you had to guess which. He did his circles if there were squirrels and he did them if there were wolves.

"Frizzely needs us. Let's go!" shouted Tinsel and Hillary together.

CHAPTER THREE – The Ravenous

Jackets were on in a flash and a shin high lace up hiking boot came tumbling down the stairs as Hillary and Tinsel sat at the top trying to get them on. Sparks grabbed the boot that had gotten loose in the flurry and had bounced and left a scuff mark on the wall at the bottom of the stairs. He bounded up the stairs and dropped it at Hillary's feet, as she was waiting to throw it on. They sounded like thunder rumbling down the stairs. They raced to the front door, not even stopping as they grabbed their peculiar backpacks. Sparks could hardly keep up, and there was no way he was going to be left behind.

Mama and Papa knew by the hurried flight that their ten-year-old stars were onto something important. They had learned by now not to even ask, but just to trust. Their trust felt like it was a thousand years old. Mama and Papa closed their eyes and stretched out their hands to their little streaks of lighting and said, "We love you," as they flew.

Off the porch, skipping all four steps in one jump, their bodies moved almost faster than their legs could keep up. Then Tinsel's body did move faster than her feet. She felt herself falling forward and thought, *now is the good time to move wildly!* She made use of the forward fall to throw her hands at the ground and launch into the biggest front handspring she had ever done. Bigger even than in the 5 years of gymnastics she had been taking. The judges would have given her a 9 on this one for sure! One handspring became two and then three.

"Tinsel, quit showing off. You're falling behind!" half joked Hillary. Hillary judged her a ten for the handsprings.

Now huffing and puffing, Tinsel joked, "You only wish you could spring and fall so far behind."

Geologists say Lookout Mountain with all its hidden caves and tunnels and drains is millions or maybe billions of years old. Once there was an active volcano that is now sleeping. Maybe it will sleep forever. Now it sleeps in the form of a vast, two thousand foot deep Raven Crater, the lake formed where the Raven River falls a thousand feet of crashing waterfall onto its rocky shores. Sleeping or awake, the hidden openings to the secrets of the Lookout Deep are known only to a few. All of the creeping and burrowing and caving animals know them. Those animals don't tell their secrets. Only a few trusted girls and boys have the eyes to see them. Some see them easily. Others have to work hard and learn and earn the trust to see them. Seeing always came easy to Hillary and Tinsel.

Arriving at the Eastern Lava Tube, Frizzely was frantically pacing back and forth in front of the ivy and branches hiding the opening. She didn't even notice Hillary and Tinsel at first. Alongside her was just one of her furry babies. The girls had seen at least four or five babies in the recent past.

Tinsel and Hillary grabbed each other's hands. Sparks knew what to do. Sparks Barks were needed to get Frizzely's attention.

"Bark, bark, bark, bark, bark, bark, bark!" caught Frizzely's ears and she came to a frozen stop and turned her head. Tinsel jumped at the barks and tried to grab Sparks' mouth shut, but one quick Sparks Circle and he was free to unleash another fit of ear splitting doggy protests. Frozen in her tracks, Frizzely locked onto Hillary's eyes first, then onto Tinsel's. As the air surrounding them began to warm and glow, Frizzely seemed to breathe out a sigh and the look on her face was friendship and hope and rescue.

Hillary and Tinsel could see Frizzely's fright. They could see her worry and why. They had images of water and dark spaces and crying and hungry little furry babies. They had thoughts of days without warmth and tiny trapped spaces. Frizzely tried to scamper into the lava tube entrance, but just as quickly as she broke into and through the tangled vines, she bounded back out soaking wet and mad and sad. Her eyes spoke as if she were calling to Tinsel and Hillary for things that she couldn't do herself. *My babies, my babies, alone and cold. And wet and drowning in this hole that's closed. I can't go in; they can't come out. Help, help, please help me now.*

Hillary and Tinsel had been to the deeps of the Eastern Lava Tube before. They breathed a slow breath and both of them thought that this was not going to be easy, especially since Frizzely had already failed to get in and she was strong and smart. Even during the dry season, the lava tubes were hard going.

Off and on for the last week, hard rains had been washing the over and the underground. Flash floods had turned The Raven River into The Ravenous River. And The Ravenous continued to feed the caverns which are the drains to the deep. The brave girls were almost afraid of what they would find once they opened the viney door to the tube.

Into their backpacks they reached. Out of their backpacks they pulled. Luminous lamps. Lights that strapped to their heads like they were parts of their bodies that fit so well. They were lights, very good lights, that Papa had bought them from a very good store. The kind of hardware store that only sells good stuff. But though the lights were good, they weren't the best. Papa knew this when he bought them. But he also knew they would get better. Everything he gave to Hillary and Tinsel got better. Everything Hillary and Tinsel put into their backpacks got better.

Good gets better, and better gets best, when in hands of goodness they're placed and rest.

On in a flash, their lamps added brightly even to the daylight outside the lava tube. It was like a second sun.

Lava tube low spaces where you have to crawl and duck and turn always have bumpy sharp ceilings. In the dark, ceilings jump out and leave a big bump and a need for a bandage. Out of their backpacks they pulled their hard-shell spelunking helmets. Lightweight and sturdy strong protection against jagged rocks, they fit neatly down around their luminous light straps.

Bravely, they strained and pushed aside the thick wall of viney branches to see what they would find. They loved to spelunk for fun, but this time it could be for life or death.

Entering the outer cave mouth, the girls peered into the inky black dark, for a moment seeing only slight glimmers and reflections off of the dripping, jagged, rocky walls. From years of their shared bond, Tinsel and Hillary's eyes would get used to the dark much quicker than anyone else's. Anytime a friend came along, they had to wait much longer for friends' eyes to adjust to their 'night eyes'. What they saw in a moment was exactly what they were hoping not to see.

They were stopped immediately at the entrance by slowly draining pooled water left over from The Ravenous River. The Eastern Lava Tubes were huge and deep. The water was deeper. There was so much water the ground could not take it all quickly. Sometimes several days passed before the waters would allow passage. That was Frizzely's big problem. When The Ravenous would rage, the waters rose quickly so that sometimes there was no time to get out of the way. Frizzely and her furry babies had been foraging for their favorite, muzzle mushrooms. Muzzles only grow deep in the ground where the air is still and wet and cold. They are a rare treat for critters that are brave enough to search and brave the deep.

When The Ravenous began pouring her treacherous waters into the ground, Frizzely knew she could not get her slow and helpless furries out in time. They would all drown if she tried to get them all out at once. She had climbed and placed all but one on a high shelf pocket in the side of the tunnel where she knew they would be safe from the water until it drained away and she could run for help and return. She had managed to bring just one of her kits with her by the scruff of its neck in her gentle teeth, but she had only one mouth and raccoon hands are good for reaching through your fence and opening your gate and reaching into secret holes for treasure, but they are not good for carrying babies.

The Ravenous was overflowing non-stop and ran for days. Frizzely could find no help and now it had been two days since her babies had food or water or warmth.

At the back of the cave entrance where the lava tunnel began to dive into its depths, the tunnel disappeared under water and there was no way in. No way in that most would know of.

"We need our rain jackets," said Hillary.

Hillary and Tinsel both quickly removed their climbing jackets, and out of the depths of their backpacks pulled waterproof rain jackets. They waterproof zipped both their jackets together into one large parachute looking blanket. Throwing it high overhead, it caught the air and floated like a balloon down upon them. Grabbing the corners and fastening them securely to their waistbands, they soon had what looked like an air balloon billowing over them. They snatched up Sparks between them and began the soggy wading into the deep.

The Ravenous often left the caves and tunnels bitterly cold. Tinsel and Hillary had become tough in their journeys through the deep. The water crept up coldly to their ankles, then knees, then chest. Soon they were sinking beneath the flowing stream, protected by their air bubble. The current began to pull them down into the deep dark.

"Tins, hold onto Sparks tightly! It's going to get rough. We're nearing the corkscrew drop!"

"I'm ready. It's going to be a crazy, dropping, spinny, watery, splashy rollercoaster!"

The corkscrew drop is always dangerous even when it's dry. Now Hillary and Tinsel were dropping through it completely submerged like a submarine. Under the water in complete darkness, the water was swirling around them. They looked like a jellyfish with their parachute canopy lit up from their luminous lamps like a glowing ball in the watery dark.

Frizzely had waited behind on the wet shore of the lava tunnel entrance, nervously pacing the shoreline in the dark waiting for her rescuers to perform the miracle that she couldn't.

Tinsel and Hillary had seen from Frizzely that her terrified babies were trapped in an air pocket in the second echo chamber beyond the corkscrew drop. The water was flowing and dropping quickly now. They could feel themselves sinking fast, deeper and deeper now one hundred feet underground. That's how deep the muzzles grow.

"We'll have to jump quickly when the time comes," said Tinsel.

"We'll need to work together so we don't miss the dry air pocket," agreed Hillary. "If we sink past our one dry pocket chance, who knows how we may get back around from being carried farther into the deep."

As Hillary and Tinsel sank, the tube got smaller and smaller. As it got smaller the water shot faster, like out of a small garden hose nozzle. The submarine began to pitch wildly from side to side in the tiny tunnel. The girls knew they would be ok. They had faith in their ability and training, but it was not always without danger. The tunnel became almost too small for their underwater rescue boat to make it through, and suddenly the girls heard a loud scraping scratch.

"Sharp rocks! Torn a gash in our sail!" was all Hillary could cry out. "There it is! It's on your side! Not that big but it'll sink us if we don't make dry air in time. Cover it with your hand! Cover it!"

"I can do better than that!" shouted Tinsel over the roar of the falling water. "It needs fixing for good or we will never make it back out!"

It wasn't easy with the raincoat bubble wrapped about them, pressing in on every side. Her arms were barely able to move in the tight space. Tinsel wrestled a roll of the best wide rubber tape out of her backpack. Ripping off a six-inch piece, she pressed it against the gash the best she could with all the being thrown about and water splashing in their faces. As she held it in place, the girls closed their eyes and held hands and rested. Everything became calm inside them. It was like they were inside a bubble inside a bubble. Tinsel's hand grew warm against the rubber tape, and then hot and then very hot. Rubber became soft and liquid and flowed together. Tape became jacket and jacket became tape. Soon you could barely tell where tape left off and where jacket began. There was no longer a gash. All that was left was a trace of a scar where the horrible rip had been. For a moment Tinsel and Hillary stared at the scar. Their eyes watered a little and their hearts watered a lot. They looked at each other and said so many things without a word.

Bloop! The girl stars had popped to the surface and were bobbing in the water like a cork. They fought to the dry shoreline in the first echo chamber. With half the chamber full of air and full of roaring water, there wasn't the usual ringing echoes made by crunching shale rock under boots. In other times, this was one of the girls favorite places to spend hours taking turns being still, then taking turns stepping just one boot at a time to hear the musical reverberating crunchy echoes from the smooth high arches and walls of the echo chamber.

Sometimes Sparks would join the game by sharing one of his whip cracking yelps. Those were almost too much to handle and Hillary and Tinsel usually couldn't get their hands over their ears in time.

"Sparks!" they would say, "is that really necessary?!" And then of course Sparks would bark again and Hill and Tins would laugh.

They were always amazed at how the hoot of a small 'hoo' would come back almost as a louder 'HOO'. No sound was ever wasted there.

Sitting on the shoreline, they removed their bubble for a minute to catch their breath and prepare for their final watery drop. Sparks was glad for the moment to be back on dry airy land with his favorite girls, as he danced about them.

"No time to waste Tins. Ready to go?"

"Yes Hill. Grab your side and let's launch the bubble."

They again threw the jackets into the air to inflate them, caught the corners and fixed them firmly to their waistbands, grabbed up Sparks between them, and waded back into the quick dark waters. Many people would have turned back by now. Hillary and Tinsel never turn back. Sometimes they choose to take a different route, but they never turn back.

Swirling in a whirlpool just above the tunnel drop, down beneath the water they went like going down the drain of a bathtub. Now they were dropping through a very steep hole slanted a little like a staircase. Even when dry, unless you had four legs, this is always rough going. Ten feet, fifty feet, two hundred feet, until they final leveled out. The water spread wide as their underground river came into the gigantic expanse of the second echo chamber. The chamber was so large you would think you were on a lake, waves lapping at the shore.

The muzzle mushroom depths were low enough now that much of the earth above was wet and dripping through cracks in the ceiling. Through hundreds of thousands of years, the water had carried its precious minerals, slowly and ever so slowly forming the hanging stalactites which looked like upside-down cones and swords. Some had cracked off and fallen and were stuck like long knives in the shale beach. Hopefully none of them would crack and fall on the girls heads. The far wall across the underground lake was almost too dim to see it was so far off. Small reflections danced off of thousands of sharp, reflecting diamond-like crystals in the igneous walls formed by huge super-hot gas bubbles burped out by the ancient volcano. Hopefully they would not run into any unfriendlies. They had enough on their hands taking care of Frizzely's kits.

Chirping and crying filled their ears right away. The girls turned to the walls near them and the shore. Just about as high as they could reach, there in a pocket in the jagged wall, were Frizzely's four other kits. They were crying up a storm to see Hillary and Tinsel and Sparks. Sparks danced and barked as if Tins and Hill needed to be shown where they were.

"Silly Sparks," laughed Hillary. "Of course we see them. If we didn't, we would surely hear them!"

Hillary and Tinsel climbed the piles of rocks forming stairs to where the kits were. Slurps of water from the girls cupped palms and a handful of peanuts later, the kits weren't crying for food and water as much. Now their scared, smaller, pitiful cries were for mama.

It was time to go. But could they make it back out…?

Two kits in Hillary's backpack. Two in Tinsel's. Zipped just enough for their cute faces to poke out. This would take more effort, more power, than the girls thought they might have. But they had done things almost this huge before. They both knew what to do.

When Tinsel was two years old, she held Hillary's hand as they took a bath. Stormy days had already become one of her favorites. Her thoughts ran deep even as a small child and she saw the bathwater dancing like an upside-down rainstorm. Before either of them knew what was going on, Tinsel's joy had rained the entire tub out onto the bathroom floor. Mama was sitting on the stool with her hair dripping like she had just come out of a storm without an umbrella. Mama smiled at what she knew about Tinsel and grabbed a towel and started mopping.

This time it would take more than shared joy to get out of this water. It would take courage. It would take determination. It would take working together. It would take all these things joined.

In the deeps are pressures and heats. The deeper you go the heatier they are. From deep, deep, deep, where the volcanoes and magmas grow, Tinsel and Hillary worked together as a courageous team to make a great rock wall split and pour it's hot melted rock into the flowing underground drain water. The earth gave a violent shake as the water miles below them exploded into steam. Just like steam pushed the locomotives long ago, the furious steam bubble began pushing the cave water backwards. The stars knew it was only a matter of time until the great bubble began to surge and shake them to the surface.

"Do you hear that?" said Tinsel, frozen still with her head tilted for better sound.

Now they both heard it. Sparks heard it and didn't know whether to start up with Spark Barks or Sparks Circles he was so confused.

A growing, slapping, flapping thousand small voices began screeching all around their heads. The air was thick with thousands of wings and teeth. It was the Billowing Bats. The kits excited chirps and Sparks' barks had awakened them from their upside down beds in the chamber ceilings. They were not happy. They were hungry. If they had not been so blind as bats are, they would have easily sunk their teeth in where ever they could get hold. The worst they were able to do before Hillary and Tinsel quickly got organized was to bounce and bump off the girls heads and cause just a few bruises. If they only had more time to properly find their victims…

"Brace yourself Hillary!"

"Grab Sparks!"

"Got him!"

The second echo chamber began to rise quickly. Then it began to bubble violently. Air and water were being pushed to the ceiling and up and out of the chamber. The Billowing Bats were forced high up back into their air pocket cave homes.

"I think we're moving sideways toward the entrance we came in through," yelled Tinsel. "Watch out for the stalactites! We have helmets on but they can still break our bones!"

Without warning, Hillary and Tinsel slammed into a giant stalactite, knocking the wind out of them and almost tearing and bursting their bubble! The impact was so violent, one of Frizzely's kits was thrown from Tinsel's backpack into the water. Sparks lunged towards the little furry and grabbed her by the scruff of her neck and was able to hold on, but only just in time to be sucked under the water by the rocking waves.

"Sparks! Sparks is gone, and one of the kits! Dive, find him! Find them!" cried Tinsel.

"We're moving too fast. It's too dark. It's too late! I can't see anything at all. We're already up the stair tube and passing the first echo chamber! It's no good. We can't fight this water."

The fears and the tears began to flow. The water was too violent and Sparks and his kit had no protection or air. They could be flowing up the lava tube or they may have been sucked down to the depths.

Within minutes, Hillary and Tinsel were being spit back out onto dry ground and pushed roughly through the viney door out into the rocky forest. Water continued to push and flow out with them, until the earth was finished with its steam belching watery show.

Hillary and Tinsel quickly ripped off their bubble and began pulling the three remaining kits from their zippered pouches. They were working without looking at their hands, for their eyes were fixed on the entrance of the cave. Looking… waiting… hoping… holding back the worry.

Frizzely came bounding to the girls and was chirping and running circles of joy for her babies… but she quickly stopped. There was one little furry missing from her full family. Her eyes locked onto and questioned Tins and Hill. Their reply to Frizzely was sadness. By now Sparks should have been thrown out of the cave.

With tears and slow steps, the girls and Frizzely searched the cave opening and inside the mouth when the waters allowed. There was no beagle or kit to be found. They closed their tearful eyes and held hands and were silent for a long time.

When enough time had passed, Hillary and Tinsel motioned to Frizzely that they were forever sorry and their time there was done. They turned to slowly walk away as the sky was clouding over and it began to rain. Neither of them could speak a word. It would be a long, dark walk home.

The rain was so loudly beating down on the leaves of the trees they couldn't hear the rustling sound of the underbrush. The crispy scratchy sounds that forest floor bushes and brushes make when they are being beaten down and pushed aside by four-legged stalking and jumping and running. But they suddenly did see frantic and scary movement. Movement coming through the forest to their north side. Quick movement. They were not prepared for this danger, as they still had tears in their eyes and in their hearts. As quickly as they could, they pulled sharp sticks from their backpacks and prepared to defend themselves from the Willow Wolves that from year to year would move through the mountain ranges. When at last the beast burst through the wall of bushes just before them, Tinsel and Hillary screamed!

It was a muddy, wet, chocolate caramel four-legged beagle in need of a bandage. And carried in his gentle teeth was a little kit.

Yells and hollers for joy brought Frizzely and her furry little kits running from the other direction.

"Oh Sparks! Sparks!" hollered Hillary.

"Sparks and Frizzely's furry!" resounded Tinsel.

They all sat and rolled and rubbed nose kisses down in the mud until the tears of loss were tears of laughter and joy and mess and dirt. Frizzely and her babies pounced and danced in the mix of girls and dogs jumping and playing and gave little racoon hugs.

When all calmed down, the girls looked to Sparks for what had happened. They saw through his eyes that there had been another Sparks sized lava tube that went straight up from where he and the kit had been sucked away. They had been pushed up like a geyser through that space that was just beagle big enough and thrown like a cannonball back up to the top of the hill above the cave entrance.

Hand in hand, heart in heart; courage and faith are a wonderful start. To know what to want, and to know what to do; to wield a strong strength and to follow it through.

Hillary and Tinsel had seen so much that day. Enough to give them wonderful dreams. Dreams of darks and lights and waters and fears; sunlights and rainlights and sorrows and cheers. Sparks curled in a warm round bundle on the foot of Hillary's bed as the girls slept with smiles and deep breaths until they awoke to brilliant yellow red rays beaming into the East window of their Citadel. Long, sleepy yawns and stretches and smells of bacon filled the air.

40

Bacon that would not get cold this time.

CHAPTER FOUR – Sock Feet and Bacon

Waking to their favorite day, like most girls and boys when school is in, the twins' thoughts and talks were already whirling about what they would do this Saturday. Sleep for them was good stuff, but once they had gotten enough sleep, time for excitement was slipping away as quickly as the sleep from their eyes. By now Sparks was already clicking and clacking his nails and paws up and down the stairs like an alarm clock. At least he had waited on his Sparks Barks until they were actually awake.

Fluffy socks on Hillary's feet helped her slip and bump bump bump down one stair at a time as she held the hand rail and pulled herself down the polished wood treads. She would pull… slide… bump… pull… slide… bump… from the top to the bottom, her strong, thick legs like hammers hitting large drums, echoing through the house. Sparks always became a frenzy when she did this. "Bark, bark, bark, bark, bark, bark, bark." He didn't really know what the game was, he only knew that one of his favorite girls was making a ruckus and he had to be part of it by running from the top to the bottom of the stairs the whole time.

Tinsel would have been quickly behind, almost knocking Hillary over as usual, if not for the fact she couldn't find her slide. She always held on to the latest cardboard box that came into the house from some appliance or delivery. But only if the box were big enough to flatten and use as a sled. She always kept it under the bed. But this morning it was not to be found and she could hear that Hillary had already finished the stairs and Sparks was barking in the kitchen. She could have just walked the stairs, other than the fact that it was too boring, but now she was stubbornly curious about where her slide had gone.

Tinsel looked and looked. In the closets, under and behind the dressers, under Hillary's bottom bunk bed. There was nowhere else to look. *Where had it gone?* Since you always find what you are looking for in the last place you look, she looked again in all the same places. Only this time, under Hillary's bottom bunk she looked up instead of down. *What was this?! Why was her super slide caught between Hillary's mattress and the metal spring slats? "How strange," she thought. "I'll have to get Hillary back for this trick."* Without further thought, Tinsel wrestled the box slide out, nearly ripping all Hillary's neatly made sheets and blankets off in the process, leaving them mostly half on and half off in a pile hanging down to the floor.

Placing her slide hanging a little out into the air over the top tread, Tinsel quickly sat down, centered herself, grabbed the front overhanging lip, and bent it back like the front round end of a toboggan. Giving a few quick forward scoots, her super slide cardboard toboggan inched its way toward the point of no return. Finally, its nose began to tip downhill like a seesaw and gravity took over. Tinsel was amazed every time at how fast cardboard can go on polished stairs. That was part of the fun. And this was a new box that she had never used before. Most cardboard boxes are dull and flat, brown and rough. This one had a shiny, waxy coating with a picture of the new refrigerator Papa had brought home. The old fridge they had for at least ten years before 'the stars' had even become twins finally broke down.

Papa always liked to make something last much longer than most people. Mama never got mad, but sometimes she had to wait too long for her liking for things to get fixed. It was partly because they didn't have a lot of money. But it was more because Papa had a deep respect for metals and wires and plastics and glass. All the things that come from the ground. And all things that go back to the ground. Papa loved that you could take things from the ground and for a short time make them into useful things. But it cost the ground a lot to give these things up. And it cost a lot to put them back.

This new waxy polished box was not at all like the other boxes Tinsel had plowed down the treads on. If the first half of the ride had scared her, the second half terrified her. Her super slide had no controls and sock feet make horrible brakes! Her speed was out of control and by the time she hit the level floor after the last tread, she was shooting like a rocket past the point where rough cardboard should have stopped her.

She had no other choice. She stuck her sock feet straight out like logs, let go of the sled lip, and leaned way back, bracing for impact. Her feet slammed into the gypsum wall, which is really only about as strong as chalk, and punched two nicely feet shaped holes all the way though the wall. Luckily, she missed the wooden studs inside the wall or she would have cracked her ankles.

Everyone came running after hearing such a crash. For a moment Papa, Mama, Hillary and Sparks all stood speechless in a half circle around, her frozen and staring, until all of them except Sparks figured out what had happened.

44

"Are you all right?" asked Papa.

"I don't know...I think so," said Tinsel with her heart beginning to race.

"Does anything hurt or can you stand?" questioned Papa.

Tinsel didn't know why but a lump started in her throat and she held back the tears. Papa helped her up and she moved around without pain of any kind.

"I'm so sorry Papa," quivered Tinsel's voice.

"What are you sorry about?"

"I don't know. I'm just sorry," blurted out Tinsel. "Maybe because I knocked holes in the wall and you'll have to fix it?"

Papa thought for a moment and said, "Yes, there's certainly that. The holes that *we'll* have to fix *together*?" Tinsel scrunched her eyes just a little, but understood what Papa was saying.

"Maybe because that didn't need to happen?" replied Tinsel, thinking again.

"Did you do it on purpose?"

"Of course not Papa!"

"I know you didn't sweetie. So why are you sorry?"

"I don't know. I just am," as she began to cry.

"Come here sweetie," as Papa gave her a hug. "Let's talk about it after breakfast."

"I don't want to talk about it after breakfast. I want it over now," said Tinsel excitedly.

Sitting down on the bottom stair tread together, Papa said, "Ok then sweetie. Why are you sorry? Sit here and think quietly and let me know. What are you feeling?"

Almost a full minute went by. Tinsel began to have a feeling she remembered having before. She didn't like it. She didn't want to say it even after she knew what the feeling was. She just looked up into Papa's eyes and began to cry again.

"Tell me. I can see you know," said Papa.

Now the tears rolled and Tinsel leaned into Papa and cried hard. She didn't want to talk at all. Minutes later as she was cried out, she could just get out a whisper between the crying snuffles.

"I feel… stupid," was the only thing she could get out.

Papa let Tinsel's words hang in the air and in their thoughts long enough for them both to think and feel them. He hugged her tightly.

When he knew Tinsel was ready, he said, "*You* already told me you didn't do it on purpose. And *I* know you love to have fun. And *we* know it was an accident," then he added, "so I think you are feeling sorry *and* ashamed."

"Yes. I keep doing these things. I can't seem to stop making stupid mistakes," whispered Tinsel.

"You already said you're sorry and you'll help me patch the holes. And I think you'll be more careful next time, right?"

"Yes Papa."

"Then I think we're done here. You are not stupid. You didn't know that would happen."

And that's all they ever said about that.

Holes in the wall are patched with glue, or plaster or cement and wallpaper too. Holes in the heart are patched much the same. But the damage repaired is heartache and shame. It takes tougher stuff than mortar and nail, to fix broken hearts and feelings that ail.

Tinsel loved chewy bacon. And Hillary loved crispy bacon. And Sparks, well, Sparks just loved bacon. Any bacon that the girls snuck to him under the table. Sparks was silly to think that Mama and Papa didn't know he was getting his fill of bacon under the table. Mama always made half the bacon crispy and half the bacon chewy.

There wasn't much of the pancakes and eggs and bacon and toast left over after the eating and laughter. The Spelunkers never really remembered the food as much as they remembered the heartfelt apologies and smiles and laughter.

CHAPTER FIVE – Tinsel's Bike

The day was young and held so many possibilities. Papa and Tinsel's wall repair had to wait because Papa already had plans with friends coming over to help him work on his half-finished workshop all day. Tinsel liked that and she didn't like that. She liked that she had plans to go find Luisa to invite her to tonight's Sleepover Extravaganza. That's what they named it to add excitement. She didn't like waiting on something that would hang over her head. Especially when it was something that she had felt bad about like knocking holes in the wall.

Hillary's head was full of colors and paints and brushes and giggles and secrets. Good secrets that the best of best friends tell. Ones that aren't gossip, but ones of hopes and dreams and likes and hurts that only your best of best could be really happy and understanding for you. That was because she was expecting Elka over early that morning and she was all set up in the craft sunroom for one of her favorites - painting. Painting and sharing her deepest. She could do this with Mama and Tinsel and Papa. Of course Sparks would always listen, but he wouldn't laugh or cry as much.

Tinsel shouted goodbye to the whole house and everything and everyone in it. Everyone in the house shouted back their well wishes and love. Liking to travel lightly, Tinsel hesitated at the door for a moment, wondering if she really wanted to take her backpack. But remembering that every single time in the past that she didn't take it she regretted it. So she grabbed it in a flash and opened the front door. Quicker than she was, Sparks was outside and down the stairs.

"Oh no you don't you little sneak! Sorry, not this time."

From the bottom of the stairs Tinsel pointed back to the house with both a frown and a smile. Sparks knew exactly what she meant, but sometimes he was ornery and pretended that he didn't understand. Tinsel recognized this game and knew that he was being beagle stubborn. The game was to wait him out. She stood there not saying a word. Just looking Sparks in the eye and holding her arm out with her finger pointing up the stairs. For a minute Sparks sat down, pretending to be waiting for her, looking away. He grew impatient as dogs do after a very short time and looked her in the eye. He tried a Sparks Circle to amuse her, but that didn't work. Although Tinsel did laugh in her head, but didn't let him know that. Second by second as their eyes were locked his head slowly drooped lower and lower until his chin was almost on the ground. Finger pointing is one thing, but voices add a lot with dogs. He was being exceptionally stubborn this morning as he was now three years old and learning the most. Finally Tinsel had to break the silence as the staring was just not working.

"Sparks!" she barked at him.

That alone made him jump back to his feet and for a split second he thought it might be a good thing. Then he saw the finger still pointing and he began to squirm with maybe defeat. He still didn't completely obey, but at least pointed his wet nose towards the door.

"Sparks!" Tinsel said again, not raising her voice any more than the first time. She had learned from Papa that yelling and anger are not the way to teach your wonderful little puppy.

"Mmrrmmpphh," in a little doggy complaint was all Sparks said as he slunk up the steps, stopping for a moment at the open door to look back, then jumping across the threshold and nosing the door closed.

Good boy, smiled Tinsel.

Tinsel fought her bike out of the crowded shed, untangling the right pedal from Hillary's rear tire spokes. *It will be nice when Papa finishes his shop so we can keep our bikes in a better place.* Left foot on the pedal and shoving as hard as she could, now swinging her right leg over the seat and catching the flying right pedal as it flew in its circle, she was in high speed down the graveled road. Luisa's house was only three miles away. This far out in the country, the road was only a little wider than a single lane, so she had to move over to let a car pass.

Hillary was excited to hear tires rolling and crunching gravel in their driveway. Elka arrived in her mom's car. She ran out to meet her best of best friends and gave her a big hug, tackling her before she could even get out of the car.

"I'm so happy to see you!" exclaimed Hillary.

"Same here Hill," smiled Elka.

The girls grabbed hands and ran up the steps and inside the house, Elka's mom barely able to keep up.

Mama had already made a fresh pot of coffee for the two of them to enjoy on the sun patio.

"We just passed Tinsel on the road," said Elka.

"She's on her way to Luisa's. Let's see if we can still see her from the Citadel," replied Hillary.

They ran up the stairs together, secretly racing to see who could get to the top first, but not really caring who won. Making it to the East Lookout, they both carefully studied the road stretching away from them. About a mile off both of them spotted a tiny speck moving away on the road.

"That must be her," said Elka. "But I guess we can't really be sure?"

"We could be sure…" whispered Hillary.

"How? If that's her, she is too far away," replied Elka.

"It doesn't matter how far away she is. We can be sure."

"What are you talking about?"

"We've known each other a long time Elka. You are my best of best friends. It's time that I trust you with something because I know that I can now."

"Yes, you know that you can."

"Do you want to see better?"

"What are you talking about Hill?"

"Do you want to see better?"

"I don't know what you mean, but sure, I'd like to see down the road better. Do you mean with glasses or binoculars?"

"This is more than seeing better down the road Elka."

"Ok Hill, what the heck are you talking about? You always like to do this. I think you enjoy this. Making a mystery and then surprising me. You've done this to me for years."

"I only make fun with the best Elka. And you are my best of best."

"Then show me."

"Do you believe me... Do you trust me?"

"You know that I do."

"Give me your hand," whispered Hillary. "Look east. Hold still. Breath deep. Breath slow. Fix your eyes on the furthest tree at the end of the road. Now close your eyes. Now open them. Hold still. Tell me everything you see."

Hillary could feel Elka's heart beating.

Waiting for a moment, Elka said, "I see the valley. I see the road. I see the forest and lichen and rocks. Wait... what?... I see caves... where did those come from? I've never seen those before."

"Good. What else do you see?"

"I think that's it. Wait... I see tiny crawling movements. What are they? It's a little scary."

"Those are mice and racoons and gophers and deer and birds."

"Hillary, how am I seeing this? They are miles away."

"What else do you see? Look at the speck."

"I don't see the speck anymore. It's gone over the hill. Wait... it's her. It's Tinsel! But I can't see her. I just know it's her."

"Do you believe it's really her? Can you see her face clearly?"

"I trust you Hill. I know it's her. But I don't see her face."

Hillary let go of Elka's hand and the thoughts and movements faded quickly. Elka saw only gravel and grass and leaves and branches nearby in the yard.

Elka looked Hillary in the eyes and wanted to ask questions. But sometimes silence is the best answer between friends. Sharing was enough. She knew Hillary and knew the rest would come later.

Without a word, the bests walked down the stairs and through the house to the craft sunroom. Easels and paints were waiting.

The girls painted for hours. Elka mixed browns and greens and whites and grays. She filled her blank canvas with movement and animals and the colors of Hillary's friendship and of Tinsel and her bike riding.

****

After three miles of furious peddling and lots of sweat, Tinsel had knocked her previous best time of 18 minutes down to 15 minutes to get to Luisa's house. There was no trophy waiting for her, but Luisa did throw an old towel at her to dry her dripping face.

"Luisa, I meant to ask you last week in school, but I'm so sorry, I forgot," said Tinsel apologetically. "Hill and I are having a Sleepover Extravaganza tonight and I want you to come if you can. I know it's such short notice. Do you think I'm just horrible?"

"Tinsel!" smirked Luisa. "Quit feeling sorry for yourself."

"What?! What are you talking about? How is that feeling sorry for myself? I'm apologizing."

"You want me to feel sorry for you for forgetting and tell you you're not horrible. Well you already know that forgetting something doesn't make you a bad person," said Luisa with a snippy look.

Tinsel thought about what Luisa just said. She had nothing to say, and it hit her hard as they walked together into the house to find Luisa's mom. She was wanting attention.

After getting a yes from her mom to go to Tinsel's sleepover, Luisa and Tinsel made a backyard afternoon out of learning to roll and walk atop an old wooden barrel on its side. There were only a few skinned knees and elbows and no broken bones until both of them could walk the barrel across the yard over bumps and holes, arm in arm.

A sharp rock caught on a rivet holding the metal banding together. One of the metal bands that held all the wooden slats of the old barrel together. The barrel band broke loose and one end of the barrel exploded into wooden slats pointing everywhere like a porcupine.

"I'm going to get into trouble," said Luisa. "My dad was going to use this barrel for potting a miniature ornamental cherry tree and he just bought it. Maybe we shouldn't have been walking on it."

Tinsel thought hard for a moment. Out of her backpack she pulled a rope.

"Hold that end and help me wrap it around all the loose slats to pull them together."

The girls pushed and pulled and put all the slats back into place and used the rope to hold them there. They pulled the broken metal band back into place.

She looked to Luisa and said, "Hold my hand."

Luisa held her left hand. Tinsel put her right hand over the broken band ends. Nothing much was happening. A little heat was all. Not enough to pop popcorn. Tinsel let go of Luisa's hand and stretched it out towards home and Hillary. Hillary could feel the power go out from her. The steel band melted to form a nice welded seal between the two broken halves. The barrel was as good as new. In fact it was better than new.

"Did you see that?" asked Tinsel.

"Did I see what?"

"I didn't think so," sighed Tinsel.

"Don't criticize me," snapped Luisa. "I get enough of that from my own family."

"What? I've never seen Brad treat you badly."

"Oh you only see him at school. He pretends to be a nice half-brother there just to look good," said Luisa.

"Half-brother?"

"He's not really even that. Didn't you know I'm adopted?"

"We haven't known each other long. How would I know that?" replied Tinsel.

"Well if you're going to be mean you can just leave," pouted Luisa.

"You're really upset about this and it's not me you're mad at," said Tinsel as she put her arm around Luisa's shoulder.

Luisa began to cry and whispered, "I never knew my real mom and dad. I don't know how they could leave me..."

Tinsel didn't say a word.

Words don't need to fill the air when all you need to do is care. A hug, a why, a look, a sigh. Give a warm shoulder, just let them cry.

At home later that day, Tinsel thanked Hillary for her help as they began preparing for their sleepover.

CHAPTER SIX – Sleepover Extravaganza

Saturday afternoon marched on, and little by little the Spelunker house became louder and livelier. It always amazed Papa at how many loud outbreaks of laughter and quiets of whispers could come from The Citadel whenever it began to fill with girls... Hillary, Tinsel, Elka, Ava and Luisa. The ceiling in the kitchen, directly below the Citadel, was not meant to be a trampoline and Mama thought the five of them might come through the floorboards at any moment.

Mama hollered up the stairs, "Why don't you girls go outside and play while there is still daylight?"

Hill and Tins thought that was a great idea. They were getting sleeping bags and beds in place.

Mama was enjoying moving around the house from room to room as she was organizing and doing light Saturday cleaning. But it wasn't the working that she was liking as much as the view from each different room. As she heard laughter coming from the south of the house she moved into the craft sunroom. From that window she saw five girls taking turns double-bouncing each other on the trampoline. When she heard *'me next'* shouting from Papa's half-finished workshop, she moved to the west hall. There she saw, between the exposed wooden wall studs, the five taking turns on the two swings Papa had rigged to the open roof rafters so the girls could swing indoors. When things got so quiet that Mama almost suspected mischief, she peeked between the curtains and spied through the east windows to the front yard picnic table. There sat five girls so hungry from the exhausted playing that all you heard if you listened closely was the lip smacking of many pieces of pizza. Mama's favorite was watching the five play tag. She stood in the very center of the house in the open living room and got glimpses from all directions of red laughing faces flashing by the various windows around and around the house.

Papa saw much the same, just a different view from the top of his half-finished workshop as he nailed on sheets of roofing plywood.

The only real mishap of the afternoon was Luisa. The trampoline handled two flailing girls well enough, but when Luisa joined as a third, she got the back of Tinsel's head to her bottom lip.

"Ouch!" hollered Luisa.

"Oh my gosh I'm so sorry," said Tinsel, helping Luisa down off the trampoline.

Luisa was stunned and cried only a little, but she had bit her lip quite hard and it was bleeding more than a little. Spitting on the ground to see how bad she was hurt, she could see the red mixed in.

Hillary and Tinsel tensed up. They looked at the ground and waited. They felt nothing. It soaked partially into the ground and still they felt nothing. They looked at each other without the others noticing. Their hearts dropped a little and they felt bad for Luisa.

It was just beginning to get dark anyway, and they all went in so Mama could take a look at Luisa's lip. By the time they got into the light of the kitchen table, it quit bleeding.

Later on when Hillary would paint pictures of this day in the craft sunroom, the colors made a crazy collage of pepperonis, bouncing bodies trying not to bang heads, barking beagles chasing the heels of shoes and a touch of sadness and care for Luisa.

****

Flannelly pajamas, cottony pajamas and silky pajamas of all colors and prints jumped and bounced all around the loft room with five girls filling them. Tinsel wrestled a pair of doggy pajamas onto Sparks once, but he would never keep them on for very long. Tinsel thought maybe he didn't like the color. Hillary thought maybe he didn't like the fit. It was a little fun at least watching him wiggle his way out of them. It's hard to take your pajamas off when you don't have thumbs.

"Klix thought he was coming over today and had packed a bag with his pajamas and pillow," said Elka.

"Why would your little brother think he was invited to a girl's sleepover?" asked Hillary.

"A seven-year-old doesn't know boys don't go to a girl's sleepover. And mom has me take him with me whenever I can. Like going to play at the school playground on the weekends and stuff. He's really attached to me right now for some reason," replied Elka.

"That must be a real pain," said Tinsel. "Boys can be so stupid and annoying."

Klaus, or Klix as they called him, loved to tag along with his big sister. To him, she knew everything and was kind to him, and was protective. He liked to tease her as well.

"Oh, it's really not that bad," said Elka. "Being his only sister, when mom and dad are working I help keep him out of trouble."

"If I had a little brother, I'd make him sleep outside in the doghouse with Sparks!" laughed Tinsel.

"That's not nice at all," said Hillary. "You need to be nice to a little brother and you need to be nice to Klix."

"Well when Mama gives us a little brother, then we'll see who is going to be nice to him," grinned Tinsel.

"I love little ones and I would love to have a baby brother," sighed Hillary deep in thought with her chin resting in her hands.

Papa loves to cook and he loves to serve and treat. His surprises are always the best of crunchy and sweet, hearty and healthy, sticky and gooey. You can't buy better cinnamon rolls. Tonight he was keeping it simple and he surprised the girls with popcorn balls and slices of watermelon and fizzy water to wash it down. Up the stairs he came with a big tray of these favorites and Sparks gave him away before his head popped up into the loft. Sparks is a good guard dog. Sometimes too good. Good luck trying to play hide and go seek with your friends. It's a little difficult to hide when Sparks spots you and points right at you and goes into Sparks Barks, "bark bark bark bark bark bark bark bark." So the girls knew something was up before Papa was half way up the stairs.

"Load your catapults for an attack!" shouted Hillary.

As soon as Papa was mostly up the stairs and half way into the room, Hillary yelled, "Fire!!"

Five pillows flew like cannonballs landing on and around Papa. Three direct hits sent his tray of popcorn balls flying and bouncing. One went under the bed. Sparks grabbed one and began to bolt for the stairs to get away with his treasure before Papa caught him by the collar as he tried to squeeze by.

"Give it over boy. I'll trade you that for a sausage treat downstairs," said Papa. Sparks was a little disappointed but released his teeth from the sticky ball of popped kernels all glued together with a shell of hardened candy syrup.

Luckily Papa's first trip up the stairs was nothing spillable or breakable, only bounceable and rollable. He smiled a menacing smile that Hill and Tins recognized when he a had brilliantly teasing idea in mind. He had only lost two popcorn balls from the tray. Bending down on his knees quickly and reaching under the bed to fish for the runaway candy ball, he scooped it up.

"Hmmm girls. Looks like someone has grown dust bunnies under the bed and some of them seem to like this yummy popcorn ball," winked Papa.

He shook it off a little to pretend he had gotten the dust bunnies off. In his one hand he held high the two from the floor and Sparks' mouth. He posed there dramatically for almost ten seconds just to make the girls wonder what was going on.

Then he said, "I hope one of you girls have brushed Sparks' teeth lately," as he grinned.

"What? Why Papa?" asked Hillary

Papa turned his back to all the girls. He dramatically dropped his popcorn ball hand and you could tell he had added them to the tray of clean treats. He swirled his hand around like he was playing the shell and pea game. Then he turned back around with a devious grin on his face.

"Because one of you is going to be eating a doggy drool popcorn treat!"

"Awwwww Papa! Yuck!!" laughed and cried Tinsel. "How could you do that to us?!"

"And one of you gets a dust bunny surprise," again laughed Papa.

And then he finished with, "That's what happens when a crew of pirates ambush the cook!" And he pretended an evil laugh.

The girls all grimaced and grinned at him.

****

Their tummies full of good snacks and beginning to get tired from all the play of the day, the girls were ready to slow down and do something a little quieter.

"For some reason, watermelon sometimes gives me crazy dreams," Elka let everyone know, as she ate more than her fair share of one of her favorite foods. "But I like crazy dreams!"

"Well, if your watermelon dreams make you sleep walk," joked Tinsel, "be sure not to step on me!"

"Oh they don't make me sleepwalk," laughed Elka. "I just must have some kind of reaction to it where I seem to have the strangest wonderful dreams."

"Well then, dream away!" said Hillary.

Earlier in the day Hillary suggested to Tinsel a fun thing to do when the night got late and it was time to shut off the lights and wind down. But it involved flashlights. Many flashlights. At least one for each girl and that would make five now.

"What are we going to do about enough torches?" Hillary whispered to Tinsel.

"You know what a flashlight freak Papa is. Quit being such a shy scaredy-cat and go ask him."

"But they cost a lot and I don't want to hurt Papa's feelings if he doesn't have them."

"Ha! When's the last time you hurt Papa's feelings just asking and being honest?"

"You're right," said Hillary, her face brightening up. "I know Papa better than that. Even if he only has one flashlight we'll still have a blast."

"I'll be right back. I have something fun for us if I can find what I need," announced Hillary.

Leaving the other girls in the Citadel, she found Papa in the office working on some little sparking electric contraption. Papa liked to tinker with electrics and motors and pumps and things. He was a bit of a backyard inventor, though he had never really invented anything that most people would think was useful. But it made him happy and Mama was amused at some of the crazy things he came up with.

"Papa?"

"Yes Hillary?"

"Is there any chance you might have one or two flashlights for our sleepover?" asked Hillary.

"Just one or two Hilly-beans?" said Papa who always had fun with our names. "I never saw a game with five girls that needed any less than five flashlights!"

"Do you have more than one?" hoped Hillary.

"Silly girl. The question is not *how many you have*. It's *how many don't I have*!" said Papa hopping up with that look on his face that things were about to be overdone. Papa amused himself. Hillary smiled and rolled her eyes.

"Follow me girlie, and you had better bring something to carry things in unless you have five hands."

"Papa, you're so silly."

Hillary grabbed a basket from the kitchen and Papa grabbed flashlight number one and two from the junk drawer next to the silverware. There was one small slim black one, and one that looked like you could use it as a small baseball bat. He grabbed flashlight number three from a cabinet over the sidebar. Already Hillary's eyes and her hopes were open wide. *How many flashlights can one person possibly have?*

"My lighting to the workshop is not done yet and it's pretty dark out already. We'll need this," as he put two in Hillary's basket and kept one in hand.

"Follow me."

Papa lit up the baseball bat torch in his hand and blinded the gravel path he had put from the house side door to the half-finished workshop where he already had many of his tools stored. They went to the side of the shop where he had already put the roof sheeting on and was rain safe.

Papa dug through a big red rolling toolbox and immediately found two more flashlights. One like the baseball bat torch and one smaller. He dropped them into Hillary's basket. He went to a set of cabinets he had installed that he had gotten half off from a flea market. Rummaging around he found another that appeared to be dead. But he immediately found batteries and the lamp sprung back to life.

"Papa, that's already six flashlights and we only have five people."

"Doesn't Sparks need one?" joked Papa. "It's always good to have a spare, and I think I have a few more over here on the tool board."

"I think you're just showing off now," Hillary poked at Papa.

"Well, I just wanted you to know who you were dealing with Hilly. *Do I have a flashlight?* I don't think you'll ever dare ask me that question again!"

"Ok Papa, I get your point. I think we've got more than enough."

Back to the house and up the stairs ran Hillary with her many torches. Each girl chose their own flashlight. Sparks didn't get a flashlight because his thumbs didn't work right, but Hillary put it on the desk for good keeping just the same.

"Tinsel and Elka can you please help me push the couch from the center of the room up against the wall?" asked Hillary.

They created a large open space in the center of the loft.

"Everyone lie down on your back with your head in the center like the spokes of a wheel and leave a spot for me," directed Hillary.

Hillary went to her dresser and pulled out 20 or so clear plastic sheets about the size of a piece of typing paper. Each sheet was different. She had gotten these for free as extras from a craft fair at school. One had geometric designs of squares and rectangles with blacks and whites. Another had rainbows and colors. Others had flowers, animals, stars, galaxies, trees, clouds, houses, lines and circles and on and on. The combinations were beyond counting. Hillary gave four or five sheets randomly to each girl, then turned out the loft lights.

Next, she lay down on the floor, taking the fifth open spot they had saved for her.

"Girls, light your torches!" commanded Hillary.

"Elka, hold up your first sheet and shine your torch through it to make shadows and patterns on the ceiling," directed Hillary.

Elka pulled a sheet from her collection and shined it up on the ceiling as Hillary had told her to do. It was a mama horse and her baby foal. They were brown and black and white and it was brilliant and amazing shown on the ceiling.

"Ok now," instructed Hillary, "tell us a one sentence story."

"What do you mean Hill?" asked Elka.

"Tell us one sentence, anything, real or silly or whatever about what you see in those horses," replied Hillary.

With a breath and a moment of thought, Elka said, "Mama Horse and her new young filly galloped to the pasture one day…"

"Stop!" interrupted Hillary.

"Well that was short!" exclaimed Elka.

"Yep. Sorry. You'll see. Keep yours up there," laughed Hillary. "Now Ava, you put up a template and tell a one sentence story."

Ava lit her torch and grabbed one of her sheets in the dark. She shone the light through it and illuminated the ceiling next to and overlapping Elka's. It was rainbows. And one of the rainbows overlapped Mama Horse's hind end.

Ava giggled and told this story, "And Mama Horse pooped out a rainbow!"

"Ava!" hollered Hillary, totally starting to laugh.

All five girls roared with shrill giggles of laughter so loud it almost made Mama and Papa jump out of their kitchen chairs. Mama was reading her newest book and Papa was melting together the ends of some wires he called 'soldering'.

Sparks, who was tuckered out for the day and had fallen asleep on the end of Ava's sleeping bag dreaming of cats, jumped, confused and not quite awake, into the air and began jumping all over the girls and yapping his ear-splitting bark and doing Sparks Circles, shooting pillows and blankets everywhere until he realized there was not a cat to chase!

The girls laughed so hard, especially Ava and Elka, that their templates were shaking and it looked like the horses and rainbows were in the middle of an earthquake.

Mama and Papa were curious enough to come to the bottom of the stairs and listen to the laughter and see if they could figure what it was all about. Smiles grew on their faces as all they caught were individual words that could hardly be understood between all the laughs. *Rainbows... poops... Mama Horse... hahaha...* Not able to even begin to figure out what was going on, they went back to their books and soldering with such joy and smiles at the warm, safe fun going on upstairs.

When the horse and rainbow earthquake was finally over as the girls wiped the laughter tears from their eyes, it was Luisa's turn.

She randomly picked one of her sheets and shone a collection of rectangles and boxes that might just even look like a row of houses or barns.

Each girl had to repeat the story before them, then add their own line.

Luisa added, "and it scared the little filly so much she ran back into the barn…"

More peals and shrieks of laughter as the story became more and more absurd.

By the time the story made it all the way around the circle and all five girls had lights and shadows and colors and shapes and animals dancing on the ceiling, the story went something like this:

Mama Horse and her filly went galloping out to the pasture one day. Mama Horse pooped out a rainbow. It scared her little filly so much she ran back into the barn. Mama Horse was so embarrassed about pooping a rainbow and scaring her baby she did somersaults and handsprings all the way back to the barn. When she got there, her filly was taking a bath and eating bacon and eggs.

And that was only the first round of what Hillary called the *Charades of Light* game. Over the next hour the girls played four more rounds until their sides hurt from laughing, and Sparks finally went downstairs to get some peace and quiet and sleep.

It was midnight before eyes started getting sleepy and Elka rolled over to begin falling asleep.

"One last thing before we fall asleep," whispered Hillary.

Elka roused herself a little and said, "What is it?"

"Tinsel and I want to show you all something. Come to the South Lookout window," replied Hillary.

They all rolled out of beds and sleeping bags and bumped shins against tables and sofas as they worked their way through the dark where Hillary and Tinsel were waiting.

Hillary was to the far east end of the windowed wall. Tinsel was at the far west.

"Hold hands," instructed Tinsel.

All five girls clasped hands forming a long line of friendship from one end of the room to the other. All of them had their own good view of the Southern Lookout bouldery woods, which were barely visible by the crescent moon. Their eyes were already used to the dark, but still not much could be seen.

"Close your eyes. Breath deep," directed Tinsel.

For half a minute all you could hear was the relaxed deep breathing of the five.

"Open your eyes. Be still," said Hillary.

For another half a minute there was silence.

Hillary and Tinsel saw and felt the low blue humming of the Regeneration across the forest floor. It dimly lit the features of the forest. Brighter and brighter you could see a whitish blue cast on tree trunks and moss and boulders and caves. It shone up into tree canopies and broke out towards the stars in the clear sky.

"What do you see Elka?" asked Hillary.

"I see… I see. Well, I can just see. Even with no light other than the slight moon which is not enough."

"What do you see Ava?"

"How am I seeing the trees? An hour ago when I looked out this way it was pitch black dark."

"What do you see Luisa?"

"It's very dark Hillary. I can barely see the tree tops from the small moon."

Hillary and Tinsel looked at each other and thought harder.

Hillary asked again.

"Hold still Elka. What do you see?"

"I see small animals moving. I see field mice burrowing. I see a racoon and her babies. I see a deer and her fawn. I see underground hollows and caves and pools of water," replied Elka.

"Ava, what do you see?"

"I…I…don't understand. I think I see the moss growing. Slowly growing. How can I see that slowly?"

"Luisa, what do you see?"

Luisa was quiet. She could see nothing. She broke her hands free from the line of friends and wouldn't answer Hillary. Tinsel walked to Luisa and offered her arms out. Luisa took Tinsel's hug. Luisa didn't let go of Tinsel for a long time as Hillary motioned all the other girls back to bed. After Luisa cried for a minute, she went without a word to her sleeping bag and quietly fell to sleep.

CHAPTER SEVEN – Elka's Dream

As Elka snuggled down into her sleeping bag and buried her head into her fluffy goose down pillow, she felt like she was floating. She couldn't help the big smile that crept across her face or remember ever feeling this peaceful and warm. It was like floating in a warm ocean in a world all her own. With her eyes closed, she could see and feel the low, warm blue hum bathing her inside and out as it lulled her into a deep sleep.

She had a dream of suns, stars, time, space and deep heavens. She saw two stars that appeared to be giving themselves up, sacrificing for something great. They gave themselves up gladly and as they died out, a new peace rang out in their place. There was blinding speed across the galaxies.

She saw the earth and beneath it growing in power as the stars died and were reborn. The core went from cold and solid to hotter and then burned yellow-white. The deepest caves glowed blue. She saw new twin stars in the deepest of caves where it was so hot no one could live. She thought she recognized them, maybe someone knew them, but not quite. They reminded her of the goodness of Hillary and Tinsel. They waited there in the deepest cave a long time. Was it months? Was it years? It seemed like a million or billion years or more.

Deep within the white-hot core of the earth she had a vision and a feeling of the strongest love. Wrapped around the white core was yellow that felt like hope and joy sending out waves to the surface where the earth's dirt was cold. The yellow faded into a beautiful glow of orange that felt like it wrapped her in courage and honesty and compassion. Where the orange glow finally began to cool and meet the earth's solid crust there was a soup of loyalty and sympathy and trust and many other good things that would flow with the love through the caves to reach those that needed them and could accept them.

Elka got the impression that these emotions were no longer feelings, but choices. More like actions or tools that could be held in the hand.

Someone was taking care of the sleeping stars. But they didn't look like stars now. They looked like cocoons or boulders. The caretakers looked like climbers, but not climbers, even though they had climbing gear. More like diving, descending down gear. They wore helmets and lamps and boots and ropes. They were like people only much older. Thousands of years maybe. They looked like a mother and a father, a mama and a papa. They smiled at their stars with a purpose in their eyes. Their eyes told of a time of goodness to come to be offered to all people, especially those that had broken hearts.

The mother spoke to Elka. *For a thousand years I could not bear my own child. The stars have healed me. There will be a child. And his name will be Kai'ed. His name means witness. I will give birth to this son. The stars will have a brother.*

All these good things made it up through to the outer cold crust, but here they began to slow down. They could not make it very easily through the cold. Sometimes they could seep up and make their way into the air, and when they came, they came with a low blue hum out from the caves and tubes. But they were the most powerful when they had help from those that knew and believed. But there were not many of those kinds that were like the stars. And even some of those that could bring out the good from inside the earth had a difficult time.

Higher into the air, into the cold mountain tops, hope became less and less. There was no bad there, but there was not much good.

And finally into the black of the space between the stars where there was no earth or air or water or volcano. There was no feeling there at all.

Elka was startled awake by something falling on her. It was jumping all over her. Four paws and a doggy tongue going at her cheeks!

"Sparks!" laughed Elka, still only half awake.

She pushed him off her sleeping bag and tried to burrow down inside where he couldn't get at her in the cocoon, but he was too determined and awake and full of energy. He was like a fox, furiously digging in after a rabbit and when he got ahold of her neck, he tickled her until she was laughing and afraid of waking up the other girls. So much for sleeping in when she was down on the ground in Sparks' territory.

"Ok fine. Come here you little rascal! Maybe you're just cold and need a good place to snuggle."

Sparks curled up deep in the warmth of Elka's sleeping bag nicely against her tummy and quickly quieted down and went back to sleep.

Elka looked up and out the window and could see the clear, deep black sky with diamond stars brilliantly shining. Was it very late at night or very early in the morning? She could hear one of the other girls snoring. She thought it might be Tinsel and she smiled and lay there a long time thinking about her dream, if it was a dream.

****

"Pssst… hey Elka," whispered Hillary from her bottom bunk. "Are you awake?"

"Yes, I've been awake for about an hour. I had a crazy dream."

Hillary popped out of her bed and sat on the floor next to Elka.

"I thought you might have," said Hillary.

"What? Why would you think that?"

"Because I heard you talking in your sleep and you told me what watermelon does to you," smiled Hillary in the dark. "Do you want to tell me about your dream?"

For the next hour, Elka told Hillary all the smallest details of her dream from the beginning to the end. Hillary listened without saying a word, but just nodding her head in the dark.

She told Hillary about Kai'ed.

When Elka was finished telling her story, Hillary remained quiet.

"What are you thinking?" asked Elka.

"I think you had too much watermelon," joked Hillary.

"I don't think this was one of my crazy watermelon dreams."

"Why is that?"

"Because watermelon dreams are always confusing and silly nonsense, like cows playing pianos up on my roof. Or Klix playing jokes and floating our farm out on the ocean."

"And this dream wasn't silly?"

"No Hill. It wasn't silly at all. It's the best dream I've ever had. It was wonderful and I wish that it were real."

"How do you know it isn't real?"

"Well because it was a dream and dreams aren't real."

"Even if dreams don't make sense, aren't some of the things in dreams real?

"What do you mean?"

"If Klix is in your dream, he is real. If cows are in your dream, cows are real. They just don't play pianos on top of your house," said Hillary.

"Oh, I see what you mean," laughed Elka with a light coming on in her head. "I know the earth is real, but I don't know anything about feelings like love being down in it."

"You said in your dream love wasn't just a feeling, but you saw that it was a real and hard thing."

"Yes, Hillary, but I don't know what that means and I haven't seen that for real."

"You have felt love."

"Yes."

"You have seen what love can do?"

"Yes, I have seen it change people."

"A tool can change things," hinted Hillary.

"Yes, but I can hold a tool," said Elka slowly.

"Is it only a tool if you can hold it and see it?" asked Hillary.

"Well, no, not like that," replied Elka.

"Some people say you can't see the wind, but you can still believe in it," suggested Hillary.

"Yes," said Elka, "but that's different. We know from school that air is molecules that are physical and exist, we just can't see them."

"Love is not a molecule, but we know it exists?" asked Hillary.

"Well, yes," replied Elka.

"So how do you know it is real?"

"Because I can see it affect and change people. I can see it cheer them up when they feel sad. I can see it make them feel included when they are lonely," said Elka.

"So it can work on people as if it were a tool and a feeling?"

"Yes, I suppose. I've never thought of it like that. That seems kind of cold thinking about love like a tool. It seems more... more... loving... when you think of it as an emotion."

"How about if you think of it as both? That way you can use it even when you don't *feel* like it."

Elka glowed, "I love the thought of that."

"So it was all just a crazy dream anyway, right?" smiled Hillary.

"I don't think so Hillary. And I think I saw you and Tinsel and your Mama and your Papa there too. How can that be?"

"Oh, now I think you're just being silly," joked Hillary. "How can that be? It was just a dream."

"What if it was more than a dream?" suggested Elka.

"Tell me more about that."

"I saw the low blue hum Hillary. The same as last night when we held hands and I saw the animals in the low forest night. I think it was you who gave me that dream!" exclaimed Elka.

"That's what you think?" said Hillary with a grin.

"Oh Hillary, please please tell me. I can't stand it. Tell me the truth. What was my dream?"

"I can't tell you what it was Elka. No one can ever tell you something like that. You will have to believe and know that yourself."

"I want to cry," said Elka

"Why?"

"Because… because I think I know something bigger than me and it is too much. So much I don't know what to do with it. Help me Hillary."

"I will help you. We will help you. Tinsel and I will help you."

To love is a choice. Make it an action and give it a voice. Speak it gently to those that can hear. Chase away broken hearts and doubts and fear.

They held hands and Elka felt the warm, blue, low hum.

CHAPTER EIGHT – Pumphouse

Sparks soon had enough of this sleeping stuff! There were rabbits to chase, girls to lead, gopher holes to be sniffed out and watery caves to be explored.

Get up! Get up! Play with me! exclaimed Sparks' body as he bounced from bed to bag to couch. Flouncing ears and sharp doggy nails were everywhere.

"Ouch you little weasel!" hollered Hillary, as Sparks' claw caught her leg like a trampoline as he launched off the bed.

"Ok, we're done here as far as Sparks is concerned. Everyone up!" announced Tinsel.

Everyone roused from their sleeping bags and bedsheets, sitting on the floor and edges of beds waiting for their turn to give Sparks his attention. From girl to girl he sprang, wagging his whole body, until he had gotten his fill of petting attention from one, then it was the duty of the next girl in line to pet. Finally Sparks had spent enough energy and sat waiting calmly on the floor for Tinsel to climb down from her top bunk because she had not yet taken her turn giving him his attention. He began impatient Sparks Circles, messing up sheets and pillows and shins.

"You needy little mutt! You're just not going to let me get away with not petting are you?!" as Tinsel hopped down and Sparks gave his last bit of wagging energy to her. She rolled on the floor with him as he wet her cheeks and tickled her neck with his nose and kisses and she hugged him and laughed.

"Quick! Come here everyone!" motioned Hillary as she was standing back at the South Lookout where they had all been the night before. She could just begin to see something down in the forest.

"Tinsel, hold my hand," said Hillary.

Together the two of them could clearly see something they had not been able to see the night before, and they began to get very excited.

"What is it? What is it?! I want to see!" exclaimed Ava.

"What do you see Ava?" asked Hillary.

"The sun coming up through the trees and rocks and forest," answered Ava.

"How about you Elka?"

"The same. Nothing else really."

They didn't ask Luisa because they didn't want her to feel bad, and Luisa didn't offer any questions either.

"Hold hands everyone," said Tinsel.

All the girls joined Tinsel and Hillary's hands at the windowpane and looked intently south. Their vision became sharper together and they could clearly see a hidden entrance to the South Igneous Cisterns glowing like a ripe mushroom. Except for Luisa.

"I see a glow. I see a delicious brow bubbling thickly sliced buttery glow," said Hillary licking her lips.

"I see it," replied Tinsel.

"The Trilliums are back in season!" shouted both Tinsel and Hillary.

"I see it too! What is it?" asked Elka.

"It's the Trilliums. The Trillium Mushrooms," replied Hillary. "They are Mama's favorite to fix and ours to eat, and they only grow twice a year for a few days. Once in late winter and once in early autumn when the cold is just right and the cistern water levels are perfect. Not empty and not too full."

"What are the cisterns?" questioned Ava.

"They are the underground water holes or what we call the swimming pools of the deep," replied Tinsel. "During winter they are too deep and wet and dangerous, and during summer they are too dry and so steep. And the Trilliums grow quickly and only last a few days before they are gone again."

"Why are you so excited about them?" asked Elka.

"Because they slice and fry up thicker and juicier and yummier than any steak you've ever seen!" exclaimed Hillary. "They are a rare treat - buttery and soft inside. Mama seasons them and fries them hot and quick to crisp the outside and tender the inside. We have to go spelunking for them today or we'll probably miss them."

"I'm not going," whispered Luisa, so quietly only Tinsel could barely hear.

"What did you say Luisa?" asked Tinsel.

Luisa replied, a little louder, "I don't believe you."

"What are you talking about?" asked confused Tinsel.

And now Luisa blurted out, "You are all being horrible to me and I don't like any of you! This pretending and playing a big joke on me is mean!"

"Luisa, I still don't understand what you are talking about," said Tinsel, *though she was beginning to have an idea.*

"All this pretending about seeing animals and moss growing and secret mushrooms. It's a lie! Why are you picking on me? What did I ever do to you?!" yelled Luisa as her red face and swollen eyes began to cry. "I want to go home! Have your mom get my mom to pick me up now!"

All the girls sat back wide-eyed mouth shut. They had no idea this was building up in Luisa and it came as a total shock. They looked around at each other not knowing what to do.

Then slowly Hillary spoke, "Luisa… we aren't picking on you. We aren't playing a game."

Luisa's eyes were fixed on the ground and her tears fell to the carpet as she sat on the edge of Hillary's bed. Her shoulders were shaking as she cried inside, silently holding back the crying sounds.

Hillary sat down next to her and put her arm around Luisa's shoulder. Tinsel sat on the other side of her and tried to take her hand, but Luisa pulled it away.

Hillary said, "Luisa, the things we saw are real and I can show you if you go with us. We can show you the Trilliums and you can see for yourself that they are real."

Through her crying voice, Luisa said, "Oh I believe you can show me the mushrooms. I'm sure they're there. But you already knew that and are just pretending to somehow see them." And she pulled away from Hillary's hug. "Let me go! I want to go home."

Elka came and knelt in front of Luisa and took her hands.

"Look at me Luisa."

Luisa looked her in the eyes and didn't pull her hands away.

"They are telling you the truth," said Elka lowly and gently. "I have seen these things and have had a dream. You can trust them."

Luisa was quiet and thought for a moment. Then she said, "But what if I don't trust you? And if I don't trust you how can I trust them?"

"Luisa, sometimes you have to trust even if you can't see for yourself. If you have faith in your friends that love you, maybe you will begin to see for yourself," said Elka.

"I just can't. And I don't even know if I want to. I want to go home now," said Luisa quickly pulling her hands away, getting up and running downstairs.

Hillary followed her downstairs and said, "Mama, Luisa needs to go home. Can you please help her?"

Mama knew by the look in Hillary's eyes and on her face that there was no talking Luisa out of this and it would be wrong to try. She gave a sympathetic smile and said, "I'll take her. Go get her things."

****

The four girls sat together upstairs for a long while not knowing exactly how to feel or what to say. With Luisa gone, there was a sadness hanging in the air. Hillary and Tinsel wanted to do something to change things, but they knew some things were wrong to change and had to work themselves out.

"Everyone gear up! We're going after the Trilliums!" said Tinsel.

Tinsel and Hillary always kept extra spelunking and safety gear. Mama and Papa trusted them. And all their parents gave permission and trusted Mama and Papa.

"Hillary, I'm sorry I forgot to tell you," said Elka. "My mom and dad have to take care of some business today with my grandmother and they need me to watch Klix this morning. I can't stay."

"Oh but you just can't miss the Trilliums! They won't come again for another six months. And you'll miss the most wonderful dinner treat of your life."

"I'm sorry, but my mom will be here in an hour to pick me up," said Elka as her heart dropped in disappointment. She had no idea such a rare adventure would come up overnight.

"Hey! What if Klix comes with us? He has never gone spelunking with us before and he always seems to want to tag along with you."

"He always wants to pester along with me is more like it," said Elka sarcastically.

"Oh gosh, he can't be that bad can he?"

"Well, having a little brother is a lot different than having a twin sister," replied Elka. "But if it's a choice between going home for the day and babysitting the little rat, I'll make a little rat's nest for him here."

"Yay!" shouted Hillary. "I'll let Mama know after you talk to your mom."

And the deal was done. Klix was dropped off an hour later and immediately disappeared into the shop when he saw the swings. He was as slippery as an eel and was about as cooperative as a mule. Both wonderful traits for an eight-year-old tornado.

"If Klix is going with us he needs to get his gear on," said Tinsel. "And I hope he doesn't mind that he has to wear girls boots."

"Klix, get over here! We want to get going," hollered Elka to her sibling.

By now he was no longer in the half-finished workshop, so Elka's yelling in that direction was not doing much good.

"Where did that little brat go?!" said Elka in an angry defeated voice.

And Sparks began Circles.

"Elka, let's not let Klix ruin our spelunking adventure," said Hillary. "If he is going to come with us, we need to remain calm and try to understand him and get him interested in what we are doing."

"That's easy for you to say. You don't have to chase him every time you watch him. Or clean up his messes. Or go find the cat he let out the door on purpose or…or…or… He's only been here five minutes and I wish I had just gone home."

Sparks took off and began a non-stop rapid fire set of Sparks Barks, "Bark, bark, bark, bark, bark, bark, bark!"

By now Elka was almost in tears and sat on the porch steps with her face in her hands.

"It can't be that bad, can it Elka?" questioned Hillary.

"Uh…girls," muttered Ava, who up to now had remained pretty quiet as she got to know her new friends.

"Just a minute Ava," said Hillary.

Sparks was now a loud crazy frenzy of continuous Sparks Barks and running frantically in big circles around Papa's half-finished workshop.

"Um…Hillary…Hillary!!" said Ava raising her voice urgently.

"What is it Ava?" said Hillary, sensing her raised voice.

"Look there! Smoke coming out from behind the shop!"

All four girls began sprinting toward the half-finished workshop when Hillary yelled to Tinsel, "Go find Papa!"

Tinsel quickly turned directions and bolted towards the side door hallway entrance to the house. She found Papa taking an early morning nap on the living room couch which he often did after his second cup of coffee on a Sunday.

"Papa!" shouted Tinsel.

Papa let out a loud startled cry as he bolted upright on the couch kicking over the half full cup of coffee sitting on the floor next to him.

"Tinsel! You scared the dirt out of me! What the heck is going on?!"

"Smoke! Fire! Something out back!" was all Tinsel could get out.

Papa had heard enough even though it didn't make sense to him yet and was on the run without taking time to put his boots on. Out the side door and off the porch on the run, Tinsel was in hot pursuit right behind him. He headed right for the smoke he immediately saw coming from around back of his half-finished workshop.

As Papa and Tinsel rounded the back corner of the shop, they saw what Hillary, Elka and Ava already knew. There were flames licking eight feet up the side of the half sheeted wooden back wall of the shop. A pile of tinder sticks Papa had been saving to start fires in the pot belly wood stove he was planning on installing in the shop for heat in the winter was all ablaze.

Tinsel was the fastest runner. Papa shouted to her, "Tinsel, go throw on the circuit breaker for the well!"

Last month Papa finished the electrical and pump work on a new well he dug to supply the shop. It had a full bathroom with shower he installed so he could clean up out there before coming in the house. But it was not in use yet and only had a regular garden hose installed to the pump house temporarily.

Tinsel loved electrics just like Papa. He was always teaching her things about electricity and wiring and in fact she had given him a hand running the underground wires to the shop and the pump house. She knew exactly what and where the breaker was. Like a flash she ran through the house, past Mama who was almost thrown against a wall, to the utility room where she found break number 21/23 and flipped it to the on position.

Mama didn't even ask. She knew whatever was going on was too important and the best thing to do was just follow. On the way back out, Mama caught on to Tinsel's tail and made tracks with her out the side door and towards the pump house. Mama saw Papa reeling out a hose and saw the smoke and right away knew what was going on for the most part.

Before Papa even got the hose completely unrolled, Tinsel knew to flip the main switch in the pump house to begin the water flow.

50 gallons of water and ten minutes later, all seven people and one dog stood staring at the smoldering twigs and black charred wall.

When heartbeats began to slow down, four girls all turned to Klix whose eyes were wide open in fear. Mama and Papa saw their stares and began to figure out who probably was responsible for the flames.

Not wanting to jump at guessing, but looking towards Klix, Papa asked, "Can anyone here tell me what just happened?"

"I have a pretty good idea," chimed Elka pointing at Klix.

"It wasn't me!" sounded off Klix, dropping something to the ground and covering it with his foot, hoping that no one would notice.

"What was that?!" accused Elka.

"Nothing. Just a twig," snapped Klix.

Coming at Klix, Elka pushed him out of the way so hard he stumbled and fell down. On the ground where the heel of his left boot had been, was a pack of matches.

"Then what is this?!" cried Elka. "What have you done?!"

"That's not mine!" yelled Klix.

"Mr. Spelunker, I'm so sorry," said Elka. "My dad caught Klix two weeks ago playing with fire in our back yard and he said he would never do it again."

"Klix, what do you have to say about this?" questioned Papa.

"I didn't do it!" protested Klix.

"Klix, your sister says you were caught playing with fire two weeks ago, you have matches here now, and we just had a fire with you alone behind the shop. Is that right?" asked Papa.

Klix would not answer and just stared at the ground digging the toe of his boot into the dirt.

Papa turned to the girls. "Why don't you girls go get us some of those Trilliums for dinner and Klix can stay here with me."

"Really Papa?!" exclaimed Hillary.

Hillary and Tinsel smiled and thought what a good Papa they had.

"Are you sure Mr. Spelunker? You don't want to call my parents?" asked Elka.

"We will surely talk to them later, but there is no pressing need to ruin their plans with your grandma today. There's nothing they can do at this moment," said Papa patiently.

"Oh thank you Papa!" cried Tinsel, jumping up and down and hugging the other girls.

"Let's go! Back to the house for the rest of our gear," exclaimed Hillary.

The four friends ran back to the house where they finished tying up high boots and harnesses, backpacks and helmets. Lastly they raided the refrigerator for waters and snacks.

CHAPTER NINE – Trilliums

The entry to the South Igneous Cisterns was a half mile away to the south of the girls' Lookout Mountain home.

Along the way, Elka felt anger and frustration about Klix. There was excitement about the finding of the Trilliums from Hillary and Tinsel. There was mystery and curiosity from Ava about the whole thing. And there was delight from Sparks just to be bounding around the girls in circles and chasing the occasional squirrel.

Climbing over boulders and jumping over tree roots is fun when you are all alone. When you are with the best of friends, it is even better. A boulder becomes a contest. Who can get over faster? Who can jump off it farther? How many can fit on it at one time without knocking others off? Who can defend their boulder as Emperor of the Hill? All these questions needed answers and the girls got their hearts racing and faces red and smiling answering them all. Tinsel liked to race ahead and be the first to the boulder. Elka and Ava ran after her like they were playing follow the leader. Hillary liked to let Tinsel go out ahead. She enjoyed seeing Tinsel's excitement at finding the biggest, steepest boulders and showing off a little. She liked to walk a little slower and see the other girls arrive at the boulder to challenge Tinsel's abilities. Usually by the time she got to the climb, the other girls had scaled it and their faces were glowing with pride to be able to keep up with Tinsel.

Soon they arrived at what the girls called the *Swing Clearing*. Here Tinsel and Hillary had discovered two huge ten-foot boulders that were very difficult to climb. They were about 20 feet apart, and just to the side was a huge Ash tree with a main limb hanging out just between the boulders. It made a perfect place where the girls had tied two ropes with handholds hanging down between the boulders. They would grab a rope and climb one of the boulders. Hanging tightly to the handhold loop, if you kicked off hard enough with your foot you could swing all the way over and land on top of the other boulder.

Tinsel was first and showed Elka and Ava how to do it. She made a loud *Whoooo-Hoooo!!* as she flew through the air and lighted on top of the other massive rock. Elka and Ava were a bit shocked and hung their mouths open unable to say anything.

Tinsel said, "Elka, your turn!"

"Are you kidding me? I'll kill myself!" shouted Elka.

"No you won't. Hillary and I will help you. Trust us."

Elka felt a blue wave of trust and friendship flood through her and she couldn't hold back the deepest friendship smile that crept across her face. Holding on and kicking off, a rush of energy shot through her and even though she knew she was safe, it was a big scare and a little bit of a scream snuck out.

"Oh my goshhhh….!!! Was all she could yell as she swung the huge gap. As she approached the top of the other rock, Tinsel grabbed her around the waist to steady her on the rocky perch. "I think I'm going to faint," she laughed.

They all took turns trading ropes and yelling so loud the forest animals thought they were crazy and ran the other direction.

"Ok, ready for the next challenge?" grinned Tinsel.

"What's that?" replied Ava.

"Well, why do you think we have two ropes tied up here instead of just one?" asked Tinsel.

"No Tinsel!" blurted out Hillary. "That's dangerous even for you and me. We can't let others do it."

"Oh come on Hill. Don't be a scaredy-cat"

"Tinsel, No! Mama and Papa don't even want us doing that," cried Hillary.

"Well why don't we just let Elka and Ava decide?"

By now Elka and Ava were very curious and insisted on knowing what Hill and Tins were arguing about.

"We sometimes play a game called *Bruised Faces*," laughed Tinsel.

"What the heck?!" said Elka, scrunching up her face.

"Tinsel, *NO!*" demanded Hillary.

"It's just a joke name we call the game because one time Hillary and I both swung from opposite rocks at same time. We smashed into each other, banging our bodies hard, but at the same time our heads and cheeks. We hit so hard we bruised our cheeks. So we call it *Bruised Faces*."

"I don't like the name of that game," joked Ava.

"Well the point of the game is not really to smash faces. It's to *avoid* smashing faces," pointed out Tinsel. "Mama and Papa don't love the name of the game either, but they thought it was a little funny. At least we didn't call it *Broken Faces*."

The girls all laughed at that and agreed.

"Here, Hillary and I'll show you," said Tinsel.

"Not," chimed in Hillary.

"Oh come on Hilly. We've done it lots of times now with no bashing. That was just the first time. Just show Elka and Ava. It doesn't mean they have to do it."

Tinsel could be so relentless sometimes that occasionally Hillary would give in against her better judgement. Sometimes that was ok, sometimes that worked out badly.

Hillary climbed to the north rock with her rope. Tinsel climbed to her south rock. Hands were holding on tight.

Together they cried, "One… Two… Three… *Bruised Faces*!!!" leaping off their perches, pushing hard. Ava and Elka laughed at their battle cry. Hillary went hard to the left and Tinsel wide to the right. In a long circular arc they both easily missed each other by a long shot and made it safely to their opposite perches.

Elka and Ava hollered victory cries to see such a thing.

"Are you ready to do the tornado?" cried Tinsel.

"Oh that? Sure, we haven't done that for a while."

This time they yelled, "One... Two... Three... *Tornado*!!"

Both leaping in a similar arc as before, but not quite so hard to be able to make it all the way to the other rock. Instead they swung in wide circles around each other like on a merry-go-round. Their ropes began twisting together in a spiral and wrapping and wrapping, pulling Hillary and Tinsel closer and closer together. The closer they came the faster they spun, like an ice skater pulling their arms in, greatly increasing their speed.

Now Ava and Elka could see why they called it *The Tornado*. By the time Hill and Tins finally met in the middle they were flying so fast if they had let go they would have flown ten feet through the air! Finally they met in the middle, grateful that they were wearing helmets or they would have gotten bumped skulls and bruises. Twisted together they were five feet up in the air and gracefully started descending as they twirled, unwinding slowly to the ground.

They released their ropes and fell to the ground pretending to be exhausted, but really just entertained and quite happy with their performance. And of course all the looks and hollers they were getting from Ava and Elka, who were thoroughly impressed.

Ava and Elka both were able to swing from rock to rock after that, and the four of them entertained themselves for an hour. But neither of them was willing to do *The Tornado* yet!

The whole time, Sparks showed disapproval that he wasn't able to do the Tornado by doing repeated Bark Flips. He ran at the big boulder that he couldn't climb, jumped as high as he could up it, kicked off into a back flip and let out a single, loud, baying *BARK!*, landing successfully on his all fours. Again and again Sparks did his Bark Flips until the girls thought that earplugs would have been a good thing to keep in their backpacks.

"Let's get going troops!" said Tinsel finally. "We have Trilliums to hunt and it is almost lunchtime."

****

"Come with me Klix," said Papa.

Klix felt panic and didn't really want to follow Mr. Spelunker, but he knew he didn't have any other good choices. His only other choice would be to call mom and dad and that would be trouble for sure. Maybe Mr. Spelunker had something less scary in mind.

They went in the house and Mr. Spelunker motioned for him to sit on the couch in the bright living room. Papa disappeared into the kitchen, returning with two glasses of ice-cold lemonade and cookies. He left the room again, going into the study, returning with a big binder book.

Klix studied Mr. Spelunker's face and strangely didn't see any anger, frustration or even disappointment. But he was still a little worried.

"Have a cookie or three Klix," said Mr. Spelunker with a good smile on his face.

How could he be so nice after what just happened? And I lied to him about starting the fire. And he knows it. What the heck do I do now?!

"Klix, how did the fire start?" asked Papa.

He didn't ask me if I started the fire. He asked me how the fire started... he knows for sure.

"I don't know," stammered Klix.

"Klix, how did the fire start?" asked Papa again.

Darn it. He knows. Why is he being so calm and nice? Dad would have punished me by grounding already.

Klix was quiet this time. Mr. Spelunker didn't say a word. He always had the patience of an Elephant and the kindness of a Golden Labrador. Papa could always out wait you no matter how long you were silent. And the silence was deafening. And he knew that too.

Klix still did not want to admit what he had done, so he decided to just say, "I think you know."

Papa knew Klix needed to say the words so he could be set free from his guilt.

"You tell me Klix."

Almost a minute passed before Klix could finally change *I think you know* to, "I think you know I did it."

Papa smiled and messed up Klix' hair. Klix let out a little smile. *Why was he being so nice after what I did?*

"Let me show you something," as Papa pulled out the big binder.

Papa flipped through the many pages which Klix now realized was a scrap book or a photo album of some sort. He found the page he was looking for and handed the open book to Klix.

"What do you see Klix?"

"It looks like some black and white pictures of a forested area. And I see… a burned down house and trees," replied Klix. "Where are these pictures from?"

"I love history, geology and archaeology," began Papa. "When we bought this house 20 years ago, I was curious so I did some research in town at the history society. The historian knew about this property and found these pictures for me."

"Those burned pictures are of this property?" whispered Klix.

"Yes they are. There was a big fire here 30 years ago. It wasn't caused by people… or anyone playing with fire. This one was caused by lightning hitting the barn. It completely burned down their barn and most of the house before the rain put the fire out."

"That's terrible Mr. Spelunker," winced Klix.

"There's more Klix. Three horses and their milk cow died in the barn."

Klix looked away. Out the window to see where that barn had been and where those poor animals had died.

"The owners, their last name was Spanning, rebuilt the house, but could only stay for another ten years before having to sell the house because the memories of the fire were too terrible for them."

"I can see how sad it would be to lose those animals," said Klix, "but I don't think it would be so bad for me I would have to move."

"I agree. But you see, there is something I haven't told you. Their four-year-old son was sleeping in the back of the house where the flames leapt from the barn. By the time the smoke woke them up, it was too late…"

Klix' eyes were as big as saucers as he fidgeted on his cushion. He couldn't look at Papa anymore. He became motionless and stared at the floor without a word.

Papa was never one to say what you could figure out for yourself. He let Klix think as he went and put his photo binder away.

When Papa came back he headed for the side door and Klix knew instinctively to follow him. Without a word, they went to the shop. Papa handed Klix gloves and pointed to a shovel and wheel barrow. Klix grabbed the shovel and barrow and followed Papa around back where Papa began shoveling charred sticks into the barrow.

Klix did the same.

****

Running, skipping, tumbling and jumping their way through the remaining woods to the South Igneous

Cisterns the girls got at least a few barked shins and scrapes.

Thinking that her jump was bigger than the tree stump in front of her path, Elka leapt into the air only to catch her boots on the top of it. Flying headlong into a metamorphic shale patch, the rough edges of the rock which had crushed into gravel over time were not kind to her hands which she shoved out in front of her just in time to catch her fall. Coming to a scraping halt and almost hitting her face on the ground she let out a cry and was frozen on her hands and knees waiting for the pain to kick in or for her body to tell her where it was hurt. The only thing she knew for sure was that she had ripped the skin off the palms of her hands.

Hillary, Tinsel and Ava, who had all been following close behind, saw the whole thing happen and winced in pain just seeing Elka fall.

They approached Elka and waited a moment for her reaction. Elka lifted her left hand to find the heel of her palm torn. She put that one back and examined her right hand. It was bleeding just as bad. She put it back down and just rested there for a moment.

Hillary and Tinsel came near to Elka to comfort her. As they neared her, the ground beneath her bloodied hands pulsated a glowing red and all three of them felt the ground slightly tremble. Shocked, Tinsel and Hillary looked into each other's eyes. Nothing like this had ever happened outside of their little family.

"Are you ok?" asked Tinsel.

"I think so. Help me up," replied Elka.

Hillary pulled healing tapes out of her backpack and bound Elka's hands.

We need to talk to Mama and Papa about this thought Hillary to Tinsel.

"Are you ok to go on?" asked Hillary.

"My hands feel like new with this tape on," smiled Elka, "and I wouldn't miss Trilliums for the world."

Within minutes they were finally at the South Igneous Cisterns secret opening. Hillary and Tinsel held hands with Elka and Ava and they could see it too.

"Why didn't we see this before?" asked Ava.

"Because you were looking with your *eyes*," winked Hillary.

Sparks startled them all by launching into a sudden flurry of Sparks Circles.

"What's up with him?" asked Ava.

"Check the Southern sky," thought Hillary. *"I'll check the Northern."*

"Got it." thought Tinsel.

"Look!" shouted Tinsel frantically pointing to the Southern sky. "Krash Krows! It's a murder of Krash Krows! Get into the caves…quickly!"

Within seconds the air was filled with flapping and crashing as angry, huge Krows were dropping and dive-bombing from the sky. Slamming into rocks and trees, breaking branches and sending stones flying, wings and sharp beaks were everywhere they looked.

The largest Krow, the King Krow, crashed down on Sparks. Grabbing Sparks in its sharp talons, Sparks letting out a blood curdling painful yelp, it flapped it's dark wings as hard as it could, but could only slowly begin to lift Sparks' fifteen pound body.

Hillary never liked to hurt any creature, no matter how mean or cruel that animal appeared to be. But here she had no choice and no time for a better plan. Jumping quickly to action before it was too late, Hillary leaped and fearlessly grabbed the great black tail feathers of the attacker. The King Krash Krow refused to let Sparks go. Hillary furiously yanked side to side and ripped out all the King Krows tail feathers. With a screech, the King Krow dropped Sparks. Without its tail, it could no longer fly and began screeching and running in circles, then ran off into the Southern Woods. The other Krows dropped to follow their King and ran with him off into the woods.

Stumbling and fighting to get free from the attack from the sky, Hillary and Tinsel held back the vines covering the entrance and pulled and shoved Elka and Ava and Sparks to safety, entering the tunnel opening which was like a big hole in the ground with descending rocky stair steps.

They recovered their senses, lit their torches and counted their injuries. The Krash Krows had not scored any direct hits on the girls and the only injuries were from tripping and cuts and scrapes in the hurried fight to get to safety. Nothing several bandages couldn't take care of. Sparks was still in a frenzy of Sparks Circles, but suffered no wounds from his near capture.

When at last everything settled, Ava asked in a quiet voice, "What… was… that…?"

"Those were the Krash Krows," explained Hillary. "They come from the far south near the Willowlands where you find the Willow Wolves. There are few animals that are bad, but there are just a few."

"Why did they try to attack us?" asked Elka

"For the reason that your hands warmed and glowed and trembled today. You are an Initiate… a Regenerate. They are the Entropia. The destruction of good."

"You're scaring me Hillary."

"You are fine with us. And we know you will get stronger to protect yourself. Now we know you are an Initiate."

And that was enough for Elka for now. She trusted Hillary with her life.

****

For the first 30 feet or so they were able to walk and crawl on hands and feet. The tunnel began getting so steep Hillary and Tinsel pulled ropes out of their backpacks and secured them to the walls. Tinsel joined up with Ava and Hillary partnered with Elka. Hillary zipped Sparks safely and securely into her backpack. Safely roped together, the crew began to descend and rappel, kicking off the walls.

Tinsel and Hillary knew it was the wrong time of the year to get past the first cistern with all the rain they had been having. They stopped just short of the water, free hanging in the air. The tunnel had opened up into a large cave which was full of water all the way to the edges with no shoreline. By now all four girls had lit their helmet torches and were amazed at the huge body of underground water. It was like an Olympic sized pool. It was very still like a mirror. There was no flow like the Ravenous River. If you were to stay there for hours you would see the water level drop an inch as the water filtered back into the earth to be purified into the deep aquifers. But this is where and why the Trilliums grow.

As the water level dropped over the last day, the cistern exposed the sedimentary rock levels which could hold water only for about two days before drying out. And the temperature was a perfect fifty-five degrees.

"Look! Look just a couple inches above water level all around the pool," said Tinsel excitedly.

As their eyes adjusted, Elka and Ava pointed their headlamp torches all around the cistern walls. Slowly they began to see what looked like roundish cones about the size of softballs all around. Hundreds of them. Maybe thousands!

It finally occurred to Ava, "Are those the Trilliums?"

"You got it!" shouted Tinsel.

Tinsel pulled a square rubber box out of her backpack. Pulling its cord and throwing it into the cistern water it instantly began to unfold and expand. Within a minute it had grown to the size of a small rubber raft just big enough for the four girls.

"Climb in!" said Hillary.

The four of them tightly scrunched into the small dinghy-like craft and began paddling with their hands around the cistern walls.

Hillary gave them each a satchel from her backpack, "Gather until the bag is full, but no more. That will feed us all tonight."

"Why don't we collect more for another meal or to sell to other people if these are so wonderful?" asked Ava.

"Because Mama and Papa taught us we only take what we need for the one meal. And we are not in this to make money, just to enjoy this treat the earth offers at this moment. Besides, the Trilliums only last for a day after you pick them before they rot," smiled Hillary.

They paddled and picked for an hour until their satchels were full.

The trip back up the tunnel was more work than Elka and Ava were used to and they needed a lot of strength from Hillary and Tinsel.

Mama and Papa were amazed at the harvest of Trilliums the girls brought home. There were so many that Mama decided Papa could have half of them to try out on the barbeque. Papa had always wanted to try that out, but they never had enough to spare for his experiment. Papa was like a little kid firing up his barbeque and mixing his herbs and spices. Mama just smiled at what a little kid he could be. It didn't take much to make him happy.

Klix was pretty quiet the whole evening, but he felt better. Elka didn't ask him any questions. She sensed that Mr. Spelunker had taken care of things.

Mama hot and fast fried up the thickly sliced Trilliums. She seasoned some savory and some sweet and some sour and battered others. They melted in your mouth as buttery, flaky and crispy. She had sides of coleslaw, biscuits with bacon and sautéed greens of kale and asparagus.

Papa barbeque roasted Trilliums, corn on the cob and skewers made of pineapple and red and green peppers.

That afternoon, the Spelunkers and their friends enjoyed the Trilliums more than any other time before. Elka and Ava's moms and dads were invited over in time for dinner and there was more than enough to share. It was good to have friends that could connect with the earth.

As the dusk set across the reddening western sky, Elka asked Hillary, "What does it mean to be an Initiate?"

CHAPTER TEN – Red

The Trillium dinner had been such a success, it left the whole family with a warm afterglow of feelings for a week.

But there was still work to be done.

Mama and Papa are always hard workers. They know that honest hard work and often a spot of good timing is the way to stay ahead. And they taught this to their stars.

"Hey there Tinsel-toe," quipped Papa.

"Papa!" laughed Tinsel. "What is it?"

"Do you remember a certain slippery slide down a certain set of stairs yesterday morning that made some nicely Tinsel-footed holes in our nice drywall?"

"Um… yes Papa," said Tinsel, furrowing her eyebrows.

"And do you remember me letting you off the hook Saturday so you could have your Sleepover Extravaganza?"

Tinsel figured out very quickly that this was headed towards a wall repair. But it was almost 8 o'clock at night on a Sunday, about an hour from her normal bedtime, and she was bushed from two hard days of activity.

"Papa…" began Tinsel, but stopped short of finishing the sentence she knew wouldn't do.

"Tell you what Sweetie. The part we need to do tonight will only take a half hour. But it is an important step because it needs a first coat of mud which will take 24 hours to dry. So it can be working overnight while we sleep and we'll get all this work done just by sleeping," said Papa with a smirk.

"Papa, I know *YOU* believe what you are saying, but I'm not buying this *work while you sleep thing* as a real bonus," grinned Tinsel.

"While you were finishing dishes I got all the tools ready near the bottom of the stairs. The keyhole saw, the backers, the drywall, the screws, the drill, the tape, the knife and the mud."

Just like Papa promised, the sawing, cutting, screwing, taping and mudding only took a half hour.

Papa is a good teacher. He knows that a job well done is important, but it is even more important to do a job well with patience and room for mistakes.

Mistakes are easy to fix - broken hearts are much harder, he would always say.

"Papa, I think you know how to do everything," smiled Tinsel.

Papa hugged her, gave her a kiss on the cheek, and shooed her up the stairs to bed.

"Mama and I will be up to chat and say goodnight after I take the tools to the shop," hollered Papa.

Papa bundled all the tools in his arms in one load and made for his half-finished shop. Coming in the side door after putting his tools to bed, he motioned to Mama and they scaled the long stairway to the Citadel where Hillary and Tinsel were just climbing into bed with their favorite books.

Tinsel and Hillary could tell by Mama and Papa's faces this was no ordinary good night.

"Did you girls want to talk to us about something?" questioned Papa.

"What do you mean?" chimed Hillary first.

"We felt something while the two of you were out with Elka and Ava today. We haven't felt something like that for a long time, and we know you want to talk about it," responded Mama. "We know it didn't come from either of you."

Mama and Papa were patient and could wait until after company left, but they weren't willing to let this go until after school tomorrow. This was too important. Hillary and Tinsel knew that.

"It was red Mama," whispered Tinsel.

"Yes, we felt that."

"We didn't touch her either."

"Yes, we felt that too."

"What is it Mama?"

"It is the Initiation. And it's the first time we have seen it since we have been here…for a very long time," explained Mama.

"Why was it red Mama?"

"That is what happens when someone first learns. It is red. Because it is from the core and it is the first feelings. Later on it will grow to yellow and finally blue as the deeper things come on. The Regeneration."

"But why now?" asked Hillary.

"We didn't expect this so soon," explained Papa. "We thought it might be Elka when it happened, but we didn't expect it for years. You girls are our blood so we expect the Regeneration from you, but she has only shared your feelings for two years."

"What does it mean Papa?" asked Hillary.

"It means she trusts you..." paused Papa. "It means that she has seen and is starting to believe in the good that comes from the Earth and by you. It means that her belief is strong enough to begin to stand on its own without you supporting her."

"You know you shouldn't say anything to her except to answer her questions," added Mama. "When you can, answer best with your actions, when you can't, with your words. You know you must not lead her. She has to search and find her place with us on her own."

"We know Mama," replied their stars.

"Last night Elka had a dream," said Hillary.

"We felt that, but didn't have any detail. Tell us," said Mama with a calm smile like she expected it.

Hillary shared Elka's dream and how she believed her.

"We believe her," said Papa.

"How old is her dream Papa?" asked Tinsel.

"You know we are old. Her dream is a thousand years in the making Sweetie," answered Papa.

"Tell us more about the Initiation," said Tinsel.

"Mama and I have only seen it a few times now. Twice when we first came to you and when you two were six years old. We were the first two and you were the second two."

"Tell us about it again. How you found us," said Hillary.

"You are our daughters by blood and by earth," reminded Mama.

"We know Mama. We want to hear again," smiled Hillary and Tinsel.

Mama continued. "It was a hard time for people in the tenth century. We didn't have all the modern conveniences like electricity and running water. But because Papa and I always worked hard and fought any challenge, we had enough to eat and drink and a decent home close to here."

"Was it on this same property we live on now that you bought 20 years ago?" asked Tinsel.

"Yes, it was. Just over by the top of Lookout Mountain higher up where the Raven River spills over," replied Mama.

"It was a time of Kings and Emperors. There were still many nomadic invaders that our land had to watch out for. It was both a time of great poverty and of great wealth. Papa and I were not wealthy, but because we worked hard we had good stores of food and supplies. There were new taxes put on us and the land all the time that made everything we had taxable where it had not been before. The greedy in charge wanted everything. They would have taken almost everything we had and left us starving. Many people were starving already."

"Oh Mama, that sounds horrible," exclaimed Hillary.

"It was honey. We were farmers and didn't have any other skill or trade. We were scared and didn't know what to do about the unfairness of it all. So we decided we would move to the caves for protection and to hide until things got better. The longer we stayed on this land, the more we began to see the caves. At first they were hard to find and almost invisible. But as we hoped and searched and looked for good and rescue, they began to appear to us more and more."

"That sounds scary Mama," added Tinsel.

"At first it was. The Eastern Lava Tube was our best hope. It went deepest into the earth as far as we could tell from previous trips. At that time there were no spelunkers. We were the first. We had to learn ways to climb and descend. We didn't have helmets and got lots of bumps and scrapes on our heads!"

Hillary and Tinsel laughed.

"You think that's funny, huh!? Well!" laughed Mama. "There was a lot to learn. We had to learn what water was ok to drink and what was too acid or too lye. That's how

I learned to love the Trilliums and all other kinds of mushrooms. Some lichen is edible, but not the phosphorescent glowing lichen. The glowing lichen is good for lighting when torches are short in supply. Sometimes we would live high in the caves so we could come out at night and find fruits and vegetables and trap game. Sometimes when we knew marauders, poachers or tax collectors were in the area for longer times, we had to descend into the caves and tunnels, sometimes very deep to avoid getting caught. We became very good at spelunking. Better than anyone else and we were never caught. No one else could go as deep and we could wait them out for months if we had to. We kept supplies deep, deep, where no one could reach."

"Is that why we are so good at spelunking Mama?" queried Tinsel.

"Yes. And you are better than Papa and me because you are daughters of the deep caves. You are naturally born to it."

"We couldn't farm anymore for a long time," said Papa. "We learned to live on very little, coming out into the woods when we needed to, but spending days and weeks learning and mapping and diving deeper and deeper. We hoped daily for the land and the people, even the people who would take everything we had. Eventually we learned that we didn't even need to leave the caves anymore and felt a strong call to the deepest."

"Tell us about the call Papa," interrupted Hillary.

"Well… it was you Hillary… and you Tinsel," and Papa paused… "Or something like you. It was you before it was you. The goodness and the power below were reaching out to our good and telling us that you were on the way. You were already here, but not like now. We were so close to the goodness, and we stayed there for years. After many years we noticed that we were not even getting older anymore."

"That's incredible Papa!" exclaimed Tinsel.

"Yes, it is a wonder. We felt chosen and called. But we still hadn't found what we were looking for after three years. Until we found the Dome of the Deep. You know the place I am talking about. It is the largest of all caves and the center focus of all that is good in this part of the Earth. It is near the border of the crust and the first mantle. And it is hot. We could only stay there after years of slowly getting stronger and stronger."

"Tell us about the Geodes!" blurted Tinsel.

"You're stealing my story Tinsel-beans!" laughed Papa.

"And the Mantle River!" added Hillary.

"Hah!" retorted Papa. "I'm getting there!"

"We were amazed at the size of the Dome and it's secrecy. It was so secret because only we could go there. And it is the size of a small city. And every rock structure you can imagine. It is too deep and hot for the surface ground water to seep all the way down. The stalactites hanging from the Dome are quartz and sapphire crystal. They act like mirrors and glass and prisms. When any light is shown on them, they light up like the sky, but it is a colored light show of a sky. Reflecting brilliant colors and beams from torches and phosphorescent lichen and the Mantle River."

"Tell us about the river!" exclaimed Tinsel.

Papa smiled because he knew the Mantle River was their favorite.

"There is a crack in the mantle that has been there for millions of years or more. The spinning of the Earth causes liquid melted core to flow from one side of the crack to the other, going straight through the cave of the Dome of the Deep. It is why the cave and tunnels above it are so hot. We could never stay in the Dome Cave more than a few hours at a time before needing rest and water. The Mantle River flows thirty feet across at its widest. And it is red and yellow melted hot. The river is so bright you can hardly look directly at it for long. The light casts to the crystalline roof 500 feet overhead and broadcasts brilliant rainbow colors all throughout the Dome. And there is only one place to cross. At the Stone Arch which is a natural underground stone bridge spanning across the Mantle River, arching 30 feet into the air and connecting the ground on both sides."

"What about the Geodes?!" said Hillary with excitement.

"What about them?"

"Aw Papa! Don't keep us waiting."

"Ok, ok. The floor of the Dome Cave is littered with millions of closed and fractured geodes. Round rocks the size of a softball or baseball. They are like eggs. When you crack them, they contain quartz and sapphire and all kinds of beautiful crystals and gems. They are beautiful beyond telling. If you toss a geode into the Mantle River, in a matter of seconds the outer sedimentary rock melts and cracks and explodes. The severe heat from the molten river throws them off in a shatter show of firework glassy crystal light. Hot molten shiny crystals fly everywhere, sometimes almost reaching the crystal ceiling above and coming down in a fire shower. It is a good idea to wear your helmets!" exclaimed Papa.

"Now the best part of all," smiled Mama. "This is where we found our little stars. Among the geodes, near the shore of the Mantle River, we found two geodes the size of large watermelons. We could tell from the melted igneous stone swirl patterns covering them that they come from deep below, formed in the flowing mantle and coming by the Mantle River. And we knew they were different."

"What happened next Mama?" anticipated Hillary, almost shouting.

"That's when we saw the first Initiation. And it was us. By now we had been years in the caves and so close to the mantle and had spent many hours in the Dome of the Deep. We had already noticed increasing connection with the tunnels. And we had started noticing that we could find the best water any time we wanted to, almost just by calling to it. It would appear to us and we felt connected and in power with it."

"That is when we found them," continued Papa. "We found you. What we called the Macro Geodes. When we first found you, as we approached you, the ground began to hum and vibrate and we knew this was something special. Then it happened. We touched them… touched you. And our hands and the ground and you geodes, glowed red. Then we knew we were your caretakers. For more than a thousand years we waited. Time passed by without worry or care. We continued living as before. Still venturing out over time into the forest."

"Mama, didn't you ever get bored or tired of spelunking?" asked Tinsel.

"No Sweetie. To us it seemed like a day as we lived our lives. We no longer made friends or had family above ground. All the people we ever knew eventually passed on. And even though we were now alone as the centuries passed, we felt our purpose with you as so important that we were never unhappy and never felt the need to hurry. Spending time near you told us more and more of the good in the Earth. And we had dreams. Older dreams than Elka's. Dreams of good coming here from far away to help people."

"And what about us now Mama?" asked Hillary.

"Yes. About you now. It is not your time yet, but it is sooner than we thought because of Elka. And now maybe even Ava. We know that whenever there is an Initiation, it is the beginning of a great change."

"What does it mean?" asked Tinsel.

"We don't know for sure. But we do know you are here for good. And where there is good, the greater the good, the greater the bad. We don't know where the bad comes from. Whether it is from the Earth or from the people or from the stars. That we will have to wait and see," replied Mama.

"When will we know?" asked Hillary.

"We just keep doing what we are doing Hill, and it will come to us. We will know it when we see it," smiled Papa.

"You don't seem very worried Papa," commented Hillary.

"Being worried and fighting a battle are two different things Hill. We don't need to worry. Worrying won't help us. Doing the right thing at the right time every time will."

"But that seems so hard."

"Yes, I never said it wouldn't be hard."

"What if it is painful?"

"The fact that it is painful is not a good reason not to do it," smiled Mama.

"I don't know if I can do that Mama," whispered Hillary.

"That's why we are always here for you," finished Mama.

"Will you go with us? Down to the Dome of the Deep?"

"Not for a while," replied Mama.

"Because of Kai'ed?" asked Hillary cautiously.

"What? Who?" said Mama, stunned.

"Elka seemed to tell me in her dream that you would have a son, that Tinsel and I would have a baby brother. And you would name him Kai'ed, which means witness."

Mama and Papa looked at each other with shocked eyes.

After a long, thoughtful pause, Mama smiled and said, "We were just about to tell you girls. We found out this week. It seems Elka has chosen his name for us."

The girls squealed with excitement and celebration. Mama and Papa hugged the girls with elation. Their family, their wonderful family, was going to increase with an unspeakable joy.

"What does is mean Mama?" asked Tinsel.

"We'll find out in less than 9 months Sweetie."

"That brings up a new point," said Papa, pausing until he had everyone's attention. "Elka…she knew about Kai'ed. She could be a *Sayer*. She will have to go through her own vision in the Dome of the Deep at the Stone Arch. But I'm guessing she is a Sayer."

A *Sayer*… pondered Hillary.

CHAPTER ELEVEN – Tetherball

Luisa sat in the very back row in Mrs. Caroline's class. In the last two days she had gone through the crying. Now she was going through the anger. She watched as Hillary and Elka and Ava laughed and shared special secrets before class began. And her anger grew.

Homework assignments were all turned in as class began. Now it was *Weekend Share Time,* as Mrs. Caroline called it. Each Monday, Mrs. Caroline asked for volunteers that wanted to share anything wonderful or difficult or exciting to come up to the front of the class and tell it like they were narrating a story.

Ava shot her up hand immediately, eager to impress Hillary.

Mrs. Caroline smiled and said, "Well I guess Ava is going to be our first *teller* this Monday." *As she would call each volunteer speaker.* And she called Ava to the front and center of class.

"I hope she is nervous and scared and messes up," whispered Luisa to Olivia.

Ava told stories of mystery and caves, underground mushrooms and rope swings and skinned palms and glowing earth, all to the amazement of her classmates, and to the scorn of Luisa.

"Ava, those are some pretty interesting stories, you think?" asked Mrs. Caroline.

"It happened just as I said," replied Ava. "I promise."

"How about instead of a promise, you give us *this is my fantastic memory of what happened instead*," suggested Mrs. Caroline with a forgiving smile.

"But Mrs. Caroline, that's exactly what happened." insisted Ava.

"Lying just like this weekend. And now she's trying to fool Mrs. Caroline," whispered Luisa.

"Ava, I think that is going to be a great start of a fiction story for you to write for our first writing assignment later this week," Mrs. Caroline said to her with a smile and a nod to take her seat.

Ava walked away looking defeated and embarrassed, whispering to Hillary on the way back, "Why didn't you help me? Why don't they believe me?"

Hillary had been there before. When she was younger and before she could keep a secret she had tried to tell others about her adventures, but they always thought she was making it up. And she soon realized that she didn't want or even need to tell anyone. That her secrets were for herself and the other Spelunkers and should be kept that way. *Ava would have to learn that on her own. No one can tell anyone that and have them understand until they go through it themselves. It was always a hard lesson.*

Luisa leaned over to Olivia with an ugly whisper, "Ava is always lying to get attention. It's good that she's embarrassed. It serves her right. You shouldn't be her friend."

Olivia looked at Luisa and into her eyes, which seemed sincere and friendly, but didn't have anything to say.

"Just look at her trying to show off for her friends up there. She hasn't even known them for a week and she is already trying to be the teacher's favorite," whispered jealous Luisa.

"I haven't even met them yet," said Olivia. "They don't seem so bad. Why are you trying to make me hate them before I give them a chance?"

"You just watch Olivia. When we go to recess, Hillary will deny it and you'll know Ava is a liar."

Next, Hillary went to the front of the class and told a different version, which was the truth, but very close to Ava's story. She told of playful jumping in the woods and swinging and of course a wonderful mushroom dinner. But of course, those are things that everyone did without connection to the earth. That is how Hillary told her stories of good things so people could believe them. But that didn't do much good for Ava. In fact, it almost made things worse.

****

The bell rang and it was first recess. Hillary couldn't wait to see Tinsel on the playground, as Tinsel was in Mr. Mueller's class. They met at the tetherball court for their favorite recess fun.

Tinsel and Hillary are so closely matched that it is mostly luck for whoever won between the two of them. But it is skill that made them so good, and almost no one could ever beat them and everyone always wanted to try. They are the rulers of the tetherball court. Of course it helped a lot that Papa built them their own tetherball pole at home and they spent countless hours perfecting their skills. But they are such good sports about it, no one really gets mad about mostly getting beat. Except Luisa.

The only person that often beats Hillary and Tinsel is Luisa's older brother Bradley, or Brad as they call him. Brad can beat them because he was born on the wrong day. The wrong day for school anyway. Brad was born on September 1st and had to start kindergarten when he was five instead of six. If he had been born just one day later, he would have started school one year later. He struggled badly through his first year because many of his classmates had better reading and friendship skills than he did. That made him mostly sad, but sometimes made him a little mad. For a long time he thought it was his fault and sometimes he even felt stupid, and it didn't matter what his teachers or mom and dad told him. The result was always the same. Bad report cards and not many friends.

After Bradley's first year in kindergarten, mom and dad did the hard thing, but the right thing. They had Brad stay in kindergarten for another year. Brad soon realized that when anyone found out, they would wonder if maybe something was wrong with him. And Luisa didn't help at all. She called him names like *Sadly* or *Badly*, or anything she could think of hurtful that rhymed with Bradley.

But really Brad was right where he was supposed to be, and now that he had been held back a year, he had caught up and was bigger and knew more than his classmates. But he never bragged about it or made anyone feel less. He was quiet and strong and hard working. And he never called Luisa names.

After Hillary beat Tinsel, next up was Ava. Hillary wrapped the rope all the way to the ball in less than five seconds. Ava stood there both dumbfounded and impressed with Hillary's victory.

"I wonder what it would have been like to touch the ball just once," joked Ava.

She was beaten so badly that she just laughed and walked off the court. And it wasn't to be mean, but Hillary didn't let people win just to make them feel better.

"Brad, play me!" hollered Hillary.

Brad had been staying off to the side so he could enjoy watching, but he was not in line. Sometimes it made him feel uncomfortable to be bigger and draw attention.

"Why don't you play Luisa. She's in line next," sheepishly smiled Brad.

"Luisa has played the last three times at recess, and you haven't had a chance at all," replied Hillary.

Luisa glared at Hillary and said, "Yeah, go ahead and play *Badly*, oops, I mean Bradley! Someone needs to teach Hillary how to play."

Hillary smiled on the outside but didn't fall for Luisa's trap. On the inside she was starting to feel angry.

"And after you beat her, you should teach that brat Tinsel how to play too!" taunted Luisa.

Hillary's blood began to boil. *You make fun of me all you want. I won't like it but I'll take it. But you hurt my sister and you're going to pay for it,* thought Hillary.

Luisa continued to tease and taunt. She stepped out of line and did a low bow and motioned Brad towards the court like a butler.

"Come on Brad, let's just play," said Hillary trying to relax the situation.

"I'll play just to teach Luisa she can't bully me," whispered Brad.

And he walked to his half of the tetherball court.

Hillary served a surprisingly easy first volley. Brad easily punched the tethered ball right back at her, but with a friendly hit instead of a winning hit. A friendly feeling rushed through both Hillary and Brad at the same time. A feeling that nothing could beat them, not even Luisa's poison. They both realized at once that they would never beat fire with fire. They needed to win Luisa over with friendship. And that didn't mean beating her, it meant not letting her beat them and their happiness.

This round went slowly, as the ball just floated in happy circles around Hillary and Brad's smiles. Sometimes they let it pass them on purpose so the other could have a second hit. Sometimes they launched the ball back on a low, easily caught course. Most games last 30 seconds. This game had gone on for three minutes already. And no one was winning. No one wanted to win.

"What's going on here?" came one puzzled voice from the crowd.

"How come no one is winning?" came a second confused voice.

Finally, Brad caught Hillary's eye and winked at her and shoved his shoulders forward in a powerful jerking motion, pretending to slam the ball hard enough to knock it off its leash, which was his way of hinting to her to hit a hard one and get it over with.

Hillary gave a knowing thank you smile. On the next go-around, her closed fist met the ball squarely on center with one of the hardest knocks Hillary had ever given. The ball exploded into a high circle so far above both their heads they couldn't have reached it with a ladder! In less than four seconds the ball came to a stop tightly wound around the pole at the very top, then began it's slow victory circles, descending back to the bottom of the pole.

Everyone looked at Brad to see defeat on his face, but were surprised instead to find a sparkle in his squinting, smiling eyes that were looking at Hillary. She smiled back.

Tinsel understood what had happened.

"I know what the two of you are doing," said Luisa with cruelty and heat. "I know that game. I can play it too. Of course I could beat everyone if I had my own tetherball court at home."

"Why don't you come over to my house and play with us any time you want and get better?" offered Hillary with a true smile.

"Oh I wouldn't want to do that. It kind of feels like cheating to me," said Luisa with a fake smile.

Hillary could see where this was going, but didn't quite know what to do about it. She didn't really want a silly argument that no one could win. And she didn't really care about winning in the first place.

"Why don't you play Tinsel?" Hillary offered.

"Oh, she's an even bigger cheater than you are," snapped Luisa.

"Don't say that about my sister," said Hillary raising her voice a little now.

"Hillary, it's ok," said Tinsel.

"See Olivia, I told you they were liars and cheaters," whispered Luisa, purposely just loud enough for Hillary to hear. "Especially that Tinsel."

Few things made Hillary's blood boil, and someone picking on her sis was one of them…and Luisa knew that. And Tinsel knew it.

Klix, who was standing right behind Tinsel, decided it was a good idea just then to pull Tinsels hair braids. He didn't know if he was doing it to be funny or to be mean, but it just felt like the right thing at the time. One thing is for sure, he didn't mean to pull it as hard as he did. He jerked on it.

Tinsel wheeled around furiously and wanted to lash out at whoever had yanked her hair. Hillary had already rushed up behind Tinsel and put her hands on Tinsel's shoulders. Elka and Ava both saw the blue glow between Hillary and Tinsel, and they saw Tinsel melt into tears.

Klix shrank back, instantly sorry for his poor choice. "I was just joking. I'm sorry. I don't know why I did that…"

"Klix, back off!" shouted Bradley, as he stepped between Klix and Tinsel and Hillary.

"It's ok Brad. It's done. Tinsel and I are ok," said Hillary.

The recess bell rang. Hillary and her best friends lined up and went back to Mrs. Caroline's class together. Tinsel and Brad returned to Mr. Mueller's class. Klix, Luisa and Olivia lagged behind and returned to their classes.

"I didn't really see Hillary or Tinsel lying today," offered Olivia.

"Oh you wait and see," replied Luisa. "It's either them or me. You have to choose. You want me as your friend don't you?"

"Please don't make me choose Luisa. You might lose and I'm just getting to know you."

Luisa scrunched her eyes at Olivia then ran ahead, leaving Oliva behind as if she had done something wrong.

Back in class, Mrs. Caroline gave her students the next hour to write notes to create a rough draft on the writing assignment she had mentioned earlier.

Hillary's mind was stuck on what had happened on the playground. And she really got stuck thinking about

Brad. How they had connected without a word on winning the tetherball game, and how he had stepped in to calm the fight between Tinsel and Klix's hair-pulling meanness. He didn't have to do that and risk maybe getting himself in trouble if the playground monitor for the morning, Mr. Adder, had stepped in and taken kids to the office. *Why was he being so nice and protective?* She had known him since the first grade and he had never shown interest in her or Tinsel. But it made her feel good that someone else had seen Klix and Luisa's tricks and had stuck up for them.

She thought about it and decided to write him a note that she would give him at lunch recess.

Dear Brad... she started. Then she crumbled the paper up. Even though she had seen Mama start letters that way, it seemed too... too...well, too something. It just didn't feel right.

Hi Brad.

There, that sounded ok she thought.

Hi Brad,

thank you for being nice to me at tetherball. And thanks for letting me beat you. Yes, I know you did. I don't know exactly why, but I know we needed to show Luisa she couldn't get to us.

And thanks for sticking up for Tinsel. I was so angry at first. That's something really hard for me, when someone does something wrong to my family.

Do you like to explore, or do you like the forest and hiking around and going into caves? If you do, maybe you would like to go with me and Tinsel some time?

Your Friend, Hillary

She thought that sounded friendly enough. So she folded the note and put it in her side pocket until she could find Brad later on the playground.

****

Hillary ate lunch quickly. It was one of her favorite meals. Spaghetti with a mini baguette and green salad. It was her favorite because spaghetti sandwiches were her favorite. And to her, baguettes were far better than garlic toast. She took her spoon and shoved it into the end of her baguette and burrowed down to make a deep hollow space. Then she put spoonful after spoonful down the bread rabbit hole until it was stuffed full. The perfect mix of bread and spaghetti all packaged into one hotdog-like work of food art. It didn't last long though. She had three reasons for finishing quickly. First, the quicker she finished, the quicker she could get to the playground for a longer recess. Second, she wanted to get to the tetherball court before the line was too long. And lastly, she wanted to find Brad as soon as she could to give him her note.

Her class was first to the lunchroom today, and she was the second one out to the playground, so the whole place seemed very empty. The only other person to beat her to the playground was Olivia, who was waiting by herself at the tetherball court.

Perfect! She said to herself. And she ran with a huge smile.

"Anyone have this game?" smiled Hillary.

"Um… not that I know," replied Olivia, not realizing Hillary was joking.

"How about you beat me in a match then?" offered Hillary.

"I saw you play earlier and I know I can't beat you," replied Olivia shyly. "Maybe I should let you play someone else."

"Nonsense!" Shouted Hillary, sensing Olivia's embarrassment. "In fact, I'm not playing with anyone except you today. And we'll keep playing until you beat me."

"Well then we may have to play for a very long time," said Olivia starting to feel at ease and smiling just a little.

That was something that Hillary did. When someone was new and feeling alone or without friends, Hillary made them her new best friend.

They played three matches before other kids began to line up for their turn. When Ava and Tinsel arrived and joined the line, they were playing their fourth game.

After Hillary beat Olivia for the fourth time in a row, it was Ava's turn up. Hillary walked off the court with Olivia.

"Where are you going Hillary? You own the court until someone beats you," said Ava.

"You and Tinsel take the court. I told Olivia I would only play with her until she beat me," smiled Hillary.

Olivia stopped and looked at Hillary. "What do you mean *only play with me until I beat you*."

"That's what I said."

"But you gave up the court and we're done playing," Olivia said more like a question than a statement.

"Yes, we're not done. And I'm not playing anyone else until you beat me," grinned Hillary.

"I don't understand. You mean for this recess, or for today."

"No, until you beat me."

"I'm so confused Hillary."

"If it takes you all year or ten years, I will only play with you until you beat me. We will stand in line together with you behind me. When I win the court you will be up next and then I will only play you. If you lose, I will give up the court," explained Hillary.

"That's crazy Hillary. I'm terrible. You'll hardly ever get to play! You can't do that. That will take all your time. You don't even know me."

"By the time you beat me, I'll really know you won't I? And by the way, I have a tetherball at my house and you can come try to beat me there."

Olivia didn't know what to say. She couldn't say anything anyway because the lump in her throat was too big. She didn't know just why, but tears began to well up in her eyes. She had the strongest feeling that she just wanted to give Hillary a hug. Hillary beat her to it and gave her a hug. Hillary gave lots of hugs. A tear fell from Olivia's eye and wet Hillary's shoulder.

"I have something I have to give Brad, and I see him over by the swings," said Hillary.

"Thanks Hillary."

Hillary winked at her and ran toward the swings.

Hillary had not noticed that when she was jumping around at tetherball, her note to Brad had fallen out of her pocket.

Sneaking up behind him, Hillary hollered, "Brad!" Brad nearly jumped, and Hillary nearly laughed, because she had done it on purpose.

"What the heck Hilly!" said Brad, having heard Tinsel call her that before.

"I have something for you," said Hillary, searching her pockets and coming up empty.

A small panic came over her as she said, "I've lost something and I have to go find it. Sorry!"

Luisa picked the note up off the tetherball court and snuck it into her pocket.

Running and searching and retracing her steps, Hillary couldn't find any trace of the note.

She stood there a little worried and completely confused.

The recess bell rang.

****

The next hour would be *Mrs. Caroline's Spelling Bee*, which was every day just after lunch. And the first 15 minutes was word study to prepare for the competition. Hillary loved spelling bee. She loved spelling and reading and writing. But not today. It was hard for her to focus. She had lost the note, and Brad had not gotten the note. It was a double loss.

Luisa watched Hillary searching her pockets and binders and scanning the floor around the room. Luisa grinned.

Luisa unfolded the note and smiled deeply as she read it. She folded it up and slipped it under her speller. She pulled it out and read it again. She smiled again.

By now Olivia had noticed Luisa reading a paper again and again and smiling. "What is that?" Olivia asked.

Luisa pretended not to notice her, but was having extra fun now teasing Olivia with wondering what the note was. Finally she looked in Olivia's direction.

"Can I help you?" she asked Olivia.

Olivia looked away quickly and turned pages in her speller.

"Here," said Luisa, reaching out ever so slowly like she was handing the note over.

Olivia looked at Luisa, then at Mrs. Caroline, then back at Luisa.

"We aren't supposed to be passing notes," whispered Olivia.

Luisa sat there with her hand out. Long enough for Mrs. Caroline to notice.

"Luisa. What is that?" came Mrs. Caroline's voice across to the back of the room.

"Oh, it's just a note," said Luisa, smiling cleverly. "Do I have to read it out loud to the class?"

"No Luisa, you know I don't make my students do that. Just bring it up to me please."

"But I really think I should Mrs. Caroline. It can be part of our spelling bee," said Luisa.

Mrs. Caroline was curious now and wondered if maybe Luisa really did have some new words or at least something for the class.

"This is a little out of order Luisa but if you think it would be good for the class to learn from."

"Oh yes Mrs. Caroline. The class would love to hear this," said Luisa with an excited grin.

"Ok, then please come to the front of the class and we'll begin *Mrs. Caroline's Spelling Bee*."

Luisa unfolded the paper as she approached the front of the class and Hillary had a fright run through her as she thought she got a glimpse of what was hand-written.

She tensed and prepared for…well she didn't know what she was prepared to do.

Luisa cleared her throat and began, "Hi Brad, thank you for being nice to me in tetherball."

"Luisa!" blurted Hillary. The words coming out of her mouth before she could even think about it, and much louder.

Hillary's yell startled Luisa so badly she dropped the note, and Hillary snatched it up before it hit the ground.

The room was so quiet you could hear a pin drop. Everyone knew something dreadful had happened but weren't quite sure what it was.

Mrs. Caroline gave the matter a few seconds of thought and let the room come back to normal, then said, "Luisa, please tell me what that was."

"Well obviously it was a love note from Hillary to her boyfriend Brad," smirked Luisa.

Hillary's face went from a light pink of somewhat embarrassment to more of a beet red of infuriation as she shouted at Luisa, "You know it's not you liar!"

She had done it. Luisa got exactly what she wanted. Hillary had lost control.

"Come with me please Luisa," directed Mrs. Caroline. She escorted Luisa out of the room and to Ms. Porter's principal's office where Luisa was perfectly content to study her speller for the remainder of the day. It had been worth it.

By last recess, through hall passes and secret meetings in the bathrooms, word had spread to Mr. Mueller's class and to Brad about the '*love note*'.

Hillary had already destroyed the note by the time she finally saw Brad at last recess.

"Hillary I heard a rumor, and I'm very sorry you had to go through that," fished Brad.

"It wasn't a love note. I'm so mad and embarrassed. That stupid Luisa!"

"I know. Don't worry about it. What did you want to tell me?" asked Brad.

"I just wanted to thank you for being nice with tetherball and ask if you would like to hike caves with me and Tins sometime out at our house."

"I love hiking, but I have never been in a cave. It sounds fun and I think I would love it. When?"

"Let me ask Mama and Papa tonight and you get permission. And if they all say yes, how about Wednesday?"

"That sounds great Hillary. I'm sure my mom and dad will say ok," smiled Brad.

"Then bring hiking boots. I don't have any your size. I have everything else," smiled Hillary.

CHAPTER TWELVE – ClausterBox

"Mom!" hollered Brad from his room. "I can't find my boots and I have to have them for after school today."

"Goldfish! Try looking in the utility room closet. That's right where you left them after your rafting trip last fall," hollered mom right back at her goldfish boy. Mom had nicknamed Bradley *'goldfish'* because he was always moving so fast he didn't pay attention to where he left things or where he had to be next. So she would tell him he had the memory of a goldfish.

"Mom," smiled Bradley as he ran by her room on the way to the utility room closet, "don't you dare call me that in front of my friends or that's gonna stick!"

There they were. Just as mom had said. And not wet like they were when he threw them there. They were scrunched and wrinkled from being wet, and the wet socks he had crammed into them were still wedged in and crinkly like stiff cardboard. And the smell!

Brad forced his socked feet down into his shrunken water-dried boots. The high tops were flared out and he had to wrestle his feet and the laces to get his boots into proper place. He looked down when he was finished and shook his head, and quietly said to himself, "I guess it'll have to do. They're my only pair. Maybe no one will notice."

"Come on guys. I'm going to be late to work if we don't get moving," said mom.

"I'm ready mom, but David is playing his game and doesn't even have his shoes on yet," replied Brad. "C'mon David, you're going to make mom late."

Luisa was already waiting in the car. She had decided to wear her favorite shiny black tap shoes from when she had tried taking dance last year, but had given up because it was too hard. She hated dance, but she loved the shoes, and she loved the sound they made when they brought her attention.

Finally, three grade schoolers and mom pulled away from their house, David with shoes still in his hands, wrinkled smelly boots on Brad's cramped feet and shiny tap shoes not fit for school on Luisa's feet.

Pulling to a stop in front of the school drop off, Luisa hopped out first. *Click-clack click-clack* said the metal soles and toes of Luisa's shiny black dance shoes.

"Luisa, come around to this side of the car," raised mom's voice.

Warily, Luisa made her way to the front of the car and stopped. "Yes Mom?"

"Come all the way over here where I can see you…"

Rolling her eyes, Luisa tip toed around the front corner to Mom's door window.

Now it was Mom's turn to roll her eyes.

"Luisa... I've said no to those shoes every time you ask me if you can wear them to school."

"But you didn't say no this time," squirmed Luisa.

"That's because you didn't ask me this time," replied Mom. "Well it's too late now. You're stuck with them. I've tried to save you the embarrassment and you just won't believe me. I'm not going to be able to get away from work to come pick you up when you go crying to the office. I'll see you all after school this afternoon. Dad will be picking you up."

Luisa noticed other kids walk by looking down at her feet, then point and whisper and laugh. Suddenly strong panic ran through her head and down through her body, making her feel faint and shaky.

"Mom! Take me home!" panicked Luisa, realizing she should have listened to mom all along. "I feel like I just came to school in my underwear."

"Luisa, it's too late. There's no way I can take you home now. I've been late twice this month already and I might lose my job," sympathized Mom.

"Dancer, Dancer!" yelled bratty little brother David jumping up and down around her pointing at her feet. "Do a tap dance for us, dancer!"

"Mom!" cried Luisa.

"David!" yelled Mom. "Both of you get to the sidewalk and wait for me."

Mom parked the car and quickly walked Luisa to the office as time was getting later and later and she was getting closer and closer to getting fired.

"Good morning Mrs. Mueller," as Mom greeted Mr. Mueller's wife working in the front office. "Do you happen to have any extra girls shoes in the lost and found that would fit Luisa. Or any other ideas. She seems to have worn the wrong shoes to school today and I don't have time to go all the way home."

"Well good morning. Let's see what I can find here," said Mrs. Mueller, pulling out a large cardboard box from under her standing desk station.

"We have one girl's leather shoe that looks her size. How about that?" offered Mrs. Mueller.

"What am I supposed to do with one shoe? That's worse than two tap shoes!" cried Luisa.

"And we have this worn-out pair of size ten boys tennis shoes," came another offering from Mrs. Mueller.

"I could swim in those!" said Luisa. "And they'll never stay on my feet and they look like they were worn by a pig."

"And we have this pair of knitted gloves with one thumb missing."

Luisa couldn't hold back anymore. She grabbed Mom's leg and slid down to the floor, crying. "I want to go home… I just want to go home…" was all she could keep saying.

"Luisa, get up. I have to leave right now and I can't lose my job because you wore the wrong shoes and won't listen to me. I'm sorry, you're stuck with them today," whispered Mom, with as much sympathy as she could muster with the rising frustration.

Principal Porter walked by and held her hand down to Luisa, helping her up. Mom explained to Ms. Porter all that had happened and what a bad hurry she was in now and just didn't know what to do.

"Let me take her for you," said Ms. Porter. "You go on to work now and relax. This is all going to be just fine."

"Thank you so much. You're so wonderful. You may have just saved my job, and for sure you just saved my feelings," thanked Mom.

Mom kissed Luisa and watched Ms. Porter take Luisa's hand and walk her back to her office. Now she just barely had time to make it to work.

****

Ms. Porter went and got a cup of hot chocolate from the cafeteria and let Luisa sit quietly in her office as she shuffled some papers around. She gave Luisa time to sip hot chocolate and quiet her tears before she offered a walk together to Mrs. Caroline's class.

"I just want to go home," was Luisa's reply.

"Come on dear. It'll be just fine. I'll make sure of that," reassured Ms. Porter with her calming, almost musical voice.

Luisa's eyes began to light up. She sat up straight with a smile and could only say, "Allright."

"Good girl," comforted Ms. Porter.

****

All eyes were on Luisa as Ms. Porter opened the classroom door.

"This is worse than if I had just come straight to class with my ridiculous tap shoes," Luisa whispered to Ms. Porter. "Now the whole world is going to stare and make fun of me."

Everyone loved Ms. Porter. She was the most fair and relaxed person in the whole school. If you ever got sent for trouble to the office, you wanted her to decide any consequences, not the Assistant Principal, Mr. Martin. It's not that Mr. Martin is mean or even unfair. It was just that you almost wanted to go see Ms. Porter even though you were in trouble. Some kids might even get in trouble on purpose just to go see her.

"Good morning class," smiled Ms. Porter. "Luisa was running a little late this morning and is feeling a little under the weather about a shoe choice. Raise your hand if you have an idea on how to help her out."

More than a few eyes noticed the shiny black shoes, but no one dared disappoint Ms. Porter by trying to draw attention to them or by making fun.

Hillary's hand went up.

"Yes Hillary?" called Ms. Porter.

"I could trade seats with Olivia and be a supporter for her."

"Luisa?" asked Ms. Porter.

"That might be nice," stammered Luisa, not quite sure.

Olivia got up without asking and walked toward Hillary's seat and they passed each other in the aisle.

Just as she sat down, Olivia's hand went up.

"Yes Olivia?" said Ms. Porter.

Without a word, she stood up, walked around the desks and to the door where Ms. Porter and Luisa were standing. Still silent, she put her foot with her red round-toed suede flat right alongside Luisa's shoe and judged that they looked about the same size.

"May I?" asked Olivia.

Luisa, still not quite sure what was going on, hoping it could only be better than her stupid tap shoes, answered, "Yes."

Olivia removed her right flat. Then she removed Luisa's right tap. They traded right shoes. Each now had one tap shoe and one red flat.

Facing Luisa, and looking down at both of their feet, Olivia said, "Oh look, we wore the exact same matching pair of shoes to school today!"

Olivia could see that Luisa's eyes were starting to shine with tears.

Turning around to the class, Olivia asked everyone, "Does anyone want to make fun of our *Ridiculous Monday Shoe Choice*?"

No one wanted to. Half the class wanted to laugh with a healing joy. The other half wanted to cry with a healing joy. They all shared the same feeling.

Everyone cheered Luisa and Olivia as they smiled and walked back to their seats and their shoes went *click-clump, click-clump*.

Luisa didn't care and neither did Olivia. They both smiled proudly. In fact, they became famous on recesses all day long. And by the end of the day at least half the students throughout the whole school were wearing mismatched shoes. There was a lot of explaining to do that afternoon at home for those that forgot to trade back.

Olivia and Luisa decided to keep their mismatched shoes and from then on it became their *Ridiculous Monday Shoe Choice*. Every Monday for the rest of the year until they had finally outgrown the shoes to the point that they were either falling apart or just too tight, they wore their *Ridiculous Shoes*. If ever one of them forgot on a Monday, Mrs. Caroline's class was disappointed as well as some of the kids on the playground.

Laugh at their expense or go to their defense. It's a choice to make or feelings to ache. Go one direction it's healing, go the other heartbreak.

****

Two feet jumped and crunched on the gravel. Then four feet. Then six. Then eight. There standing on the gravel road at the bottom of Lookout Mountain were Tinsel, Hillary, Brad and Olivia.

Then six eyes were looking at Olivia as the bus pulled away, leaving a trail of dust.

"Ummm…" was all Tinsel could say.

"Well it looks like Olivia is joining us today," said Hillary right away smiling.

Tinsel wanted to say something, but Hillary had already answered the question well enough with just accepting that Olivia had invited herself.

"What are you doing here Olivia?" asked Brad politely.

"Well I overheard you all talking yesterday, and…well, Hillary said I could come over any time and play tetherball with her, so my mom said it would be ok and she would pick me up later," replied Olivia. "Maybe I should have asked?"

"Sounds fine to me!" grinned Brad.

"Let's get to some tetherball then!" said Hillary, spinning around on her heels and bolting like an excited horse up the hill. "Last one up is a rotten egg!"

"No fair," hollered Tinsel. "You head started!" as she took off after Hillary.

Tinsel was always faster and recognized Hillary's trick. She still beat Hillary to the tetherball court. They dropped their backpacks and waited for Brad and Olivia who didn't have the practice of running up their hill one hundred times before.

Olivia dropped to the ground and took off her red toe and tap shoes. She traded them for boots from her backpack. She had planned for this trip.

"Why didn't you just give Luisa your boots today Olivia?" asked Tinsel.

"That would have fixed her tap shoe problem, but it really wouldn't have taken her sadness away would it?" replied Olivia.

"You joined her in her sadness to take it away Olivia," smiled Hillary. "Now get those boots on and play me first up!"

Hillary beat Olivia in one minute, then turned the court over to Tinsel and Brad.

"Let's go get gear and snacks while they play," said Hillary.

Into the house and to the spelunking equipment room, they picked helmets and harnesses that fit Olivia, and ones they thought would fit Brad. They didn't really have 10-year-old boy gear though, so it was either Papa's huge floppy gear, or girl's gear. They thought it would be more fun to choose the girl's gear.

A quick drop into the kitchen and they filled a satchel with oatmeal bars, crackers, carrots, almonds, beef jerky and bottled water.

Up to the Citadel, and back down they came, arms loaded with Hillary and Tinsel's gear and boots.

Back to the tetherball court where they dumped their overflowing arms in a pile and started digging in to show Olivia and Brad how to wear torches and helmets and harnesses.

Brad geared up and looked very pleased with himself and he stood as tall as he could with his hands on his hips, puffing out his chest, trying to impress the girls.

"I think I'm going to be the best climber ever!" proclaimed Brad.

Hillary almost laughed, but instead paused for a moment before she said, "Well then… you better go find your climbing team, because we're going spelunking."

Brad looked puzzled, then said, "What's spelunking?"

"Climbing is mountains, spelunking is caves," chimed in Tinsel.

Brad dropped his shoulders and chest a little.

"Don't feel bad Brad, most people don't know what spelunking is. Everyone knows what climbing is," smiled Hillary.

"Gee thanks Hilly for not making fun of me."

"Everyone looks ready! Let's go so it doesn't get dark on us," directed Hillary.

"Here," said Tinsel, handing out a small jingle bell on a carabiner hook to each person. "Attach these to your harnesses. They alert animals to us being there."

"Where are we going?" asked Olivia. "I'm afraid of wild animals."

Tinsel clipped 2 of the little bells to Sparks' harness. Sparks instantly tore off to the nearest tree where he did three bark flips, making the bells jingle like a reindeer.

"We're going over the top of Lookout Mountain to Spanning's Well," suggested Hillary to Tinsel. Tinsel nodded with approval. But before we do that, there's one last thing we need to do. Tins and I call it the Clausterbox."

"What the heck is a Clausterbox?!" frowned Brad.

"Come with us into Papa's half-finished workshop," directed Hillary.

They walked to a corner of the shop where there was a low plywood box and if you thought about it too long it might look a little like a coffin. Only the top was fixed, and the one end facing them was open.

"Show them Tins," motioned Hillary.

Before Tinsel could demonstrate, Sparks cut her off, diving deep into the box and letting off a series of Sparks Barks.

"Sparks doesn't even know the word Clausterbox," laughed Tinsel, and she had to bribe him out with a piece of beef jerky.

Sparks out of the way, Tinsel got down on her hands and knees, then fully down on her belly with her head facing the opening in the box. Doing an Army trench crawl, she used her elbows and knees to scoot herself head first into the Clausterbox. The box was so low and tight, Tinsel had to turn her head sideways to fit in. And once her shoulders were in, her elbows were hitting the sides of the box. She wiggled and wriggled like a centipede or a snake until just the soles of her boots were showing from the end of the box.

The whole time, Hillary was secretly watching Brad and Olivia's faces. Brad was grinning ear to ear and was bouncing on his heels. Olivia looked like she was turning pale, and didn't even realize she was using her heels to slowly sneak backwards. Brad was obviously going to be ok. It was to be seen if Olivia could do it. Hillary had seen worse reactions from other people, but they were still able to work through their fear.

"W…w… why do you call that thing a Clausterbox?" questioned Olivia.

"Do you know what claustrophobia is?" asked Hillary.

"I think so," Olivia replied in shaky voice.

"It's panicking when you are inside a tight space if you think you can't get out," explained Hillary.

"Then I have claustrophobia, because I'm about to faint just watching Tinsel," stammered Olivia.

"You don't have to do it, but we'll have to take a different route today."

"No, I don't want to ruin it for everyone," said Olivia trying to sound brave.

"Pull me out now," came Tinsel's muffled voice from deep within the Clausterbox.

Hillary grabbed Tinsel by her boots and with a quick heave, slid and launched her five feet across the shop floor.

"That was fun!" laughed Tinsel. "I used to have a bit of claustrophobia, but then Papa built me this box to practice and now I can stay in there for an hour and even fall asleep."

That seemed to put a small smile on Olivia's face.

Without even being told, Brad dropped to the ground and plunged into the Clausterbox. He crawled so quickly he didn't pay attention to how far he had gone and banged his head on the far inside wall.

"Good thing for helmets!" hollered Brad. "Leave me in here."

"Oh you just wait!" yelled Tinsel into the box. "Ready Hilly?"

They both grabbed handles and began to lift the open end of the Clausterbox until it was about a foot off the ground.

"Hey! Hey! What's going on?!" came Brad's excited cries.

"There's a steep downhill we have to crawl in the tunnel. This is to make sure you don't panic. We have to know before you go," laughed Hillary.

"Lift it higher then!" dared Brad.

"Showoff," chided Tinsel.

They held the box there 30 seconds then let it down and yanked Bradley out by his stinky boots.

"That was awesome!" exclaimed Brad.

"Olivia?" questioned Hillary.

"Ummm... I don't know Hill."

"How about this. Just lie down in front of the box. Don't go in it. Can you do that?"

"Sure."

"Just rest there for 30 seconds. Breath and relax."

Olivia remained calm and did as Hillary told her.

"We're going to take baby steps," said Hillary very gently.

"Baby steps? I'm not a baby," reacted Olivia.

"I don't mean that as an insult Olivia, but that is how babies learn. When they are afraid they take very small steps to keep themselves safe. Does that make sense?" said Hillary calmly. "And we're going to keep you safe."

"Well ok."

Hillary bent down and firmly grabbed Olivia's ankles.

"What is your favorite food Olivia?" asked Hillary.

"I'm not hungry. I'm nervous," replied Olivia.

Hillary laughed and repeated, "Just tell me, what is your favorite food?"

"Ravioli."

"Ok, say the word *Ravioli*."

"Ravioli."

Before Olivia could finish the word, Hillary strongly pulled her backwards a foot.

"See how that works?" smiled Hillary. "Use the panic word *Ravioli*, and we'll have you out before you could eat one Ravioli."

Olivia seemed to relax a little more at that moment.

"But I'm afraid you'll play a joke on me and hold me in," said Olivia.

"I would never do that Olivia. I promise," said Hillary with a reassuring voice.

"I...I trust you. I know you would never be mean or lie to me," said Olivia.

"Go one body section at a time," encouraged Hillary. "Take as long as you like. We're not in a hurry."

Olivia pushed forward until her head was in and stopped. She waited there fifteen seconds.

She crawled forward until her shoulders were in and her elbows just touched the box sides. Hillary could see and hear Olivia begin to breath harder.

"Breath slow and deep and think about tetherball Olivia," offered Hillary. "Move when you're ready."

Olivia trench crawled up to her waist.

"Hillary…" Olivia's voice quavered, "I'm starting to panic."

Hillary pumped Olivia's ankles to remind her she was in good hands.

"Ravioli! Ravioli!"

In one second flat Olivia was out of the box and Hillary was rubbing and patting her back. Olivia lay there, her heart racing, not talking until her breathing slowed.

"I feel like a big baby," lamented Olivia.

"None of us think that. We all have things we are scared of. Rest there and decide if you want to try again. Either way is fine. Just remember I will always quickly pull you out."

Olivia decided she would do this thing. Into the hole she crawled a second time. This time right away up to her waist.

After about a minute with no sound from Olivia, "How are you doing in there Olivia?"

"Um…"

Hillary could sense the panic creeping into her voice and offered to Olivia, "Ravioli?"

"Yes! Yes! Hurry!" Olivia cried.

Out in a flash, Olivia sat up right away and buried her face in her bent knees and was able to hold back the crying sounds, but her body was shaking from the sobs.

"Oh Olivia. I'm so sorry. I hope I pulled you out fast enough," sympathized Hillary.

"You did. It's not your fault. I wish... I just wish..." and Olivia couldn't speak anymore.

"You wish what Olivia?"

"I just wish it was my dad helping and pulling me out," sobbed Olivia.

"I'm sorry Olivia. Maybe he can help out some time," offered Hillary.

"He can't help. He can never help again," blurted out Olivia between the tears.

"What? Why not?" asked Hillary.

"He... he's dead. He died 3 years ago in a work accident. I was only 7 and I feel like I'm even forgetting his face," sobbed Oliva.

Hillary and Tinsel both sat down next to her and put their arms around her and just let her cry until she sat silently.

"We're so sorry Olivia, we didn't know," said Hillary. "Is there anything we can do?"

Olivia sat quietly letting their hugs relax her as the sobs stopped and her body moved with normal breathing.

When she was finally calm, Oliva said, "Help me back into the Clausterbox. I can do this."

Hillary and Tinsel smiled and patted her on the back. They knelt beside her as she dove in up to her waist, then trench crawled all the way in.

"Tip the box! I'm crawling downhill," ordered Olivia.

Hill and Tins smiled and tipped the box high for a minute and then set it back down. Olivia flew backwards in a fury of trench crawl and popped out of the Clausterbox all smiles.

"Let's do this thing!" announced Olivia.

Hillary and Tinsel thought to each other, *something big just happened*.

CHAPTER THIRTEEN – Stinky Boots

Hillary led the troupe in a northwesterly direction towards the mouth of the Raven River. In line were Olivia and Brad. Tinsel brought up the rear. Hillary and Tinsel always flanked their group to keep them as safe as possible.

Along the route, Hillary and Tinsel pointed out Spruce and Fir, lichen and moss, fern and mushroom, and a whole host of other plants and small animals as they saw them. Neither Brad nor Olivia had ever spent much time in the forest. Brad had been camping a few times, but not Olivia.

Sparks put his nose on everything the stars pointed out. Sometimes he nibbled, but he was not a natural vegetarian. He did lift his leg and pee on everything he felt he needed to claim as his own.

"Are there any dangerous animals out here?" asked Olivia.

Hillary and Tinsel immediately thought of the Willow Wolves. The Willows had not been seen in these parts for years.

"I don't think so," answered Hillary. "There is the occasional sighting of black bear, but they mostly mind their own business unless a mama has cubs. And our bells will tell them we're coming and they'll move away from us. And we have bear spray."

"A bell might be fun at a party, but I don't feel very protected from bears," replied Olivia.

The day was beginning to get hot as the sun beat down on the south side of Lookout Mountain. And now a breeze was beginning to flow over the top of the Lookout Mountain from the cold north side. When the hot and cold air met near the top of the mountain it always made swirling tornados of wind. Alders are not the strongest trees, and when the wild wind hit their treetop canopies, the large, weak branches sometimes snapped off sending huge daggers of branches hurtling towards the ground. The four spelunkers could hear the snapping and cracking of massive limbs but couldn't see which tree it was coming from.

Bang! A sharp widow-maker slammed into the ground just 15 feet away from them to the east of their trail to Spanning's Well. They all four jumped wide-eyed.

"What if that had landed on one of us?!" exclaimed Olivia.

"Run!" yelled Tinsel. "We need to get to the well tunnel. It's too dangerous out here in the open. If one of those hits us it will skewer us like a sword from the sky!"

Hillary bolted into a run as fast as she could without leaving Brad and Olivia behind. Tinsel was bringing up the rear and using her hollers to speed Brad and Olivia like a horse buggy driver whipping the reins.

The hike to the Spanning Well that normally takes fifteen minutes only took five as the spelunking team arrived panting and unable to speak and ducked into the cave mouth as Hillary directed.

"No one told me I would have to dodge wooden lightning bolts trying to kill me from the sky!" exclaimed Brad, who had a smile on his lips, but scare in his eyes.

"Oh Bradley! Don't pretend you didn't love dodging the danger from the treetops," quipped Tinsel. "I saw the way you dove into the Clausterbox and almost didn't even want to come out."

Brad grinned.

Olivia looked worried, but was not complaining.

"Torches on! Gloves on!" said Hillary.

The Spanning Well began as a ten-foot cave opening. The ground ran horizontal for 20 feet before beginning to take a sharp dive downwards.

"Why do you call this a well," inquired Olivia. "It just looks like a cave."

"You're right Olivia," explained Hillary. "It is just a cave, but a very specially formed cave. And it was perfect 20 and 30 years ago for Mr. Spanning and his family. Before modern well drilling like the one we have at my house, people had to rely on natural wells. It's hard to get water to a house up on a mountain. That's why our house and the Spanning house were built right where they are today. At the bottom of this well, about one hundred feet down is what we call a horizontal lava worm tube. It's only a few inches around in diameter, but it flows sideways and comes out of the mountain close to our house. Papa found out from the town historian that Mr. Spanning had built a sluice gate from the Raven River to redirect water to the well to refill it when it got low. The sluice gate has rotted and disappeared over time. That's where the Spanning's got their water from, the horizontal lava worm tube. And it came right to their house."

"That's amazing! I want one at my house," exclaimed Olivia.

"Follow me everyone. And keep your eyes overhead," warned Hillary. "Helmets can only do so much and there are nose-breakers everywhere."

"Are you serious?" asked Olivia. "I don't really feel like busting my nose and teeth."

"Want me to lead the way?" offered Bradley.

"Why, because you're a boy?" jabbed Tinsel.

"No!" retorted Brad, "I just want to do my fair share."

"Well unless you want to lead us off a cliff, stay behind Hillary. She has one thousand times the spelunking experience that you do," rebuked Tinsel.

"Tinsel!" warned Hillary.

"What?"

"Be nice. Bradley is just trying to help."

"He's trying to show off like a dumb boy," blurted Tinsel.

"I am not."

"Tinsel!" reminded Hillary.

"Alright, alright, I'm sorry *Bradley*," said Tinsel sarcastically rolling her eyes. All the time thinking to herself, *this is why I don't like boys going with us.*

Be nice! thought Hillary to Tinsel.

I don't hate boys; I hate when they try to take over! thought Tinsel right back.

"My leg!" exclaimed Brad. "My leg. Your dumb dog just peed on my leg. He just lifted his leg and peed on me and now my pant leg and sock are all warm and wet! What the heck?!"

Tinsel began laughing so hard she couldn't breathe or speak.

"He only marks people he likes," said Tinsel, "if that makes you feel any better."

"That doesn't make me feel better. I wish he didn't like me so much. Now I'm going to spend the next couple hours with a wet pee sock."

It's what he deserves, thought Tinsel.

Tinsel, be nice. Brad is a good guy, thought Hillary back at Tinsel.

All right. All right. Fine!

"Everyone stay within sight of each other at all times. There are hundreds of miles of tunnels and you could get lost forever down here," said Hillary. "Soon we'll need to tether off to each other anyway."

"Why is that?" asked Olivia.

"Because the Shale Slides are coming up," warned Tinsel. "Underground slippery slopes steeper than you can imagine. You could get lost down in the Shale Shards. And the edges of the Shale Shards are razor sharp so if you slip don't dig your elbows in or you'll cut them to ribbons. Use your glove hands and knees."

"Um… tie me in please. Quickly," said Olivia.

"When we get to the Cross Winds Tunnel coming up," replied Hillary.

Rounding the corner and descending a ten-degree slope that went one hundred feet, the spelunkers came to where the tunnel widened and intersected another tunnel running crosswise to their path. The second tunnel was two feet lower than their tunnel so it intersected like a big dip in the road. The big problem now was the Cross Winds Tunnel was flowing with overflow water from the Raven River and it was rushing by fast at two feet deep and fifteen feet across. And there was a strong cross wind flowing by from the left to the right that might easily blow you over and send you downstream.

"Ok, well I didn't expect this," remarked Tinsel.

"What? What's wrong?" implored Olivia.

"By this late in the winter, the Raven is usually not overflowing to the Cross Winds Tunnel," pointed out Tinsel. "But the bigger danger is the cross wind. Gusts of wind coming over the top of Lookout Mountain hit the opening of the Cross Winds Tunnel and increase speed quickly until they reach us here. An unexpected gust can knock you downstream in a heartbeat. You can never come here alone. You have to have someone else to tie off to so if one of you is knocked down the other one can pull you out."

"Do we tie off now?" asked Olivia.

"Yes," answered Hillary.

"But of course that's not even the biggest danger," started Tinsel.

"Tinsel," said Hillary. "Don't scare."

"What?! I'm not trying to scare. They have to know. They came with us. It's only fair," snapped Tinsel.

"Go ahead but don't scare," warned Hillary.

"Ok ok. It's the Tunnel Tornadoes," began Tinsel.

"I think I wanna go back," muttered Olivia.

"It'll be fine Olivia… they wouldn't bring us down here if we were in any real danger," interjected Brad.

"That's pretty much true," said Hillary.

"Pretty much true?" exclaimed Olivia. "Not totally much true?"

"Well you can never one hundred percent predict the underground weather no matter how safe you try to be. There's always some element of danger, but that's what adds to the excitement," said Hillary trying to reassure, but not helping Olivia much.

"I think I want safe, not excitement," replied Olivia.

"We are all going to be just fine. Tinsel and I have been down here one hundred times and we know the earth. Trust us."

"This is going to be a blast," Brad proclaimed calmly.

"I wish I were as brave as you Brad, and that Tinsel would stop trying to scare me," said Olivia.

"Ok, tie off at ten feet apart. I'll help you with the special fording knot I invented," announced Hillary.

"What's a fording knot?" asked Olivia.

"It's a knot you can tie using a single rope without cutting the ends and keeps us all on one line. And its fording because we're crossing water and some knots when they get wet they can't be untied. This one gets tighter the harder you pull it, but even wet it opens up quickly with the quick release loop. Here I'll show you."

"You know so much about knots, and you tie them so quickly and they look amazing," complimented Olivia. "Maybe sometime you can teach me knots?"

Hillary smiled and nodded yes.

"And we're tying off at ten feet apart so that no more than two people are in the water at any time," added Hillary.

The spelunkers finally all tied in, Hillary led the way, wading in leg deep. Struggling just a little for balance against the fast water, when she was half way across Olivia began to wade in. Hillary made it to the other side safely and took up the slack as Olivia progressed. Only once did Olivia's boot slip off an underwater rock and she almost fell over, but caught herself and proudly emerged on the other side safely.

By this time Brad was in the middle of the ford. A sudden gust of wind and a surge of water around a big rock hit Brad at the same time and in a moment his legs were swept out from under him and his entire body disappeared under the water for a moment. His helmet crashed against the rock that had tripped him and he fought the current to stand again but was forced downstream a few feet. His rope, now tight, tried to jerk both Tinsel and Olivia off their dry tunnel bank, but they had seen him fall and braced and held tight. When he finally stood against the current he was dizzy from the helmet hit, but thank goodness not injured.

Hillary and Olivia reeled him in and Tinsel took up her slack to steady him.

"Are you ok Bradley?" asked Tinsel.

"I…I think so. Yes, I'm ok," said Brad a little shaken.

Once she heard he was ok, Tinsel really couldn't help herself.

"Good thing three girls were here to pull you out," taunted Tinsel.

"Tinsel!" admonished Hillary.

"What? Oh come on. I'm just toying with him. Bradley knows that," Tinsel replied playfully.

"Oh? Do I know that Tinsel?" snapped Brad. "You've been toying with me all day now."

A moment of regret hit Tinsel. *Sometimes maybe I go too far. Maybe this is just like throwing my body around and not being careful with other people. Either their bodies or their feelings… but now was not the time to deal with this. Too much going on and too many people…*

"Whatever," was all Tinsel would say.

And that was the end of Tinsel's complaining about boys for that trip.

"Let's go," commanded Hillary. "Shale Shards straight ahead."

****

Within one hundred feet the tunnel roof began dropping down towards them. Within another hundred feet they found themselves crawling on hands and knees the ceiling was so low, still tethered together as Hillary had told them to remain tied.

The ground became all loose shards and they were slippery and their hands and knees sunk six inches in. They were like bark chips, only hard and sharp. The disintegrated rock is a lot like large, sharp gravel, only flatter. The ground became very steep and sloping forward until they had to keep their arms locked out in front of them to keep from falling over as they continued to descend.

"These shale shards would make a good souvenir," said Olivia excitedly to Hillary.

"I can see why you think that Olivia, but we have a few hard and fast rules. One is that we never leave anything behind that we brought in with us, like trash. Another is that we never take out anything we didn't bring in...like shale shards. That way we respect the tunnels and leave them always natural."

"Sorry, I feel stupid for asking," said Olivia.

"You didn't say anything at all wrong Livvy. If I were you I would want a souvenir too," smiled Hillary.

Olivia smiled. Her new nickname made her feel special.

Olivia's arms were getting tired and weak from going downhill in the cramped space for so long. Her left arm finally gave out and she fell forward. She had not realized that she was following Hillary so closely. As she fell forward, her helmet smacked squarely into Hillary's bottom end, shooting Hillary forward and landing flat on her chest.

"Ugh!... Oh gosh Hillary. I'm so sorry. Are you ok? I'm so stupid!" lamented Olivia.

Turning around and sitting upright in the shale, Hillary turned her helmet torch to Olivia.

"You're not stupid. And if you wanted me out of the way you could have just asked," laughed Hillary. "I'm fine. It's not the first time I've eaten dirt."

Olivia cracked a little smile and said, "thank you" to Hillary for being so understanding.

But this all made Brad stop as well and now Tinsel crawled right up to him. Almost on top of his legs as his boots stuck back out towards her.

"What is that smell?!" howled Tinsel.

"I don't smell anything," said Hillary, a little worried because dangerous smells might mean underground explosive methane gas.

"I think Brad farted!" hollered Tinsel. "And right in my face! Disgusting!"

She punched Brad in the rear end.

"Hey! I did not!" retorted Brad, embarrassed.

"Then what is it? It smells like an animal died or pooped on you!" said Tinsel still very excited.

"I noticed it a while back but I didn't want to say anything," said Brad flustered. "It's just my boots. I think they are rotting and moldy from being put away wet for six months."

"Oh gosh Brad. Is that really any better than farting in my face?! You need new boots. Let me in front of you!"

"Tinsel, we need to flank our inexperienced spelunkers. Calm down and trade spots with me," said Hillary.

So the two traded places. As Hillary and Tinsel passed each other on hands and knees, Hillary thought to Tinsel, *we'll talk about this later.* Things calmed down and soon Brad's embarrassment disappeared as Hillary was not a hothead. Tinsel led on down the Shale Shards path.

The tunnel narrowed to a hole that they called the Shale Door, just the width of your shoulders and sloped steeply downhill. Tinsel wriggled through quickly like a snake disappearing into its underground den. Olivia was glad now that she had gone through the Clausterbox training and made it through fairly easily. Finally all four made it through and the tunnel opened up into a great hall.

"We call this the Halls of Shale," announced Hillary.

Tinsel was being a little quiet now, realizing she shouldn't have embarrassed Brad even though he was a smelly boy.

The Halls of Shale are three large chambers that had been formed by massive lava gas bubbles that expanded within the molten lava and then cooled. Over millions of years large shale deposits had formed and time had broken them into many sharp shards.

The three large chambers are connected by small round bubble-like openings the size of a car. The passage from the second to the third chamber is on ground level so you can easily walk through it, but getting out of the first chamber is no easy task. That opening is ten feet in the air and smaller. The piles of boulders and shale formed a rough stairway that crumbled and shifted under your feet as you climbed. Sometimes you take two steps up and slide back down one.

The chambers are huge in size. About the size of a football field. It would be difficult to see well in there because the walls are so high and the torches are not that bright if it was not for the SilicaSuns and their reaction to the twin stars. SilicaSuns are the tiny gold-like microscopic drops the size of a grain of sand lodged in the igneous and sedimentary rock brought up from the center of the earth that begin to burn, brighter and brighter when near Hillary and Tinsel. Their connection to the earth reacts with the SilicaSuns. The brighter the girls need, the brighter they glow. Sometimes as bright as the sun to brilliantly light the chambers, and sometimes a low glow like a beautiful sunset barely lighting the sky just at dusk.

The SilicaSuns now lit the first Shale Hall to an early morning glow. A brilliant glow with a little blue sky mood added to it. They turned off their torches and enjoyed the brilliant diamond reflections from the wet hall walls and the pools of still waters gathered here and there like wading pools. Some cave-dwelling fish even stocked the ponds and enjoyed bites of crackers right out of the spelunkers hands from their stores of snacks.

Tinsel stayed far away from Brad because he still smelled like he stepped in dog poop.

This was the best part of the journey, and the spelunkers had only been in the first hall for ten minutes when a breeze picked up. After another minute or so the breeze turned stronger. One more minute and it was a light gale. Water began whipping into the air like the ocean wind whipping waves into your eyes and face.

"Follow me!" ordered Hillary sounding a little urgent now.

Tinsel's face turned quite serious.

"We can't go back the way we came," yelled Hillary over the howling gale winds and water. "That's where the wind is screaming through the Shale Door. We could never get back through there now!"

"We have to get out of this chamber before the winds hit hurricane speed!" yelled Tinsel over the clamor. "Quickly, up the shale stair and through to the second chamber."

This was no place for a loose beagle. Hillary quickly picked up Sparks and zipped him safely deep into her backpack. He didn't appreciate being locked inside the depths of a backpack when there was so much adventure to play in. As hard as he tried, a backpack is a very small space for Sparks Circles. The best he could do was muffled barks and bulging bumps throwing Hillary from side to side.

Almost before she could get the words out of her mouth a monstrous circular vortex whirlpool of wind began screaming in the center of Shale Hall.

"Too late!" screamed Hillary. "The Tunnel Tornadoes are forming."

Boulders and shale shards began lifting off the ground and hurtling like train cars against the walls and smashing and exploding into thousands of flying knives. Sparks of light and shards of shale and rocks were flying everywhere including towards them.

Hillary and Tinsel pushed Brad and Olivia towards the shale stairs without words because it was louder than a jet engine now and no directions could be heard. They began pushing them up the stairs and stood between them and the shale storm. Brad was pushing Olivia up the hill towards the shale chamber door ahead of him.

Brad paused for a moment to look back and check on Hillary and Tinsel. His dumbstruck face told a story.

"Olivia, look," he yelled loudly into her ear. "Am I seeing what I think I'm seeing?!"

Several feet below them, Hillary and Tinsel were facing the raging shale storm holding their hands out towards it. A blue glowing globe was encompassing all of them. They could see through its transparency. The shards of shale smashing into bits against what he could imagine was some kind of protective shield made out of transparent blue light.

Hillary looked over her shoulder at him and yelled, "Brad! Move it! Get through the door! Get yourself and Olivia through!"

He could barely hear her but could certainly make out what she meant, and he quickly resumed their ascent.

Pushing too quickly, Olivia wrenched her ankle on a strong rock just below the surface of the moving shale. Her leg gave out from the red hot pain shooting through her leg and she fell backwards just in time for Brad to catch her from falling down the hill. It was no use. The ankle wouldn't work any longer. It was sprained badly beyond use. Brad tried to help and even carry her but it was no use.

"Climb on my back!" he yelled in Olivia's ear.

He turned sideways and she came around and climbed on.

"Hold on as tight as you can!" he yelled. "You have to stay on yourself. I can't hold you. I need my hands to climb!"

Choking from Olivia's bear hug around his neck and almost falling back down the stairs himself, Brad eventually fought his way up to the shale door and helped himself and Olivia through, with Hillary and then Tinsel close behind.

Climbing down the shale stairs on the other side, they finally rested on some large boulders, drank some water and shared some snacks as they let the scare and disbelief wear off. Well, Brad and Olivia anyway. Hillary and Tinsel didn't look shaken at all. They could still hear the roar of the storm in the next hall, but it was dying down quickly.

"What the heck was that?" asked Brad.

"That," explained Hillary smiling and wide-eyed, "was a Tunnel Tornado. Which created a Shale Storm."

"No. I mean the blue. The shield. The glow. Whatever that thing was!" exclaimed Brad.

"Oh, you saw that? The Blue Refractory?" said Hillary.

"How could I not!? It was as plain as day, protecting us... you... all of us?" asked Brad.

Hillary exchanged knowing glances with Tinsel then said, "We'll talk about that later. We have to move now."

"You act as if nothing dangerous just happened!" exclaimed Olivia.

"We were never in any real danger," laughed Tinsel.

"What about my ankle then?!" asked Olivia.

"Well that could happen on any old rock anywhere, even on the playground at school. It wasn't the storm's fault," explained Tinsel.

"Well I certainly wouldn't have almost had my head taken off by exploding shale at school!" exclaimed Olivia right back at her.

"I told you. You were never in any real danger," said Tinsel quite calmly. "Besides, you could always fall off the monkey bars and break your neck."

"Tinsel!" snapped Hillary. "Stop it."

"Awe Hilly-beans, I was just having fun with her," grinned Tinsel.

"Now is not the time," warned Hillary. "We have to get moving so Olivia can get her ankle looked at. And since we can't go back through the Shale Tunnel, we'll have to go out through the backside of Lookout Mountain and have a two hour hike back with a bad ankle."

Tinsel frowned but kept quiet. *I'm stuck with a stinky boy and a little baby with a broken ankle. Not the fun I had in mind!*

Tinsel, Hillary sadly thought.

If Olivia could trust…if she could believe…maybe we could help her with her ankle, thought Tinsel.

I thought of that and tried already, but she is too afraid, thought Hillary. *It doesn't take much, but there has to be the smallest belief in the Regeneration for us to help. We can't do it all for her. No one can do it all for another person.*

It took the spelunking troupe another hour to maneuver the remaining tunnel which was mostly bare rock at this point and fairly easy to traverse. But it was slow going as they all had to take turns being Olivia's crutch.

Finally exiting the backside of the Spanning Well Tunnel on the far side of Lookout Mountain it was just approaching sundown. Hillary was just a little concerned at that point.

"We need to move faster so we don't get caught in the dark. That is a hard rule. Don't get caught in the dark," warned Hillary.

"I'll piggyback carry Olivia," volunteered Brad. "Ok Olivia?"

"Um, I guess so, if Hillary says we have to move fast and get back before dark. I can't put any weight on this foot at all and I can't hop two miles over rocks and roots."

"It's settled then," as Brad turned around and bent his knees.

Olivia hopped on and they began making their way. This time Tinsel led the way with Pony-Brad and his rider

Olivia, with Hillary bringing up the rear. They did make it home easily by dark, Brad looking worn out, but something happened along the way. Something Hillary had never experienced before…

    Now and again she would get side glimpses of Olivia's face. Olivia was smiling. Then she would get a peek of Brad looking up over his shoulder to check on his rider and he would smile. This went on again and again and they whispered and laughed and smiled at each other. And Hillary began to feel something. Something in her gut. Something she had never felt before. She didn't like it. It made her mad.

    It made her… *jealous?*

CHAPTER FOURTEEN – Corkscrew

Days turned to weeks and to months. And finally…

"I won! I won! I beat you! I beat you! I beat you!" yelled Olivia dancing and jumping around the pole and yelling so loudly everyone on the playground stopped what they were doing and looked in the direction of the tetherball court.

Olivia was beginning to wonder if she would ever beat Hillary, the reigning Tetherball Queen. And, almost worse, she had been worried that Hillary was getting tired of playing just her.

"You can finally play someone besides me!" apologized Olivia.

"Don't you dare apologize to me Olive-Oil," as Hillary had begun affectionately calling her. "You won fair and square and I have enjoyed every single game with you immensely. I'm actually sorry our competition is over."

"You're not tired of me then?" asked Olivia.

By now half of the crowd on the playground had gathered around them in a circle to see what the commotion was.

"Are you kidding?! This has been one of the best journeys of my life seeing you stick to it in all honesty," said Hillary. "I have to say Olivia, you were defeated a thousand times and never gave up. And I never let up and played easy on you. I saw the willpower grow in you, not weaken. You are amazing."

Olivia was blushing now in front of so many of her classmates.

Cassie broke into the conversation, "Finally I get to play Hillary again. Get over here Hillary!"

"No! I get to play her," butted in Kori.

"Sorry Cassiopeia and Koriander, we have a new reigning queen and this is her court. You twins have to win it from her before you can play me," smiled Hillary looking over at Olivia.

Now Olivia really blushed, held her head up, swallowed down the lump in her throat, and walked confidently over to the server's court. Her proud eyes spoke a thousand stories of friendship as she looked at Hillary, then grabbed the rope and said, "First up!?"

Friends make better and friends make best when you never give up and you're put to the test. The truest care of a caringest friend, even when difficult makes you better in the end.

****

Over these same months, afternoons and weekends at Lookout Mountain became busy with adventure. As often as they could, Hillary and Tinsel, Elka, Ava, Brad and sometimes Olivia would meet to play and plan, spelunk and explore, skin knees and bump heads.

Very rarely Luisa and Klix would accept an invitation. And even then they didn't play or talk much. When they did come out, it felt as if they were only there to watch… or to spy.

Hillary and Tinsel explained more about the blue Regeneration and the red Initiation. Brad and Elka and Ava saw the Regeneration more and more in the forest and caves and in the Citadel as they began to connect and understand.

****

By the beginning of Spring, the Eastern Lava Tubes were drying out for the most part. The Ravenous River was no longer threatening to wash the spelunkers down the drains to the center of the earth. Occasionally the Raven River would spit a smallish stream in that direction during heavy rains, but nothing so dreadful that would require raincoat balloons to breathe.

It was only two weeks until Spring Break. This was always one of Tinsel and Hillary's favorite times to explore and spelunk. So much beauty was blooming and so many interesting critters were about. The caves were becoming dryer, but just wet enough to grow the necessary mosses and lichens on wet glistening walls. Water seeping through the sedimentary layers of earth to the depths so their drips and drops could be heard splashing and draining and creating their stalactites and stalagmites. The cistern pools needed just enough dripping year round to make homes for the salamanders and newts and tadpoles.

Frizzely's kits were becoming more independent and able to take care of themselves and could be seen frequently foraging on their own without mama. They were learning how to get into trouble of their own. Now and again they felt the need to raid Papa's garbage bins at night, turning them into a mess strewn about the yard. Sometimes in the middle of the night you could hear Papa's feet pounding the floor as he ran to see what the noise was banging about in the yard. It was always the kits and Papa would say that someday he would build a keep for the bins. Mama always laughed and rolled her eyes when he said that. She knew Papa's heart couldn't stand in the way of nature.

It was Saturday morning and the spelunking troupe had all been dropped off by their parents just before lunch. The idea was for the seven of them, Hillary, Tinsel, Elka, Ava, Olivia and Brad, and of course Sparks, to have lunch in the Second Echo Chamber down in the deeps of the Eastern Lava Tube. Elka, Ava, Olivia and Brad had never been a mile deep into the earth before and they were all very excited and maybe even a little nervous.

All geared up, it took the spelunker seven only 15 minutes to arrive at the tube entrance.

"Here we are," announced Hillary.

"Here we are where?" asked Brad. "I don't see anything."

"Right there," pointed Elka to the viney twiggy door to the tube.

"What?" questioned Ava.

"Right there. Are you kidding me?" joked Elka.

"They can't see it yet Elka," whispered Tinsel.

Elka went over to what Brad, Olivia and Ava saw as just a thick wall of vines and rocks. Sticking her arm deep into the thicket and pulling hard to one side, she revealed for the rest of the troupe a dark gaping hole behind the viney tangle.

"What the heck?!" muttered Brad, scratching his chin and looking around. "Am I the only blind one here?"

Tinsel laughed and said, "Yep. Boys are blind."

Tinsel! thought scolded Hillary. *Behave yourself.*

Sorry Hill, thought laughed Tinsel again.

"It's not funny," said Brad.

"Oh, it's a little funny," teased Tinsel.

"Tinsel! Maybe you need to go home?" scolded Hillary.

"I'm done teasing. Sorry Brad," said Tinsel only half apologizing.

Brad didn't say anything.

After final gear checks and torches on, they made their way through the viney entrance as Hillary and Tinsel directed them.

"Tinsel, would you like to lead and I'll bring up the rear flank?" asked Hillary.

"Sure sis," replied Tinsel. "Forward ho!" she shouted to the troupe. "And watch your step. There's no shale, but there's lots of round river cobble carried in here from the Ravenous that would love to roll and break your ankles. Slow and steady on the feet."

Though no one could see, Hillary rolled her eyes and thought, *I wish that Tinsel wouldn't always be trying to scare and excite. Sure footed is safer than scare footed.* By now everyone was getting to know that Tinsel was always exaggerating and they didn't take everything she said seriously.

"Bark, bark, bark, bark, bark, bark, bark, bark!!" shot out into the air suddenly and startled the whole spelunking troupe. They all stopped and wheeled around to see what the commotion was. Sparks was Sparks Circling and Sparks Barking all at once.

"This isn't good," said Hillary with eyes scanning the woods. "When Sparks does both at the same time I know it's danger. Everyone in the tunnel quickly."

One hundred feet out in the distance, half hidden by a Giant Spruce, frozen solid, head held low in a stalking hunting position, Hillary could just make out the head and shoulders of a wolf. A Willow Wolf. Now that he had been seen he would surely attack.

Tinsel held open the tangled viney mess which was obstructing the tunnel mouth and grabbed hands and pushed shoulders as quickly as she could through the entrance without actually hurting someone. Elka, Ava, Olivia, Brad. All being rapidly pulled and shoved into the inner tunnel mouth, tripping, stumbling and falling into the dark.

Hillary and Tinsel would have to be last in to guarantee the safety of their troupe. They were responsible for their safety, and all future trips hung on what happened here now.

The Willow Wolf began leaping and bounding at them. One hundred feet became ninety. Ava was safe. Then eighty feet. Olivia was safe. Seventy. Elka was safe. Faster and faster and now Hillary could see fangs and glaring eyes. Furiously sharp Willow Wolf paws and claws throwing up needles from the forest floor. Forty feet and Brad was in safely. The Willow was so close now Hillary could see the fur hackling up on the back of the Wolves neck and its mouth began to open wider. Thirty feet and Tinsel sprang in through the tunnel mouth. Twenty feet and Hillary had a grave decision to make. Sparks was still Circling and Barking. If she tried to get to him, they would both be lost to the Willow's teeth. She had no choice and Sparks was not paying attention no matter how she called. Ten feet to go. The last thing Hillary saw as she slammed the thick viney mesh behind her was the front legs of the Willow Wolf attack-leaping into the air. Then the thwump of a flying one hundred and fifty pound predator body slamming into the viney door.

Through the thicket door, the spelunkers heard a crying beagle howl. A whining, whimpering, doggy screaming. Through small gaps in the thick vines, Hillary could just barely make out the reason for the beagle howls. The Willow Wolf had Sparks by his right hind leg and was dragging him off into the woods out of sight.

"Everyone hold hands, quickly," said Hillary.

The quickest circle of hands formed. Hillary and Tinsel closed their eyes. Brad, Elka and Ava did the same.

Heat flowed. Concern flowed. Anger and purpose flowed. Red and blue went out.

Sparks' whines stopped. The Willow Wolf stopped. He dropped his beagle meal as something strange began to happen.

Sparks' broken and mangled leg was bleeding badly. Dripping and dropping onto the forest floor and into the ground, into the earth sparking and crackling. Now Sparks' hackles stood tall on the back of his neck. And he stood. He stood tall. He began to grow. To the Willow Wolf, Sparks had grown twice the size of a wolf. And twice as angry. Red molten drops were flying from Sparks' right hind leg as it strengthened and healed. Hillary and Tinsel focused even harder as Brad, Elka and Ava added to them.

And now Sparks had twice the fangs. The Willow Wolf began to slowly back away from a fight he knew he could not win and slowly turned away and try to run. With one quick snap, Sparks had the Willow Wolf's right hind leg in his mouth and gave it a good hard bite, half crushing his bones. The Willow Wolf could not run after that, but did a three legged hobble as fast as he could get back to the Willowlands. Over time his broken bones healed, but he was left with a permanent limp to remind him of Sparks and the power of the Regeneration.

By the time Sparks returned to the mouth of the tunnel, he appeared to have shrunk back down to his perfectly beagle sized, cute as ever self. The other spelunkers had not seen what happened, but Hillary and Tinsel always knew what really saved Sparks.

****

The first slope was easy and they walked without too much effort for the first quarter mile. It was much easier without a flood of water trying to drown you.

Tinsel could tell by the echoes that they were nearing the Corkscrew Drop. She stopped everyone 20 feet from the drop entry.

"Ok everyone, we're going to stop here and rope up," directed Tinsel.

Brad and Oliva knew the routine from their adventure through Spanning's Well, and they were eager to teach Elka and Ava the fording knot Hillary had taught them. But Hillary stopped them.

"Sorry guys," interrupted Hillary. "The fording knot is not the right knot for this descent. It's too easy to get caught on gear in this situation and come loose. We don't want to lose anyone to a one hundred foot fall. I've got a new knot for you. It's called the 'Spelunker Special' and it uses a double loop and a carabiner so you can easily attach and detach when you don't need it. Here I'll show you on Tinsel."

All the troupe was impressed by Hillary's new knot. Hillary let them all tie their own knots at five foot intervals on the rope and attach their carabiners to their harnesses. Then Hillary double checked them for safety. A cinch here, an adjustment there, Hillary was gentle with her corrections, but in the end they all got it right.

"Why are we tied at five foot intervals instead of ten like in the Spanning Well?" inquired Brad.

"Awesome question Bradley!" quipped Hillary. "At the Crosswind Tunnel, ten feet kept two people on the shore all the time. Five feet here means that we will catch you before you fall one hundred feet into the Corkscrew Drop."

"Um…yikes," was all Bradley could say.

"You'll be fine," winked Hillary.

Brad didn't look so sure.

Hillary took off her backpack, zipped both sides down and set it on the ground. Sparks knew just what to do. Within two seconds he had jumped and wiggled in and awaited the zipping. As Hillary zipped him in securely, he kissed and licked her hand thank you. He was thankful that he had not been left behind this time. And he was thankful he wasn't at the vet getting shots.

"Ok, everyone follow me slowly," directly Tinsel. "Use sure feet. Papa says *slow is steady and steady wins the race*, and he's right every time."

The Corkscrew Drop is a huge hole about twenty feet around. It drops one hundred feet straight down and the edges are very jagged and very bumpy which is a very good thing. Millions of years ago as hot gasses escaped up from the middle of the earth, they bubbled up through this passage making a giant wormhole. As the gasses rose they spun in circles causing huge two and three foot gashes in the walls spinning up in circles like stairs or foot paths spiraling from the bottom to the top of the tunnel. The whole one hundred foot drop is a spiral staircase. All you have to do is hug the wall, grab rocky handholds sticking out along the way, and secure to pitons as often as Hillary and Tinsel had permanently installed them into the walls.

"This descent will take us about an hour," said Hillary from the rear. "Take your time. Be safe. Have fun. Don't tense up. We'll be fine."

So, six spelunkers and a pup began their treacherous descent into the Corkscrew Drop.

"If I fall and kill myself I'm holding you responsible," Ava joked to Hillary as she peeked down the center of the monster's throat. Her torch could not even see the bottom of the drop from this height.

"Oh gosh Ava, don't even joke like that!" smirked Hillary. "But if you do fall, try not to take me with you."

"Ok you two, now you're scaring me," chimed in Olivia.

"Ok, everybody. Backs against the wall for a viewing," said Tinsel. "One torch can't see the bottom, but all combined we get a great view."

Everyone tied together at a five foot rope interval nearly completed the circle around the drop now that they were all within the tunnel on the spiral stair.

"Now carefully bring your toes to the edge," said Tinsel.

"Are you kidding me?!" said Elka.

"Stay clipped to the wall and you'll be fine," reassured Tinsel. "Ok everyone ready? Go."

All six carefully made it to toes on the edge. Five of them had to wait a little longer for Olivia, as she was inching her way out, one tiny shuffle after another.

"Heads and torches down and center to the bottom of the drop," directed Tinsel.

All six looked down. The reactions ranged from pure thrilling excitement to pure terror.

"I think I'm going to faint," swooned Olivia.

"I think I'm going to barf," choked Ava.

"I think I'm going to fly!" hollered Bradley.

"I think I could stand here forever," longed Elka.

The circular walls glistened and glowed. Sparkling and jagged. Steep and ominous. Wet and dark and dripping. Moss and lichen and SilicaSuns. A sheer terrible drop of sudden death from a sudden stop at the bottom is what it would be if not for the secure ropes. The very bottom was now visible with six torches focused. It was not flat at all like some imagined. It was sharp and chunky boulders heaped in a pile. It would not be a nice landing at all.

"Isn't it funny how things are magnified when danger is involved," offered Tinsel.

"What do you mean Tinsel? What are you saying?" asked Elka.

"Well, if you were in your front yard and painted a big circle on the flat ground, you could dance and jump up and down outside it and even be careless and you would never fall past the painted circle into the center, because you're not afraid and there's no danger if you did fall. But here you would never do that because the risk is too terrible even though it's the same as the circle in your yard."

"Are you crazy Tinsel?" exclaimed Ava. "It's not the same thing at all. The chance of falling makes it totally different."

"To-may-to, to-mah-to" said Tinsel, making a smirky smile no one could see in the dark.

"Tinsel. Stop," pleaded Hillary.

I'm just having fun. Fine, I'll be good, thought Tinsel to Hillary.

About half way down there was a section that had broken out. It was a four foot gap in the stairs which Tinsel jumped across. Olivia, who was second in line just behind her, let out a little scream of panic and quickly sat down. The terror at the thought of jumping that gap locked her legs in place and they refused to let her move.

"There is *absolutely no way*, I am jumping across that gap," whispered Olivia.

When Tinsel heard Olivia scream she turned around and immediately and actually felt bad. *Darn it, I should have warned her what was coming up. My showing off is just too much sometimes.*

"Make way, make way," said Hillary as she carefully worked around the others to the front where Tinsel and the gap were.

"Stand by everyone. We'll take care of this," said Hillary. "We knew this was coming up and Tinsel should have warned you. This isn't the first time we've gone across here."

Hillary and Tinsel both removed their backpacks and Hillary handed hers with Sparks in it over to Tinsel. The two stars now stood with their heels to the gap, back to back. Tinsel secured their backpacks with a rope to the tie off.

They counted together...*one*...*two*...*three*...*go*. Both allowed themselves to fall backwards, where their backs collided in the middle and they interlocked arms. There was a strong blue glow between them that held like a glue and they were rock steady across the gap. They slowly lowered until their legs were straight out and they formed a solid spelunker bridge.

"Now climb across," said Hillary.

Elka, Ava and Brad seemed ok, even impressed and excited.

Olivia said, "Are you nuts?! There is no way I'm going across you!"

"Then we'll all have to go back," said Hillary.

"Come on Olivia, I'll steady you," offered Brad. "I can reach all the way to you once I'm across and hold your hand."

"Maybe..." said Olivia, "Go over first and then I'll see."

Carefully and safely Elka then Ava then Brad made it across. Brad held his hand back out to Olivia.

"Grab it," said Brad. "I've got you. We're still tied in and there is no way I'll let you fall."

Carefully Olivia reached out and grabbed his hand, then his forearm, and they locked arms. Slowly and steadily she climbed across Hillary and then Tinsel until she was on safe ground, where she grabbed Brad and hugged him and wouldn't let go.

Tinsel gave Hillary the signal and they both pulled up on their tether ropes and swung to the safe side with their companion spelunkers. Olivia still would not let go of Brad as if she were frozen in fear.

"You're ok Olivia," said Hillary, not meaning to sound snippy. "You can let go of Brad now."

"I'm sure that's the scariest thing I've ever done in my life," laughed Ava. "Can we do it again?"

"I think we've created a real thrill-seeking monster here gang. What do you think?" joked Tinsel. "Let's get moving!"

Over the next half hour, the spelunkers went round and round and round and round. Thirty-seven times in all to be exact. That's how many spirals it took to get to the bottom.

Finally arriving at the Corkscrew Drop floor, the spelunkers took a well needed break. Their minds were tired from so much danger. Their bodies were ready for a snack.

And Sparks showed that he was dog-tired of being cooped up in a backpack! He had six spelunkers to dance around and jump on, and just as many faces to lick. Of course not everyone likes wet dog germs so there was just a little complaining, but not too much because his excitement was so entertaining.

The scariest part of the journey was over. The hardest part was ahead. There were many ups and downs, but mostly downs because they would end up a mile underground. All lava tunnels are difficult and full of surprises. The ups and downs were zapping the spelunker's energy and tiring them out. There were lots of tired groans and sweating. Even the downs take a lot of work to keep yourself from falling forward on your face.

Brad was sweating so badly he took off his helmet as his hair was soaking wet now and dripping down into his eyes. Hillary noticed and was not too happy about that.

"Bradley, you should put your helmet back on," she said.

"I'm too hot and the ground is flat and the roof is high here," complained Brad.

"Bradley, it's bad form not to wear your helmet. You really need to wear it all the time," Hillary said much more insistently.

"Awe, come on Hills. I'll put it back on in a few minutes when sweaty rivers are not pouring out of my head," joked Brad.

Brad had barely gotten the words out of his mouth when a sharp, dark stalactite came out of nowhere and slammed into his forehead just near his right temple. He slammed into it at full marching speed and it knocked him to the ground. He let out an agonizing yell and clutched at his head which immediately began bleeding badly through a gash.

The blood dripped through his fingers. Elka saw each drop fall in slow motion. Elka and Ava both saw each drop hit the hard rock ground. As each drop hit the tunnel floor, it instantly melted the rock into tiny drop sized pools of orange molten golden fire. Drop after drop of the precious liquid melted small fiery red holes that began to look like a fields of stars in the sky and they began lighting the tunnel passage like orange firelights from the ground. Brad was in too much pain, moaning with his eyes closed, to see the spectacle.

"Hillary, what is going on?!" said Ava. "The floor…what is happening?... I want out of here."

"It's ok Ava. Come here quick! I need your help," said Hillary. "Shine your torch here on Brad's head and help him put pressure while I get bandages."

Ava could see where Brad was failing to apply pressure. "Brad, move your hand, let me help."

Ava was not squeamish. She gave her hand a quick wash from her water bottle, then pressed her right palm hard against his gash and put her left hand on the other side of his head so she could squeeze it a little like a vise.

"What…what is going on?" exclaimed Ava as her right hand began to glow red and heat up.

Ava jumped back as Hillary and Tinsel looked on, both a little startled, but mostly with excitement.

"Get back to him now!" ordered Hillary.

Ava was startled right back into action with Hillary's intense orders. She jumped right back to Brad's aid and applied her palm compress. Again her hand and now Brad's temple glowed red and heated almost too hot to touch.

Hillary and Tinsel were both frantically ripping their backpacks apart to find the healing gauzes. Besides just the gash and the bleeding, they were both very worried that Brad had a concussion and bruised his brain. They had never had anyone die on them during all their spelunking and they weren't about to let Brad be the first.

When Ava calmed a little she was able to ask, "What is the red? What is the glowing? What is the heat? What are the dripping lava drops on the ground?"

"It's the Initiation. It's stronger down here in the caves and it's amplified because you are close to us," answered Tinsel. "You are conducting the good power of the deep within the earth because of us. We'll explain more later. We don't have time right now. Just trust us ok?"

"I trust you," was Ava's quick and confident reply.

"What are you talking about?" asked Olivia finally. "What's this red and glowing and lava you're talking about?"

"You don't see it?" asked Tinsel.

"Don't see what? Are you kidding me?" cried Olivia. "All I see is Brad's broken head bleeding through Ava's fingers."

"Then you don't see it," Tinsel said as a fact this time.

"What are you trying to pull on me?! What kind of game is this? Is Brad's head really even hurt, or is that just some kind of joke too?!" exploded Olivia.

"It is no joke Olivia. I'm sorry. You can't see it," said Hillary politely but hesitantly. "It is the good healing power. I have to help Brad now."

Hillary had found the large healing gauze kit in her backpack, ripped it open along with cloth tape, and rushing to Ava's side, "Take your hands away Ava."

Ava released her tourniquet grip so Hillary could do her job, but kept her bright torch in just the right spot on the gash.

Hillary moved to place the gauze, then stopped. She pulled back away and said, "Well look at that Ava."

Ava looked and had to blink twice to see if she were seeing correctly. There was no blood. There was no gash. There was only a long, somewhat rough looking scar where the horrible gash had just been. And Brad had quit moaning at least a minute ago.

The melted drops on the ground had disappeared into cold little rough spots. Sparks sniffed them, but couldn't make anything of them.

Tinsel had been watching all this time and realized that Ava had been Initiated. She was one of them now. Or at least becoming one. One of exactly what she herself didn't exactly know.

"Brad, how are you feeling?" inquired Tinsel.

"I've never felt better!" and he turned to his newest rescuer friend and smiled and said, "Thanks Ava."

"I'm not sure what you're thanking me for Brad," replied Ava. "I know something happened through me, but I don't really know what it was."

"You really made my skull burn there for a minute. I thought maybe you were going to fry my head off, until the throbbing pain in my temple started going away," replied Brad. "And then I knew I was safe in your hands."

"If everyone is ok, let's keep on the path," said Hillary.

"Wait just a minute," interjected Olivia. "I wanna know what kind of trick you all are playing on me. Why am I the butt of your joke? I think I'm starting to see what Luisa was talking about now."

"I told you Olivia, I'm sorry, there is no joke. You just don't trust us. That's why you aren't seeing the workings," replied Hillary.

"So you're just gonna keep up the joke then. You're going to keep on with ganging up on me and being mean? What have I done to you all?!" said Olivia.

"Calm down Olivia, please," said Hillary.

"Don't tell me to calm down!" shouted Olivia. "And I think maybe you're just jealous that Brad likes me better than you."

"What? Brad? What does he have to do with this?" answered Hillary.

"You're jealous because he shows me attention and he's only here because he really just wants to be around me, not you," replied Olivia.

"You're talking crazy Olivia. Brad is both of our friends."

"Yeah, but he doesn't want to be your boyfriend," snapped Olivia.

Brad dropped back and leaned against the tunnel wall, very surprised and without a word to say.

"I don't care what you do or where you go!" yelled Olivia. "I'm going back. I want to leave now. I'm going home!"

"If you won't change your mind Olivia, we'll all have to go back then. We can't leave anyone behind," pleaded Hillary, trying her best to be an honest friend.

Olivia reeled around and set off on a quick pace without waiting for the others.

"Olivia! Wait! You can't go alone. It's too dangerous. We have to be roped together to make it back up the Corkscrew."

Olivia went faster and began to run.

Hillary chased her and grabbed the back of her jacket and jerked her to a stop.

"Let me go!" scowled Olivia.

"Olivia I don't care how angry you are. You can do whatever you want when we get out, but you placed yourself in my care and that's exactly what I'm going to do."

In a flash and without her permission Hillary tied and cinched the lock knot, which is extremely difficult to get undone by anyone except the person who tied it, around Olivia's waist. Then she tied and cinched it to her own harness. Olivia fought and twisted at the knot until her eyes were angry enough to burn holes in Hillary.

"Now we wait for the others and go up together," concluded Hillary.

"I hate you Hillary Spelunker," hissed Olivia. "I will never speak to you or play tetherball with you again."

And those were the last words Olivia spoke the whole trip up the Corkscrew and through the East Forest back to the house where she would not come inside. She pouted very loudly by running ahead and out of earshot of the rest of the spelunkers.

"Well that's pretty disappointing," muttered Brad.

"Yeah what a rip-off," added Ava. "I was super looking forward to a picnic lunch a mile down in the earth. Not many people can ever say they've done that."

Tinsel and Hillary looked at each other and thought, *should we tell them and invite them now?* And they both agreed they should.

"We've got something to tell you," announced Tinsel to the group. "Well, an invitation really."

"What is it?" asked Elka eagerly.

"Well let me just say this," hinted Hillary. "The disappointment of today will be nothing compared to what we have planned for spring break if you're all in on it."

"You're killing us Hillary. Tell us!" blurted Ava.

"Ok, ok," laughed Hillary. "Tinsel and I have seen you all experience the Initiation. That means that we can trust you…now and forever…with the deepest and best of secrets. Tell them Tins."

By now, Brad, Elka and Ava stopped walking and stared with silence and intensity.

"Ok, so it takes a few hours to get to the Second Echo Chamber where we were going to have lunch," began Tinsel. "It takes three days to get to the Dome of the Deep…where we were born."

The three stood silent for a moment before Elka finally had the courage to speak and say, "Um…what? Where you were born…what are you saying? What are you talking about?"

Tinsel continued, "You all know already we are different, but you don't know why and you haven't asked.

We didn't come about in the usual way. Mama and Papa did help bring us into this world, but not in the way you think."

The three companions didn't ask many questions about the story.

"I think we were all beginning to suspect something like this anyway," said Elka.

"Yes, agreed," added Ava.

With the Initiation came a calmness that doesn't need answers right away because it knows the answers are coming and they can wait until the right time. Now was just the time to listen and to trust.

"You'll need to ask your parents to go on a weeklong camping trip over Spring Break. That's how long the journey to the Dome of the Deep will take," finished Tinsel.

There was a loud silence the remainder of the way home.

They arrived at the Lookout Home to find Olivia sitting silently on the porch, not looking at anyone, or talking, until her mom came to get her.

At last, just as she climbed into the car, she paused and shot one last hateful glance at Hillary, then ducked her head into the car and didn't look back.

As the car drove away Hillary held out her hand towards Olivia in one last gesture, but Olivia could neither see nor accept the Regeneration.

CHAPTER FIFTEEN – Pandemonium

First bell just rang and kids began draining away from the playground into the school. Hallways were filled with a crowded sea of smiles and shouts, dragging backpacks and jackets in arms, horseplay and friendly shoves.

Mrs. Caroline's class filled quickly and seats were mostly taken. Mischievous kids were sneaking to the whiteboard drawing funny faces and putting their friend's names next to them.

The classroom door opened again and Mrs. Caroline joined them. She quietly stopped for a moment to smile and enjoy the chaos. Only one or two students had noticed her come in and they were already in their seats.

"A-hem," said Mrs. Caroline loudly as if clearing her throat.

A quick rush of guilty looking students began running for their desks. Kori sprinted to his desk from the front board, running into a front row desk as he turned the corner. His legs got so mixed up with the chair legs that both he and the desk flipped over and ended up in a tangled mess on the floor.

"Are you ok Kori?" asked Mrs. Caroline.

Kori, who was trying to untangle the mess of legs replied, "Yes Mrs. Caroline. I'm sorry."

"Please right yourself and the desk and take your seat," was all she said back to him.

"I can see it's already beginning," said Mrs. Caroline with a sly grin.

Ava raised her hand.

"Yes Ava?" said Mrs. Caroline.

"What's beginning?"

"Pandemonium week," replied Mrs. Caroline.

Before Mrs. Caroline could explain, Ava's hand was back up in a flash.

"Yes Ava?"

"Um… pandemonium… does that have something to do with pandas?" asked Ava.

Half the class wondered the same thing and the other half laughed at Ava's question.

Mrs. Caroline did smile, but she didn't laugh at Ava.

"No Ava. Pandemonium. That's chaos, disorganized, panic. It's Spring Break Madness when students can't control themselves and draw funny pictures on the board and trip over desks," smiled Mrs. Caroline.

Kori grinned a half way goofy and half way embarrassed smile.

"It's when it's the last week of school before Spring Break," continued Mrs. Caroline, "and students have so much energy they can't control themselves because they are so excited about their fun plans for vacation. It happens every year."

Mrs. Caroline was ready for the pandemonium again this year just like she was last year and the year before that. In fact for the last ten years since she realized you have to beat these kids at their own game.

She thought to herself, *trying to keep the excitement in these kiddos under control is like shaking a bottle of soda; it's going to explode if you try to keep it contained.*

"Ok, everyone stand and push the desks to the back of the room," she instructed.

Her kids were used to clearing the room like this for the various fun and sneaky activities Mrs. Caroline would always spring on them, so they had the room cleared in record time.

She pointed and said, "Boys on this side and girls on that side."

As they separated, Luisa and Olivia were right next to Hillary, Elka and Ava.

Luisa grabbed Olivia's hand and whispered, "Come with me and put the other girls between us and Hillary's gang. I don't wanna be near them."

Olivia did have an 'excited for the game' smile on her face until Luisa reminded her they were at war with Hillary and her gang.

"I am so angry at them," said Oliva, "after all the tricks they pulled on me down in that stupid Corkscrew Tunnel."

"Ok class, repeat this chant after me," said Mrs. Caroline. "We want Spring Break!"

All the class said together with her the second time, "We want Spring Break!"

"Oh that was pretty weak. That wouldn't wake up a sleeping baby," chided Mrs. Caroline. "Again now. One…two…three."

And the whole class yelled at the top of their lungs, "WE WANT SPRING BREAK!!"

"Ok that's much better," smiled Mrs. Caroline, knowing for sure the next door class could hear them and would wonder what the heck was going on. She thought to herself, *that's not nearly enough energy to tire them out though so we can get some real classwork done.*

"Ok now, with each word jump, and when you land, stomp both feet and say it. One jump for each word. Got it? Ok…one…two…three…"

It went something like this.

"We…" *STOMP!*

"Want…" *STOMP!*

"Spring…" *STOMP!*

"Break!…" *STOMP!*

Now Mr. Adder from the next door's third grade classroom was peeking in the door window. He already had a good idea from years past what was going on, though he didn't much approve of Mrs. Caroline's antics because he would never do anything like that in his class. He frowned and walked away…although deep down inside he wished he knew how to have a fun class like that.

"Ok now, we're going to add activities to your Spring Break. Boys jump and yell *We want Spring Break*, then girls jump and respond *We're going to the lake!*" directed Mrs. Caroline.

They went through several rounds of that and faces began to flush a little pink.

"Ok everyone. Girls yell *Going out in a boat*, and boys respond with *Hope you don't forget to float!*"

And it went something like this.

"Going…" *STOMP!*

"Out…" *STOMP!*

"In…" *STOMP!*

"a…" *STOMP!*

"Boat!..." *STOMP!*

"Hope…" *STOMP!*

"You…" *STOMP!*

"Don't…" *STOMP!*

"Forget…" *STOMP!*

"to…" *STOMP!*

"Float!..." *STOMP!*

Mrs. Caroline had the energy packed kids go through this chant ten times before some of the kids began to slow down and most of them had trickles of sweat running down their faces. She figured that had about done it. At least now no more desks would be turned over.

"All right class, pull your desks back to their marks."

"Wait Mrs. Caroline," shouted Luisa as she jumped up and down with her hand raised. "Can we do one more? I've got one more chant."

"Well ok Luisa," said Mrs. Caroline turning to the class. "Does everyone want to do one more?"

They were all excited at what Luisa might have for them and many "Yeses!" and "Yays!" filled the classroom.

"Ok Luisa, you've got our attention. Teach us your chant."

"Ok," began Luisa, with a nasty grin now crawling over her face. "Repeat after me…"

"We want Spring Break; Hillary is such a fake."

A few seconds of shocked, tense silence hushed across the room. In another few seconds half the class broke out in a laugh. The other half looked back and forth with mortified faces between Luisa, Mrs. Caroline and Hillary waiting to see what terrible thing might happen.

The first thing that happened was Mrs. Caroline pointing at the door as she looked at Luisa.

Next, Mrs. Caroline directed, "Continue on with putting your desks back on their marks. Luisa and I have business in Ms. Porter's office."

Luisa smirked at Mrs. Caroline, then she turned and smiled at the whole class as she walked towards the door. She made sure to stop her eyes right on Hillary.

Hillary smiled back at Luisa. But it was a true smile. It was a smile that felt sorry for Luisa. It was a smile that still hoped to have Luisa as her friend one day. Mama and Papa and Tinsel and the Regeneration gave her the strength to know that Luisa didn't really hate her. Luisa didn't like herself.

In an hour, Luisa finally returned to class. She tried to smile again at the class and at Hillary, but it was easy to see that this time the smile wasn't sneaky. It wasn't proud. It wasn't boastful. No, this smile was covering up something that looked like it would cry if she let it.

No one saw Luisa at first recess, or lunch, or lunch recess. A rumor floated around that she was enjoying Ms. Porter's company for study hall and lunch as she thought through what she thought was her wonderful and witty rhyming activity for Spring Break.

Luisa was allowed to join the rest of the class for final recess.

"I'm glad to see you," said Olivia. "I've been lonely and Hillary has been trying to be my friend. But after what she did to me down in that Corkscrew Tunnel, I'll never speak to her again."

Luisa grew a despicable smile, and said, "Let me tell you some more of Hillary and Tinsel's lies."

At last recess of the school day, Hillary was talking to Tinsel and the other spelunkers.

"We have just one week until Spring Break and I want to try one more time to patch things up with Luisa and Olivia," said Hillary.

"Aww.. why don't you just give up on that Hill," said Ava. "They are making it pretty clear they don't want anything to do with you."

"That may be true, but I'm not completely sure. Until I am I'll keep trying."

"You should just give up," said Brad. "They are a lost cause. I see what you are trying to do, and it's nice of you and all, but their kind can never understand the Regeneration."

"Brad, you don't understand the power of the Regeneration. It never gives up. It can change the most closed mind, the hardest heart, the saddest feelings. It can heal relationships better than any medicine or counsellor. It never gives up, and I will never give up."

"Tinsel, just you come with me. I don't want them to feel like we are ganging up on them."

Hillary and Tinsel approached Luisa, Olivia and Klix, who were hanging out on the swings by themselves. The spelunkers had plans for this Wednesday afternoon and they decided to invite Luisa and Olivia.

"What do you want?" snapped Luisa before Hillary could say anything.

"Well, we're getting together Wednesday after school to play and hike and ride Bushwackers on the Lookout Mountain Trails. We have miles and miles of them. And then Papa is going to barbeque a good dinner for us. Would you like to join us?"

Luisa and Olivia were so surprised they didn't know what to say for a moment. But Klix did.

"I'm coming," said Klix.

He didn't even realize he hadn't been invited, but it made Hillary chuckle anyway.

"Ok Klix, you can come," said Hillary.

Tinsel thought to Hillary, *why did you say yes to him? He's a brat. He's a third grader. And worst of all, he's a boy.*

Tinsel! thought Hillary right back. *He's Elka's brother and he's not so bad when he's not being a brat.*

After staring at each other for a moment, Luisa spoke for both herself and Olivia, "Let us talk about it... alone."

"Ok, just let us know as soon as you can so Papa can make enough food," replied Hillary.

"Actually Hillary, I have decided. We will come," said Luisa confidently.

Olivia glanced over at Luisa with a surprised look and leaned and whispered, "What the heck?! I didn't say yes and you didn't even talk to me about it."

Luisa whispered back, "I know what I'm doing. Trust me. I'll fill you in later."

"Ok then! It's all set. If it's ok with your folks and Olivia's mom, just take the bus with us out to our drop-off Wednesday afternoon."

After Hillary and Tinsel returned to the other spelunkers, Luisa lowered her head towards Olivia, and with whispers that not even Klix could hear, began making a bent plan.

CHAPTER SIXTEEN – Bushwackers

Permissions were gotten and proper boots were worn to school for Wednesday afternoon's activities out at Lookout Mountain.

"Good morning Hillary," said Luisa with the best smile she could pretend, as the bell rang and everyone headed into the school.

"Hey Luisa!" welcomed Hillary. "Are you excited about this afternoon?"

"We can't wait," as she glanced over to Oliva, who returned a weak smile.

Throughout the day, during the recesses and lunch and free library time things appeared to be going ok. There were no mean words. There was no taking sides. But there was just something that Hillary couldn't quite put her mind straight on.

Every now and again if she looked rather quickly in Luisa's direction she would see whispers between Luisa and Olivia. Whispers and smiles. Not evil smiles. Just grim or suspicious smiles that quickly turned into smiles that she couldn't quite trust.

****

All the spelunkers and Luisa, Olivia and Klix would take bus number 49, the long bus ride going all the way out to Lookout Mountain. It was the furthest route out. Any further and moms and dads had to provide the ride to and from school.

The spelunkers were so excited, they made it out to the bus first and grabbed the seats near the front of the bus. Hillary saved a seat for Luisa.

"Tinsel, save a seat for Olivia," said Hillary.

"I don't want to sit by Olivia. I didn't even really want them out to the Mountain today," said Tinsel.

You can do better than that, thought Hillary to Tinsel.

Maybe I don't want to do better than that! You're always telling me to do better…to be like you, thought-snapped Tinsel right back.

I'm not telling you what to do Sis. I'm just reminding you of the Regeneration power in you, that we share, that can be fragile if we don't share it right. Maybe it's a little selfish, but if I don't have your help, I can't be as good or strong, thought-pleaded Hillary back.

Tinsel thought a moment. Hillary saw a sad and regretful look come across her face and maybe even in her eyes. Then she gave Hillary an agreeing smile and slid across the seat to the window, placing her books on the seat next to her to save the seat.

You're such a good Sis, thought Hillary.

It's a lot because of you Hilly-beans.

Hillary laughed out loud at the name Papa liked to call her.

Mr. Rossi was just beginning to close the bus door.

"Mr. Rossi," said Hillary, "can we wait just another minute or two? Luisa, Olivia and Klix are supposed to join us today."

"We're going to be running behind schedule Hillary. Parents get worried when I don't show up on time. And many of them have tight schedules that we need to respect."

"Please, please, please, Mr. Rossi," pleaded Hillary in her sweetest pleading voice.

Mr. Rossi enjoyed seeing Hillary more than any of the other wonderful kids on the bus. Secretly she was one of his favorite reasons for driving. If he was ever having a little bit of a down day, her loyal smile gave him strength and he wished that everyone was as nice as she was. In fact, he wished he could be more like her.

The difficult thing about Hillary being his favorite was that he absolutely found it impossible to disappoint her.

"Yes, please, please, please Mr. Rossi," chimed in Tinsel as well.

Mr. Rossi could not resist the one-two punch of the Spelunker twins.

"You girls are going to get me fired," as he re-opened the bus door with a defeated but happy smile. "Two more minutes. That's all."

"Thank you!" cheered the Spelunkers.

Almost two minutes passed and finally Luisa, Olivia and Klix came out of the front school doors together. Hand in hand they looked like they were almost trying to walk as slowly as possible. At one point, when they knew many eyes were staring out the bus at them, they stopped and faced each other and whispered something, then Luisa laughed and they continued their walk.

Tinsel jumped across the aisle and whispered to Hillary, "Look at them! They're trying to make us wait. They're doing this on purpose."

At that point Hillary began to agree and whispered back, "You may be right about that Sis. In fact I know you are. But I don't know what to do. They're already invited and have no other ride home now."

I just want to punch that Luisa in the face! thought-yelled Tinsel.

Hillary didn't even want to answer Tinsel. She understood the frustration. She held onto the hope that Luisa and Olivia could still be better. She had faith in others before when they seemed they had no hope and was able to love them and had seen things change. *Why not Luisa and Olivia?* No, until they flat out told her to leave them alone, she would never give up. They could never make her give up hope.

Tinsel, just prepare yourself for them. Then they won't upset you so much, thought Hillary.

The three climbed the bus stairwell, then stood in the front and center like a King and Queen and Prince with their noses in the air looking over their kingdom.

Hillary ignored their poses, looked Luisa straight in the eyes with a smile and patted the empty seat next to her.

Tinsel met Olivia's eyes and thumped her seat once rather hard.

Luisa turned her eyes straight down the aisle, grabbed Olivia's hand and quickly pulled her to the back of the bus. Luisa tried to start some talk with her, but Olivia's attention was towards the front of the bus. Her face said that her feelings were torn and that she didn't know what to do. She almost looked like she could cry.

Mr. Rossi closed the bus doors and stepped on the gas pedal. Tinsel jumped over to Hillary's bench. Tinsel had two ideas. She could either go throw a book at Luisa or she could heartache with Hillary. She decided to put her head on Hillary's shoulder.

****

The sound of Hillary, Tinsel, Elka, Ava, Brad, Klix, Luisa and Olivia tromping up the gravel sent Sparks into Bark Flips, bouncing and barking and flipping off the walls. It was bad enough when the pup knew it was just Hillary and Tinsel. But this time his alert ears knew that there was much more here than normal.

Mama and Papa had to cover their ears. An inside barking voice was something that the family beagle just had not mastered yet at only a few years old. Mama opened the door earlier than normal just to get his ear splitting yaps out of the house.

Mama could see Sparks' four paws throwing up a dust trail going down the hill, and many feet making another dust trail coming up the hill. The thought of some kind of explosion happening when the two met in the middle made Mama laugh.

Mama warned Papa that he needed to either put on his earmuffs or spend the rest of the day out in the half-finished workshop if he wanted to keep both his sanity and his hearing because half the school was just arriving and it would be chaos the rest of the day.

"Oh you think you can handle it and I can't?" toyed Papa.

Mama winked and laughed.

It was an army of sixteen feet tromping uphill. The four feet of Luisa and Olivia hung out at the back of the troupe. The further Hillary lagged behind to try to join them, the slower Luisa dragged her feet. She was determined to be last. Olivia was caught just between the two of them, and she really wanted to walk with Brad.

The more kids Sparks saw, the faster he ran. It was like the group of kids was a swimming pool and he was about to jump right in. Sparks plowed right into a sea of shins, not really caring who he greeted first. What he actually greeted first though were Brad's legs. Sparks is not a big dog, which is why it surprised Brad that this medium beagle took his legs right out from under him. Brad lashed out with his arms flailing, trying to find anything he could grab to slow his fall. He caught ahold of Olivia's jacket and it did slow him down a little, but it made her go a lot faster. Right down on top of him.

No one was hurt. But Olivia did stay on the ground so that Brad could help her up.

"Brad, can you help me up please," asked Olivia, reaching her hand towards him.

Brad grabbed her hand and pulled her to standing. Olivia walked fine for a few steps before she said, "My ankle is hurting. I think maybe it's sprained. Brad, I think I need your help."

Hillary thought, *Oh gosh Olivia, you were fine just a moment ago and now you're faking a sprained ankle.*

Brad offered his arm and Olivia put her arm around Brad's waist and leaned against him and pretended to limp her left leg. They arrived at the front porch where Brad helped her sit on the steps.

Hillary thought, *I know what will fix Olivia...*

"Well that sprained ankle is too bad Olivia," mentioned Hillary. "I was going to put you on a Bushwacker Bike with Brad. They hold up to three riders, but you're not allowed to ride with an injured ankle. It's just too dangerous."

Olivia looked a little panicky for a moment, then a clever look spread across her face as she jumped up and said, "Oh, I think it's starting to feel better already. It must have only been a tiny sprain." As she hopped up with just the smallest limp on her *right* leg.

"That's pretty amazing. It looks like your limp jumped from your left leg to your right leg Olivia," said Tinsel.

Olivia again looked a little panicky before saying, "I think they must have both been sprained, but the left one is totally better and the right one is almost there."

Liar! Hillary thought-yelled to Tinsel.

Hillary, calm down. We both know she's faking, but you know it won't come to any good for her, thought-calmed Tinsel.

Since when are you the one calming me down? thought-laughed Hillary. *Thanks Tins. You know the one thing that really makes me furious is a liar.*

You know she's only hurting herself, her own reputation, thought Tinsel.

I know. You're right. Thanks Sis, thought Hillary.

Mama and Papa had set out a nice afternoon snack at the picnic table out near the well under the big Alder tree to give the troupe energy for the afternoons events. Olivia made it to the table without a limp.

Hillary sat at the end on one side and Brad sat in the middle. There wasn't really enough room, but Olivia managed to squeeze in just between them and Brad had to move over to have enough elbow room to eat. Hillary wanted to dig her elbow into Olivia's side, but just rolled her eyes instead. Tinsel saw the eye roll and gave Hillary a hug before going to the other side of the table and taking a place.

Before long, their bellies were full of snack cracker sandwiches of smoked meats and cheeses, grapes and Mandarin oranges, chocolate cupcakes and Snickerdoodle cookies, almonds and granola, all washed down with fizzy lemon water.

"Get enough, but not too much, or your bellies will hurt when you hike or ride," warned Hillary with a smile, as Klix tried to hide stuffing his jacket pockets with huge handfuls of Snickerdoodles.

"Finish up! Everyone over to the barn," said Tinsel.

****

Just out behind the half-finished shop was the Spelunker barn, where they kept their four horses and the two Bushwackers. Papa had already moved many of his tools to his half-finished workshop.

"These are Bushwackers," instructed Tinsel. "Have any of you seen or ridden these before?"

Not a one of the troupe spoke up or raised a hand, so Tinsel knew this was going to be a real training session before they could head out and have fun on them.

Bushwackers are a wonderfully odd vehicle and rare to find. They have five wheels. There are four wheels like a cart and the vehicle can pivot between these two wheels to turn very sharply. There is a single wheel out front that the driver uses to steer with handlebars like a motorcycle. All four wheels in the back are drive wheels which push the cart around. The large knobby paddle balloon tires make it impossible to get stuck even in the deepest, thickest mud. The best part of the Bushwacker is that it holds not one, not two, but three people. Everyone knows it's more fun to have three people on an adventure.

"These are unstoppable. They're very safe," continued Tinsel. "They are not impossible to flip over, but it's very difficult. If you flip them over, you were probably doing something stupid."

Tinsel! Don't say stupid, thought-scolded Hillary.

"Oh, I'm sorry," corrected Tinsel. "You were probably doing something bone-headed."

"Tinsel!" reprimanded Hillary out loud.

"Foolish…moronic…brainless?" offered Tinsel.

"Reckless," corrected Hillary.

Straighten up or I'm taking over, thought Hillary.

"Reckless it is," said Tinsel with a playful smile. "Anyway…"

"Everyone. Helmets on!" directed Hillary.

"Brad, Elka and Ava get on that Bushwacker," directed Tinsel. "Practice slow circles around the house. Each of you take turns driving. When you're driving, remember you are responsible for the safety of your passenger crew."

"Luisa, Olivia and Klix get on that one and practice the same thing. Remember everyone, safety is first, fun is second," said Tinsel.

"Me first," said Luisa as she jumped into the driver position. "Get behind me Olivia so I can talk to you. Klix, get behind Olivia."

As they pulled away for their first circle, Olivia whispered to Luisa, "Why did Tinsel separate us? Hillary said I could ride with Brad. I feel like she's trying to exclude us."

"It doesn't matter. It's perfect," schemed Luisa. "Tinsel doesn't realize she's just making our plan that much easier for us."

"Your plan," corrected Olivia.

"Our plan," hissed Luisa, gritting her teeth.

****

An hour of practice loops and Hillary and Tinsel knew the crew was safe to operate the Bushwackers on their own.

"All right everyone, we're ready to set out," said Hillary.

"Wait a minute," said Brad. "There's six of us on the two Bushwackers. These won't hold the two of you. How are you going with us?"

"Very good question Bradley," laughed Hillary. "I was just getting to that."

The barn door swung open and out came Tinsel leading two Welsh ponies. One had a shining silky silvery gray color with a jet black streak on her muzzle that traveled from nose to ears. The other had a brilliant white glossy coat with dappled chocolate spots like a leopard all over her body.

"This silver one is Seren. She is Hillary's and she loves to ride at night under the stars. And this is Brynn. She's mine and she loves to run the hills with or without me. That's only because she is a sneak and always seems to find a way out of the barn. She always comes home, but she seems to love to worry me."

"We're going to follow you," said Hillary. "Horseback takes months and years to learn safely, but the Bushwackers you can learn in an hour."

"And the Bushwackers don't have a mind of their own," laughed Tinsel. "They won't try to throw a new rider off."

"A few simple facts and rules," announced Hillary.

"First, Lookout Mountain is close to 50,000 acres. That's almost 75 square miles."

"Second, we have almost 50 miles of horse and Bushwacker trails. Stay on the wide double track trails. The single track trails are only for the horses."

"That means it is super important we stay together. No one gets out of each other's sight. If you lose the group, stop where you are and we'll find you. If you get lost out here it could take a week to find you."

"And by then you'd be shriveled up like a twig with no food or water," smirked Tinsel.

"Tinsel!" snapped Hillary. "Don't worry everyone. You won't get lost and you have food and water in your underseat packs. But you're not going to need them because we're all sticking together, right Tins?!"

"Yes Sis...," groaned Tinsel.

"Fire your Bushwackers up!" hollered Hillary as she put her left foot in Seren's stirrup and swung her leg over her pony like a pro. "Brad, why don't you lead us out. Over there to the right. That's the first trail head."

"Sure thing," said Brad proudly as he checked his passengers and slowly pressed forward on the thumb throttle.

Two Bushwackers and two horses with all their riders progressed through the trailhead and set out over the rocky, rolling, swervy, tree-rooty, tilty, slanty, muddy miles and miles of trails.

Sometimes Brad led the team. Sometimes it was Luisa. Riders switched turns so sometimes it was Ava or Elka or Olivia or Klix. Whoever was leading, there were hundreds of smiles and laughs and an occasional wild yell when something was too scary. The Bushwackers were truly amazingly powerful and nimble vehicles.

Five miles into the first trail, Hillary galloped past the Bushwackers and came to a halt in the lead. She pulled her reins back hard and came to a spinning stop and brought Seren face to face with Luisa. They all stopped there to rest by the Raven River so the horses could drink and rest and nibble at the freshly watered grass.

"That is the most fun I have ever had!" exclaimed Ava.

"Um yeah Ava, with you driving that might have been the biggest scare I've ever had," joked Elka.

"Well Elka, with you driving I think I nearly pooped my pants," added Brad with a smile.

"Oh, just like you pooped your pants in the Spanning Well Tunnel while I was right behind you Bradley?" mocked Tinsel.

"Hey, no fair!" protested Brad. "That wasn't pooping my pants, that was my stinky boots!"

"Stinky boots…stinky pants. It's all the same. Smells just as bad," said Tinsel poking good fun at Bradley.

They had many more good jokes as they rested and made plans for the next section of the trail.

"Coming up next is what we call the Forest Circle," explained Hillary. "There is only one entrance off of this trail into it, and it is a big zig-zaggy circle about a mile around and it comes back to the same entry point. Just like a big circle. Only one way in and one way out. It's pretty flat and Tinsel and I like to race the circle. Do you think you are all up to it?"

"Just one time around?" asked Brad.

"That's what we usually do. Not enough for you Brad?" taunted Tinsel.

"Well why don't we make it more interesting and say three times around?" challenged Brad.

"Why not?!" replied Tinsel. "And if we're going to make it interesting, why don't we say the losing teams have to bring the winning teams candy first day back from Spring Break?"

"You're on!" replied Brad. "The rest of you in?"

All the shouts and dares and taunts confirmed they were all in.

"Ok then, the rules are very simple," started Hillary. "Three times around as fast and safe as you can go. No running each other off the road. Stop at the entrance after three rounds. First one there is the winner. Pick your best driver."

The drivers were Elka, Luisa, Hillary and Tinsel.

"Ready?" hollered Hillary. "One… two… three… GO!!"

CHAPTER SEVENTEEN – Snickerdoodles

All four teams were off like a shot. Tinsel in the lead, followed by Hillary. Next was Elka and in the rear was Luisa.

Sparks was directing traffic from the saddlebag on Hillary's horse Seren. At least he thought he was. Sparks kept barking and the Bushwackers and ponies kept moving so he figured he was making them move according to his instructions. Hillary figured *why hurt his feelings by telling him he's not in charge.*

"We're last already Luisa!" yelled Olivia over the noise of the Bushwacker roaring engine.

"Quiet!" Luisa snapped back. "I know what I'm doing. Did you forget the plan?"

"What?... Now?... What's the plan?"

"Quiet! Just follow my lead," said Luisa.

"I want to know what you're planning," said Olivia. "I know something is up. You were driving much faster than this when we were practicing. Is this what you've been waiting for?"

Luisa's silence put a frustrated look on Olivia's face.

It took them almost eight minutes to make the first circle. Luisa had purposely fallen behind far enough that they were out of sight of the race leaders. When they arrived at the entry point to the Forest Circle, instead of turning left and starting the second lap, Luisa turned right and went out of the circle. She pulled far enough up the trail so the other racers couldn't see them if they came around again.

"Ok Olivia, where is this Spanning Well Tunnel with the Shale Shards you told me so much about?" demanded Luisa.

"What?! From here? How am I supposed to know? I've never been on this trail and I'm totally lost without Hillary guiding. You never told me you were going to do it this way," protested Olivia.

"Oh... my... gosh...," groaned Luisa. "What good are you Olivia?! How did you get there last time?"

"I have a good mind to get off this Bushwacker and tell the others what you're up to," protested Olivia. "I don't like how you're treating me."

"Oh gosh, I'm sorry Olivia. Really," fawned Luisa. "I didn't mean it. You're my best friend. I don't know what I would do without you. You can't leave me. You just can't. I'll be better I promise. Let's have fun and do this together. Look how they separated us back at the house and stuck us together with Klix. Not that I mind. Really. Because I like you so much. But they... they did it to be mean. They don't like you Olivia. Are you going to let them do that to you...?"

Olivia was silent for a minute as the look of frustration turned into anger.

"The only way I know to get there is from the house. That's where we set off from."

"Well we can't go back that way and be seen," said Luisa.

"If we go almost all the way back," said Olivia, "we can stop short of barely seeing the house and cut across from there. I should be able to find it after that and we shouldn't be seen."

"Good plan. Let's do it. You're driving from here," said Luisa.

Olivia started the Bushwacker and headed southwest back the way they came. Within a couple miles, just coming over the top of a rise, the three could barely make out the Lookout Mountain Home.

"We'll cut back and stay behind this rise and make our way directly west now," said Olivia. "That should run us right into the trail that takes us to the Spanning Well entrance."

Olivia pulled the Bushwacker off the trail into the rough and rocky forest. It was slow going trying to pick a path that wouldn't get them stuck, roll them over or drive them off a cliff. But the Bushwacker was unstoppable and slowly and steadily Olivia, Luisa and Klix wormed their way through the treacherous terrain.

Klix had been so quiet this whole time that Luisa and Olivia had all but forgotten he was the final rider on the back of the Bushwacker. Klix had long learned that keeping quiet, keeping unseen, was often the best way to both keep himself out of trouble or to get himself into trouble. Both were equally fun to him.

Within ten minutes, Olivia whispered back to Luisa, "I think I recognize where we are now. I remember this forest opening with those high rock wall faces over there. Tinsel had mentioned how fun they are to rope climb and we should do that some time. If we turn here and go North we should find the covered opening."

"What do you mean the covered opening?" asked Luisa.

"The openings to the caves and lava tubes are covered for the most part with vines and thickets and they can be difficult to see until Hillary or Tinsel point them out," answered Olivia.

"Well you better be able to find it for me," said Luisa.

Olivia bit her lip and said, "I've had just about enough of your bullying."

"I'm sorry Olivia. I was just teasing. You know that don't you?" pouted Luisa. "I didn't mean anything by it. I'll be good. I'll do better. You know you're my best friend. I would never do anything wrong to you."

Olivia shrugged her shoulders and let her silence do all her talking.

After ten minutes of rough trail terrain Olivia shut down the Bushwacker engine and said, "We should just about be at the Spanning Tunnel opening. It should be near here."

Helmets off, the three began looking around intently and running in circles around the same rock formations until Luisa began to show signs of frustration.

"How are we supposed to teach them a lesson if we can't find the tunnel?!" said Luisa exasperated.

****

After three laps around the Forest Circle, Hillary and Tinsel had almost completely lapped and caught up with Elka, Ava and Brad and watched them just starting their final lap.

Hillary and Tinsel were expert riders and horses are always so much more nimble than any mechanical vehicle. Horses are nature. Engines are not.

"They didn't even know they never stood a chance of beating us," laughed Tinsel.

"Yeah it's almost unfair if it weren't just for fun," said Hillary. "Of course we won't be able to take their candy."

Ten minutes later, Hillary could just make out the mud-covered face of Elka coming up over the final hill to the finish line. Elka, Ava and Brad arrived laughing through dirt covered shirts and grins.

"I guess we're third place after you and Tinsel," said Elka to Hillary.

"How far back did you pass Luisa?" asked Hillary.

"We didn't pass them. They must be right behind us," replied Elka.

"That's strange. We saw you take off on your last lap as we arrived at the finish line. You must have passed them," said Hillary.

"That would have been an impossible pass on these narrow trails without noticing. No way we passed them," confirmed Elka.

"Ok, I'm a little concerned now," worried Hillary. "Tinsel, you go that way forward on the trail and I'll go around backwards and meet you half way in the middle unless one of us finds them, then stay there and wait for the other."

They both heeled their ponies around and set off in their assigned directions at a fast trot. Only minutes later they met each other half way and immediately realized by the confused look on the other's face neither had found them.

"Back to start!" yelled Hillary as they both broke into a quick canter on the rough trail.

"Ok everyone, we might have a problem," said Hillary uneasily. "Luisa, Olivia and Klix are not on the trail. They may have accidentally run off the side and could be in trouble down in a ravine or runoff. We need to search on foot now and look for any sign of wheel tracks or listen for distress calls."

"Brad and Ava come with me," directed Tinsel. "Elka and Hillary you go that way. Go slow. Look and listen closely. They may have had an accident. We can't afford to miss them. And we only have two hours until dusk. Hillary and I are staying on our horses. Go!"

The spelunker search team combed every inch of side trail looking for signs but could not find the slightest hint of a departure from the trail. Fifteen minutes into the search and both parties met at the far half of the Forest Circle.

"Nothing?!" exclaimed Tinsel, seeing the empty look on Hillary's face. "How can that be?! This is weird and scary. What could have happened?"

"Brad, Elka and Ava… use the Bushwacker and head back the way we came on the main trail to the house," said Hillary. "Do you know the way?"

"Absolutely," replied Brad. "Come on girls!"

"I'm going to start a large circle sweep around the outside of the Forest Circle," said Hillary. "Tinsel, ride as fast as you can back to the house to see if they are there. Explain to Mama and Papa what is going on."

"Got it," as Tinsel took off in a flash of hooves and dust.

****

"Here it is! I think this is it!" cried Olivia.

"I don't see anything but a bunch of twiney twigs and overgrown ivy," said Luisa. "What are you looking at?"

"Here, through the brush. Push your arm. There's a big hole there," confirmed Olivia.

Luisa pushed her arm in where Olivia showed her, "Well how the heck would I ever find that? How did you know?"

"Somehow I just had a feeling it was there… like an intuition," replied Olivia.

"That's a bunch of superstition. Intuition… that's crazy. Are you trying to pull a trick Olivia? Because if you are…"

"No, really. I just felt it was there somehow," said Olivia.

"Whatever," scoffed Luisa. "It took you way too long to find it. Now we barely have time to do it and get back before they notice we've been gone."

"Do what?" asked Olivia. "You still haven't told me what we were doing once we got out here."

"We're going to swipe some of the Shale Shards and mark the place up a little to teach them a lesson not to keep secrets," said Luisa as she pulled a can of red spray paint out of her pack.

"I don't know about this…" warned Olivia.

"Don't chicken out now Olivia. You're already guilty by showing me the tunnel. Too late now. Don't make me rat you out."

"I don't know why I ever let you talk me into this," said Olivia. "You made me your accomplice by tricking me and now I'm stuck in this. Just please don't do anything too bad. Hillary and Tinsel are good people."

Luisa silently glared at Olivia, then pointed her finger at the tunnel.

With some difficulty, the three of them pressed through the thickets and Luisa turned on the torch she had brought in her pack.

"How far to the Shale Shards?" asked Luisa.

"Well if I remember correctly it's not that far once we get past the Cross Winds Tunnel… if we can get across the Cross Winds Tunnel…" said Olivia.

"Um… what do you mean *if*…" demanded Luisa.

"Well, I kind of forgot that we all had to rope up because the Raven River flows across when there is too much rain and runoff," replied Olivia.

"And you're just now telling me? You better hope we can get through."

"I never should have brought you here," said Olivia. "Why did you drag me into this? You used me to get to Hillary and Tinsel. You never cared about me. And now I've gone and shown you their sacred tunnel. You never would have found this place without my help. Hillary and Tinsel are going to hate me."

"Too late for that regret now. Show me the Shale Shards and I'll never let on that it was you that showed me. If you turn back now, I'm going straight to the Spelunkers and tell them what you've done."

After a moment of silence, Olivia finally said, "This is the Cross Winds Tunnel."

"Well it doesn't look bad to me. What were you all so afraid of?" criticized Luisa.

"When we came through it was two feet deep and raging and roaring past us. Now it's no more than a six inch deep stream. Barely enough to cover our boots. The runoff must have stopped," replied Olivia.

"Come on now. We're in a hurry," demanded Luisa.

Within minutes they had waded through the shallow water and had come upon the Shale Slides.

"Here we are. The Shale Slides," said Olivia.

"What? These? This is what the commotion is all about? A bunch of little rocks?! I'm almost sorry I let you bring me down here," lamented Luisa as she pulled a satchel out of her pack.

Before Olivia could warn her, Luisa jammed her hand down into the pile of shale to scoop up a large handful. She quickly pulled her hand back, wincing in pain, and looking down at it she exclaimed, "I've sliced my fingers. Why didn't you warn me?! This might need stitches. What am I going to do now?"

The drops of blood falling on the shale did nothing but slip into the cracks between the shards.

"Here, I do have this cloth to wrap it," offered Olivia. "But you'll have to hold it tight. I don't have any tape."

"Klix, use your gloves and shovel some shale into here," demanded Luisa. "We need to get out of here quickly."

Klix did as he was told.

They were almost back to the tunnel entrance when Luisa announced, "Olivia you're going to have to tag the wall for us."

"What are you talking about?"

"The red spray paint. Pull it out of my pack and write what I tell you on the wall."

"I don't know about this Luisa. You're not supposed to take anything out, and we're already breaking that rule. Now to leave behind graffiti, that's double bad."

"You'll do it, or the first thing they'll hear when we get back is how you showed us the tunnel and where to steal the shale!" demanded Luisa. "Besides, it's just a funny little note. More of a joke really…"

"Oh all right… let's just get this over with. I'm getting creeped out by this tunnel."

Luisa directed her torch to the side of the tunnel and directed, "Spray in capital letters… LIARS!"

"What?… no… no… I won't do it," protested Olivia, almost in tears now.

"Do it and we can get out of here. Quick now. It's not so bad. Just a joke. Don't make me tell on you…"

"I hate this Luisa!"

Olivia removed the cap… held out her arm… pressed the trigger over and over to spell out the horrible red letters.

Shoving the can back into Luisa's hand, she could just see the light at the opening of the tunnel and ran with all her might until she broke free through the vines into the sunlight.

****

A quick canter around the Lookout House and Tinsel could not find the Bushwacker or it's riders anywhere. Now she was getting very concerned.

"Papa," hollered Tinsel through the open studs of the half-finished workshop where she caught quick glimpses of him working away.

Walking out of the opening where the rollup door would eventually go, "Yes Tins? You look a little worried," Papa replied.

Half out of breath and a lot worried, Tinsel replied, "Papa... Luisa... Olivia... Klix..., we can't find them, we lost them, out in the Forest Circle."

"Calm down Tinsel. Climb down. Tell me everything you know."

Tinsel didn't have a lot to tell. She didn't know much. Hearing the excitement, Mama joined them. Within a couple minutes Mama and Papa knew all there was to know and were already saddling up their horses.

"Lead the way Tinsel," urged Papa after he and Mama were all mounted and ready.

The three of them broke into a quick canter and headed straight back for the Forest Circle. They passed Brad, Elka and Ava on the way.

"You three get back to the house and stay there," commanded Papa. "We don't want two lost parties and the Bushwackers are not good search and rescue vehicles off the paths."

"Yes sir," answered Elka, with nods from Brad and Ava.

****

"We need to hightail it back to the Forest Circle before anyone knows we were gone," said Luisa, climbing into the driver's seat and firing up the engine. "Get on! Both of you, now."

"We should mark the tunnel opening so we can find it again later," said Klix.

"Absolutely not," said Luisa. "We don't have time for that. We've been gone too long already and you're going to get us caught dummy."

Olivia reluctantly climbed on. Klix and his frown climbed on last. And the three headed back toward the Forest Circle like nothing had ever happened.

Except Klix.

Just after Luisa launched the Bushwacker back towards the trail, Klix, quiet and sneaky, worked his way to the rear of the seat. With a gentle push off the back and light feet, Klix landed on the soft forest floor without a sound. Luisa and Olivia continued on unaware of Klix's departure.

Running back to the tunnel opening, and with no tools at all, he tried to tear away the thick vines by hand but only succeeded in lifting himself off the ground by pulling down on them. He tried hacking the vines in half with rocks but there was nothing behind them to bash them against. He was about to give up, when searching through his jacket pockets he found only Snickerdoodles, and... his nasty matches that almost burned down Mr. Spelunker's half-finished workshop.

Looking carefully, he saw that there was not much else around the opening that could catch fire. This would be easy. In fact, it was really just an addition to Luisa's plan and he was really just helping her out. *She would probably be proud of me to think of such a thing.*

It took him several matches, but Klix finally got the dry twigs to catch fire near the center of the cave. And within a minute, the flame was going rather well... in fact too well. The vines were dryer and hotter than he had anticipated. They snapped and crackled and began shooting out popping sparks that went too close to other dry needles on the ground nearby.

Oh my gosh, what have I done?!

There was no water to put the fire out and the only thing Klix could think to do was use his jacket. He ripped it off quickly and began pounding the flaming vines. His heart was racing as he tried desperately to extinguish the flames. After several minutes of his flailing jacket with Snickerdoodles flying everywhere out of his pockets, it looked like he might have actually put the flames out. He continued to watch for any sign of flame but all he saw was small rifts of smoke coming through the charred vines. The fire was out and he was safe as he sat down on a rock for a moment with his head pounding from the scare. *That could have been really bad. I'd better catch up with Luisa before anyone finds out what almost happened.*

Klix took out on a run in the direction Luisa had headed. Within a few minutes he came around a corner and Luisa almost ran him over head on.

"Where have you been?!" yelled Luisa.

"I… I… I fell off when you hit a bump," lied Klix.

"Olivia noticed you were gone. What were you really doing?" demanded Luisa.

"I told you! I fell off!"

"Well, I don't believe you, but we don't have time and it doesn't matter. Get back on, and STAY on!" barked Luisa.

****

"What happened to you?!" exclaimed Hillary finding Luisa going around the Forest Circle as if nothing had happened. "We've been searching for fifteen minutes. We were afraid something bad had happened."

"Klix had to go to the bathroom and said he couldn't wait, so we went back to the house," stammered Luisa.

Papa arrived just in time for her explanation. "We didn't see you at the house. Tinsel and Mrs. Spelunker and I were all there."

One lie always led to another for Luisa. "Well… well, we got half way back and Klix was crying that he was going to wet his pants so we stopped and let him off in the woods to go behind a tree."

"Why didn't we pass you parked on the trail?" asked Papa.

"Well… well, we didn't want to block the trail so I pulled the Bushwacker off into the woods. You went right by us. I saw you," continued Luisa, lie upon lie.

Tinsel now noticed something strange about all three of them and said, "Why are all of your boots and pant cuffs soaking wet?"

There was a panicked silence from Luisa, Olivia and Klix as they looked back and forth waiting for the other to answer. Even Luisa couldn't find a good lie that quickly.

"We don't know," was all Olivia could come up with.

By now Tinsel had heard enough and realized they weren't going to get a truthful answer.

"Let's head back to the house. All of us," as Papa rounded up the whole search team. "I've got a hot barbeque ready for us all."

****

It's difficult to enjoy a nice meal and good laughing conversation when there are lies and suspicions in the air. Mama and Papa and Tinsel and Hillary all knew it. They also knew that now was not the time to try to force the truth.

The rest of the evening Luisa and Klix stayed at one end of the barbeque. Olivia tried to go back and forth between Luisa and Hillary, but Hillary could see she was unhappy. She wasn't even trying to get Brad's attention.

The Spelunkers were glad for the evening to finally come to an end. At least to have Luisa and Olivia and Klix leave. Elka, Ava and Brad had wanted to stay longer and Papa had agreed to drop them off at their houses.

Now it was relaxed. There was not a cloud in the sky and the stars came in nicely in the clear night. The full moon was shining brightly. All sat around the fire pit which Papa had gotten burning steadily orange and yellow and gold with embers of red. Now the 'smores came out to fill their sweet tooth bellies. Happy smiles flickered in the firelight.

There couldn't be a better way to end the night…

CHAPTER EIGHTEEN – Fire

Sometimes the Spelunkers agreed without saying a word. They all knew tomorrow was a school day and they should finish homework and chores and eventually get ready for bed. But sometimes the evening is so fresh and long and relaxing. They all agreed they weren't going to worry about those things. They pretended it was a Friday or Saturday night and stayed up as late as they wanted. They pretended it was a long weekend. Everyone agreed tonight. And Papa had already called parents to let them know it would be later and not to worry and they all trusted Papa and were ok with that.

The night sang along and everyone sang along with it. Papa built a big fire surrounded by round stones from the forest that were tumbled smooth from a million years of water polishing. The fire... everyone loves a fire. It sooths the heart and the imagination floats away with the images made by the dancing flames. You imagine a thousand dreams in the fire, staring so long that you forget to blink. You forget whether you are awake or asleep until someone interrupts the silence with a word or a laugh. The fire.

Mama played guitar and Papa taught everyone words to camping songs he learned when he was ten years old. There were songs about rivers and trees, pancakes and tents falling in on the sleepers. Silly songs about bears counting their toes-es and people counting their nose-es.

'Smores and more hotdogs were second dinner around nine-ish when the sky became black as ink and one hundred billion stars poked holes in the sky and peered down at them.

"That's where we came from," pointed Hillary.

"No, it's that one over there silly," laughed Tinsel.

In truth, no one really knew. That was the mystery they wondered if they would ever know. Mama and Papa didn't know.

To the north the moon was larger than it had ever seemed before. Some called it a harvest moon, some a blood moon. Tonight it was both. That only happens on peculiar nights. Papa moved everyone to the south side of the fire so they could watch the moon slowly trace its way across the northern sky.

Papa had a story about the moon he would tell only once in a while so you would forget about it before the next time he told it.

"There's a reason you only see one side of the moon," Papa would start. "There are creatures on the back side... the Terra-Rogues," he would continue. "They don't want to be seen. Not by rocket ships and not by telescopes. There is only one night every 30 days or so when She (and by *She*, he meant the Moon), turns her face away from us and the Terra-Rogues on the back side are exposed to us. That's when they use their powerful bulging eyes and telescopes to spy on us. That's when they influence the oceans to make waves. They move the earth's plates to make earthquakes. They stir up the winds to make tornadoes and hurricanes. They squeeze the earth to make volcanoes."

"They sound a little scary," said Elka. "They seem a little mean or nasty."

"Oh no," Papa would explain. "The world needs all those things. The earth needs to move and turn and grow to stay alive."

It was a strange story that left you wondering if the moon dwelling Terra-Rogues were really benevolent or if they were evil. Papa hoodwinked you so you never even stopped to wonder if they were real or not.

As Papa's story died down, so did the talking. Everyone sat by the fire hypnotized by the moon as in a dream. A mysterious cloud began rising in front of the moon that no one noticed for a time. Then finally…

"Why is that cloud black and rising from the ground?" whispered Elka.

Papa sat up and took notice. Sure enough a puffy black cloud was billowing from down below and began blotting out the moon.

"Well isn't that strange…" said Papa slowly and quietly as if he were scratching his brain for an answer. It took a minute… until he saw a single spark rise above the treetops…

"Fire!!" yelled Papa, knocking everyone out of their moondreams.

There was a panic as everyone regained their senses and began to see more sparks rising into the air above the moonlit treeline.

The flames soon became visible through the treeline at the top of the ridge and cast thin dancing tree shadows that looked like dangerous wood faeries across the house, the shop, the barn.

Mama and Papa looked at each other and both thought the same thing... how decades ago the lightning fire had swept away the house and the happiness of the Spannings. Their faces became stern and determined. Their minds turned to action.

They both knew the Mountain View Fire Department was too far and too small to be the kind of help they needed. They knew the Spelunkers had to do this or no one could. If they didn't act quickly it would all be gone. The house. The beautiful and powerful forest. The access to the Deep. Every moment they wasted was one second closer to the monstrous fire becoming so out of control nothing could stop it. But it was going to require more than Mama and Papa and Hillary and Tinsel could give. They needed all the spelunkers. Even the new Initiates.

Papa spoke firmly and purposefully, "Elka, Brad, Ava. Do you know you can help defeat this?"

They all looked at him but didn't quite know what to say.

Papa repeated, "Do you feel it? Come closer. Everyone gather close in a circle. Do you begin to feel it?"

"I think I'm starting to," said Elka.

"Everyone hold hands. Do you feel it?" Papa said a third time.

A surge of blue, bright and low and pulsating, surrounded their arms, their held hands. Now across their chests, around their necks. Up and down their bodies from head to toe.

They all felt it and Mama and Papa were sure now of what to do.

"We need to raise the Raven into the Ravenous," called out Papa. "It's the only way. Or it will be too late. If we don't, even we may not escape. Are you all willing?"

"We are Mr. Spelunker," Elka replied. "It is our time."

"Spread out in a straight line," said Papa. "We must face the fire head on. It's the only way. Up the hill to the Raven. We have to be closer."

All holding hands in a straight line. Mama and Papa in the middle. Tinsel and Brad to the left. Hillary, Elka and Ava to the right.

"The Raven is high up the mountain. Further away from the Deep and the low-lying land near the cave openings," explained Papa as they marched. "That is why it will take all of us. We won't have the power of the core melt all the way up here. It will be just the good in us drawing as much as we can."

Finally they approached the Raven. It was the last thing between them and the growing inferno. If the Raven had been much further they wouldn't have been able to reach it. As it was, the fire was so hot they could barely stand the heat.

Hillary and Tinsel began the initiation of the Blue Refractory. The bubble grew from them and went out both directions, encompassing Mama and Papa and Brad and Ava and Elka. Suddenly there was no more heat. The Blue Refractory was holding steady and reflecting all the angry blaze. The Initiates felt as if they might have just been sitting next to a cozy fire. They looked at each other with amazement and bewilderment. They looked at the Spelunkers with trust.

"Keep hands and raise them," said Mama loudly above the roar of the fire. "Raise them like you are lifting the Raven. Rolling it into a big wave. See it rolling into a big wave. Think of all the good it will do to stop this destructive burning. Think of the animals saved. Think of the life giving plants and trees saved. Think it hard."

Trees were now falling, crashing and burning and sending up huge showers of sparks as they smashed into the ground. Waves and walls of yellow-white hot fire were towering into the air threatening to fall on them like buildings in an earthquake.

"Don't be afraid," calmed Mama. "Just think hard, NOW!" she yelled.

Mama was so loud it frightened the Initiates for a moment, but they responded immediately with the strongest will and trust they could give.

The Raven began to transform to the Ravenous. It seemed like it took on a life of its own. It began to lap at the far shore like waves on a lake. Then it began to roll like waves on an ocean beach. Then it began to surge like a tsunami coming in from an earthquake. Finally it rolled up like a mountainous wall towering high above the trees and the flames.

It was like looking through a thick piece of distorted rain glass. It was the most beautiful and terrible thing they had ever seen. The beautiful water wall hung there like a protector, growing and growing larger and larger as it was building and being fed from upstream, leaning strongly towards and over the flames. Through the glass wall were all the most beautiful and favorite warm dancing colors of yellows and reds and greens and violets that would warm your heart and make you never want to leave. At the same time, these were the horrible colors that would turn a house to smoking cinders within seconds leaving nothing but destruction and tears.

The Ravenous was now a towering building many times larger and higher than the raging forest fire. But Mama had not given the command to lower arms yet. She had to be sure. This was their one chance and if it failed, more than their 50,000 acres would burn.

Finally when everyone's arms were so tired they thought they would have to give up, Mama yelled, "*DROP ARMS!!*"

Everyone obeyed, instantly dropping their arms. By now the water wall had grown to over ten feet thick and two hundred feet high and a half mile long. Just as quickly, the towering wall, which was already leaning over the flames, began to overtake, to fall, to crash and consume the raging fire. As the crash of water hit the flames and cindering trunks, there was such an explosion of steam that it almost knocked the spelunkers over. And it would have if not for the Blue Refractory which encompassed them and held them tightly to the ground.

The enormous power of the Ravenous was so large and final that every flame, every spark, every cinder, every hint of danger was instantly killed beyond rekindling. Dead smoke and steam rose to cover the moon and created a darkness in the forest that might have been terrifying if it weren't for the assurance in their hearts that the danger was completely over. Utterly vanquished.

****

The walk back to the house was like a dream. No one had brought torches, so it was slow and careful going as the moon finally broke through just enough to light their way.

One by one it began to dawn on everyone… *How did this happen?... What started this fire?...*

Most of the spelunkers thought it, but at first no one wanted to say it… *Luisa…*

Luisa and her Bushwacker team were the only ones unaccounted for today for almost a half hour. And Papa knew she lied when he pressed her for an answer. *Why would she lie if she weren't protecting something she shouldn't have been doing? I didn't know why it seemed fishy at the time, but my gut told me something was wrong…*

Back at camp, Papa asked Brad, Elka and Ava to get ready. The night had enough excitement and he was ready to take them home.

****

Returning from dropping the Initiates off, Papa was hit by a wall of questions and theories from Hillary and Tinsel, who were both agitated and hopping mad at the prospect that Luisa had anything to do with the fire.

"Yes, yes. All possibilities," replied Papa. "Until we can get up there and investigate, we're wasting our time and getting ourselves all upset about theories. We beat the fire and the only damage done is maybe a few acres of trees. We can take a look tomorrow morning after breakfast."

"You mean we can miss school?" asked the girls, exchanging excited side glances.

"I think in this case Mama and I would agree the fire takes priority over school this time," confirmed Papa.

Mama nodded in agreement.

"Yay!!" they both yelled.

"We're not glad for the fire, but we're excited to help figure this out," said Tinsel.

"How about we all hit the hay and get a good night's sleep so we can start bright and early tomorrow?" suggested Papa.

****

Sparks' bouncing and barking woke the house up well before any alarms went off.

"Ok, ok!" laughed Hillary at Sparks. "Don't lick my whole face off. Save some for later."

Sparks ran down the stairs into Mama and Papa's room after making sure the girls were getting up properly. He had learned that if he wanted Papa out of bed he had to bite and pull Papa's ears and pull pillows out from under his head and onto the floor. Papa used to buy new pillow cases, but he was spending so much money on them he learned to sleep on pillow cases that had beagle teeth holes in them.

This morning Mama had gotten up early and prepared a light breakfast of yogurt and granola with fresh apple chunks mixed in and scrambled eggs with sharp white cheddar cheese. She knew that Hill and Tins would be so anxious to get out and start investigating that they wouldn't be able to sit for a long breakfast. She was right.

"Should we skip breakfast and eat when we get back?" suggested an excited Tinsel.

"Not me," chimed in Papa. "I need my protein and my coffee."

"We'll be out there soon enough Sis," added Hillary. "The burn isn't going anywhere."

"Hey! No fair. You're supposed to be on my side," chirped Tinsel with a joking smile.

Sparks seemed to agree with Tinsel as he danced Sparks Circles and whined and scratched at the front door. Even Bark Flips off the front door didn't change his Spelunker family's minds.

It only took fifteen minutes for their light breakfast and Mama promised a more substantial brunch for when they got home.

Mama gave Ms. Porter a call to let her know there had been a fire emergency and the girls would not be in school today.

"Everyone grab a shovel and a collection bag," said Papa.

Within fifteen minutes, the Spelunkers and Sparks had climbed to Spanning Ridge. For a minute they all stood in silent disbelief at the ugly black mark the fire had so cruelly left on their beautiful Lookout Mountain.

"What a needless waste of forest life," grieved Mama.

"Where do we start Papa?" asked Hillary.

"Did Mama or I ever tell you girls that about a hundred years or so ago when the Forestry Service was established we worked for them?" asked Papa.

"What?! No. You never told us that," said Tinsel.

"Lots of thing we haven't told you Tinsel-Toe," smiled Papa. "Well, yes, we did. As part of our job of forestry conservation we were trained in locating fire start origins so we could help establish ways of preventing fires."

"Oh wow! That is perfect for this job Papa!" cheered Hillary.

"It's been about 75 years since we've used those skills, but I don't imagine the physics of fire have changed much," added Papa. "First thing we look for is V shapes and evidence of colder to hotter progression. We look at what direction the wind was travelling last night, which I already checked with the weather service this morning. It was moving South. Then we look for blackened sides of trees and ash piles. Usually by then you have a good idea of where it started. Then you start looking and digging if necessary for what actually started it."

"Geez Papa, that sounds like a lot," said Tinsel.

"This burn is pretty small Tins," confirmed Papa, "We'll have the origin within an hour."

"One thing I'm confused about," questioned Hillary, "is why the fire waited until so late at night to start if Klix and the others were here in the early afternoon?"

"Mama, would you like to tell them?" suggested Papa.

"Sure…I'm guessing this whole thing was an accident. Like Klix behind the shop. I think they may have meant to mark or vandalize, but I'm thinking they didn't mean to start a forest fire. Papa and I have investigated scores of fires and found that many started later from smoldering wood hours or even days after someone thought the fire was out."

Tinsel and Hillary watched an amazing cooperation and conversation between Mama and Papa. Never an argument or disagreement, Mama and Papa listened intently to each other and nodded heads and agreed and pointed at things and took notes and drew figures and arrows on maps.

In just under an hour, Papa announced, "I think we have it girls."

They had moved steadily north and west until they were now standing…

"That's the Spanning Well entrance Papa!" exclaimed Tinsel.

"Are you saying the fire came from there?" asked Hillary.

"We're not saying that Hilly," replied Mama. "We just know it started from somewhere near here."

Just behind Papa, Sparks was furiously digging at something. Suddenly he had picked something up and was trying to chomp it down as quickly as he could like he would at home when he got ahold of something he knew he wasn't supposed to have but wanted to get it down before someone took it away.

"Papa, grab Sparks," said Hillary urgently. "I'm afraid he might have gotten ahold of a poisonous mushroom or something else!"

Almost before Hillary could finish her sentence, Papa had scooped a startled Sparks into the air and wrenched whatever he had in his mouth out. Sparks looked disappointed and when Papa set him down he went right back to digging and pulled up another of whatever it was. Now Tinsel grabbed him and freed the object from his mouth.

"Here Hillary, hold this mutt so he doesn't get into any more trouble," said Tinsel.

"Whatever this is, it's covered with ash and is charred almost to coal," observed Papa.

It was round like a flat rock and about a half inch thick and three inches in diameter. Papa bent hard on it and it snapped right in half.

"Well whatever it is, it isn't wood or stone," said Papa. "It wouldn't snap easily like that. It's lighter in color in the middle. Kind of a light tannish color. This is strange. I've never seen anything like it in the woods."

"Papa, you better see this one," started Tinsel. "Mine is not so burned. It kind of looks like a... like a cookie... kind of like one of Mama's Snickerdoodles!"

Mama and Papa both examined it.

"I know my Snickerdoodles, and if ever I saw one, that is one!" exclaimed Mama. "Let Sparks loose."

Hillary released the anxious beagle who immediately went to work finding two more of the round treats. He seemed to act like it was unfair that every time he found one it was taken away.

"Don't you fret boy. I'll reward you with sausage treats when we get home. You're the hero of the day," joked Papa.

"Now what in the heck would four Snickerdoodles be doing at the mouth of the Spanning Well Tunnel," Papa puzzled.

Something triggered in Hillary's memory. "Um... Papa... I think I have an idea."

"What is it Hillary?"

"Well this afternoon as we were finishing up the snacks Mama made for us, I noticed Klix stuffing his jacket pockets full of handfuls of Snickerdoodles. I didn't say anything because I didn't care and I was glad he enjoyed the cookies," explained Hillary.

"Oh wow," remarked Papa. "That is circumstantial and it doesn't prove anything, but it is certainly suspicious."

"But Papa!" exclaimed Tinsel. "It *had* to be him. The cookies! Who else?!"

"It certainly makes you want to think so. What other evidence do we have?" asked Papa.

"Well," added Hillary, "They were missing for half an hour from the Forest Circle and that would have been just enough time to get up here and back."

"But why?" asked Mama. "Why would they come up here. Up to Spanning's Well?"

"The only thing I can think is that they wanted in the tunnel for some reason," said Papa. "Let's check in there."

Papa lit his torch and the four Spelunkers and Sparks proceeded into the Spanning Well Tunnel.

They didn't have to go far. Only about 50 feet before they all stopped half surprised, half in shock.

In large red letters... LIARS!

"What? Why?..." muttered Mama.

"I know *WHO!*" cried Hillary. And she spent the next several minutes explaining to the rest of the Spelunkers how she had heard rumors of Luisa telling people, especially Olivia, she was a liar and how in Mrs. Caroline's Pandemonium Week rhyming she had called her a fake in front of the whole class.

"Why didn't you tell us any of this honey?" asked Mama.

"Because I can handle it Mama. Honestly it doesn't bother me. I know it's not true. It's because Luisa is hurting so badly herself she has to hurt others."

"Oh sweetie… still… you should tell us these things just so we know."

"Ok Mama. I didn't think of it like that," replied Hillary. "I will from now one. But now she's gone too far. She could have destroyed our whole forest. She could have burned our house down. She could have killed someone. Just like the 4 year old Spanning boy."

"We don't know it was Luisa," added Papa.

"What do you mean?" asked Hillary.

"Well, Klix was the one with the Snickerdoodles. And he is also the one who almost burned down my shop," said Papa. "He is the one with an arson history if you could call it that. And the cookies place him here at the scene of the start of the fire. The thing I don't understand is why he, or they, would want to burn the entrance to the Spanning Well?"

"I just thought of one more possible piece of evidence," said Tinsel. "I thought it was pretty lame that they couldn't tell us why their boots and cuffs were soaking wet. Let's go check the Cross Winds runoff."

The Spelunkers went a little deeper into the tunnel, and sure enough, the Cross Winds Runoff was six inches deep. Just enough to soak boots and cuffs.

"So it's a good bet they came this far," surmised Papa. "And if they went past the runoff the next obstacle would be the Shale Slides. What could they possibly want with those? This just keeps getting stranger and stranger."

"I don't even know how they found the tunnel opening," said Tinsel. "Except… Olivia was with us when we went down here last. Luisa and Klix have never been. I don't know for sure, but I think there may be the slightest blue connection in Olivia, but no one, not even her, can see or feel it."

"If that is true Tinsel, it might have been enough for her to find it. And enough for Klix to try to mark the opening," calculated Papa.

"One thing is for sure," said Mama, "We have now had a direct attack on us, and on all that is Regenerative and that is good. Here on our home property. That has never happened before."

There were a few moments of quiet as they all thought about the situation.

Papa broke the silence.

"It looks like the timing was meant to be. Your journey to the Dome of the Deep next week with the Initiates seems to be our future…"

CHAPTER NINETEEN – The Journey

"Wake up Hilly!" clamored Tinsel.

"Tins! Alarm clock doesn't go off for another hour."

"I'm too excited. Last day before spring break is always like a vacation at school. Let's go ride the Bushwackers in the dark!"

"You're crazy Tinsel. Go back to sleep."

"Why do you think Luisa wanted shale shards Hillary?"

"That's the mystery. They are cool formations, but not cool enough for anyone to risk burning down a forest to get them. She could have just asked. I don't get it either."

****

Hillary arrived at Mrs. Caroline's room to find it about half full. There was Luisa already in the back of the room. She looked at Hillary out of the corners of her eyes.

Arriving at her desk, her heart jumped a beat and she stopped abruptly in her tracks for a moment when, lying right there in the middle of her seat, she found a shale shard the shape and size of a flat golf ball.

Turning her eyes slowly to the back of the room, she saw Luisa's head lower a little and her body was shaking like she was either crying or laughing very hard. It certainly wouldn't be crying. Olivia's eyes were shifting from Luisa's laughing head to Hillary's gaze. She looked either scared or embarrassed.

Hillary felt something. It was strange. Anger? Sadness? No, it wasn't either of those. Hillary started to laugh. Harder and harder. Luisa lifted her head and grew a furious look.

Hillary calmly walked back to Luisa's desk and held the shard out flat on display in her open palm.

"That's it? That's the plan? I have a million of these at home. I could bring some more for you after spring break. For what? To prove you broke through into the Spanning Tunnel and Shale Slide? We already figured that out. I would have taken you there myself and still would if you wanted to be friends. Well?"

Luisa wouldn't look up. Wouldn't move.

Through her teeth Luisa hissed, "Leave me alone. Get... out... of... here."

Hillary shrugged her shoulders, slipped the shard into her pocket and went back to her desk.

****

Tinsel and Hillary ate lunch together and the story about the shale shard was told. Tinsel scrunched her eyes at the telling. She clenched her fists as she rolled the shale evidence over and over in her tight hands.

"I'm gonna stomp her Hillary!"

"How about we take it out on the tetherball instead? Let's get out there quick to get first court."

"Ok, then I'm gonna stomp her!" said Tinsel as she slipped the shard into her pocket now.

"Tinsel!" warned Hillary.

"Hillary!" said Tinsel, sticking out her tongue and smiling.

They thought they might be first to the playground, but as they broke through the doors, there were Luisa and Olivia leaning against the brick handball wall pretending not to see Hillary and Tinsel.

"Well at least the tetherball court is free. You can serve first since I'm going to beat you anyway," joked Hillary.

Skipping over together, just as Tinsel popped into the server's court, she abruptly stopped.

"What is it?" asked Hillary.

"Look!" said Tinsel, pointing to the ground.

There at her feet was another shale shard a little bigger than the first.

Tinsel felt her face grow hot in a flash. Hillary recognized that rare look in her eyes and tried to stop her, but it was too late.

Without hesitation, Tinsel scooped up the shard, wheeled around, took expert aim and sidearm sling shot the shard at rocketing speed toward the enemy. There was a gap of a foot between Luisa and Olivia. The shard went hurtling right into the gap cutting it exactly in two. The shard met the wall with such force it exploded into a thousand pieces sending shale showers raining into enemy hair and shirt collars and jacket pockets.

Olivia gasped in fright and ran for the school doors, shaking shards from her shirt and hair all the way.

Luisa didn't flinch an inch. She looked like she had gotten exactly what she wanted. In fact, she smiled and let out a few snorting laughs.

Tinsel's aim had been exactly where she wanted it. She could have taken Luisa's head off if she had wanted to. Luisa's laugh made her feel out of control. In a dead stare with Luisa, Tinsel slowly slipped her hand into her pocket. Slowly pulled the remaining shard out. Turning it over and over in her hand, she waited for Luisa's attention.

"Tinsel, No. This is not how we do it. You know that. It's not our time yet."

"Step back Hillary. It's time for this."

The shard began to glow a low red in her hand. She shifted it from hand to hand and rocked from foot to foot.

Luisa wasn't laughing now.

The shard became orange and steaming.

Hillary tried to use calming hands on Tinsel's shoulders but it only made matters worse. Tinsel drew on Hillary's power and it threw the shard into a yellow hot spectacle of molten rock. She cupped the pool in her outstretched palm and swirled it around like quicksilver, not taking her eyes off Luisa for a second.

Luisa looked like she was bracing for something.

Tinsel drew her arm back and like a catapult shot the hot rain of fiery glowing liquid like a meteor directly at Luisa.

Luisa had been bracing. There was no change in her jet black eyes. There was no change in her stance.

The flying hot magma meteor began to break into two pieces. Then ten and fifty and a thousand glowing micro fireballs. When they reached Luisa, nothing was left but a million cold grains of sand that bounced helplessly off her jacket.

Luisa and her dark eyes smiled, stooped and picked up a pinch of cold meteor sand, dropped it in her pocket, and walked into the school building without a glance back.

Hillary and Tinsel stared at each other without a word.

****

Plans and permissions and provisions had all been made for the nine day trip to the Dome of the Deep. It would take three days down, three days in the belly of the earth and three days out if all went as planned. The journey would need to start early Saturday if the spelunkers were to make it back the following Sunday in time for school the following week.

Friends began arriving at Lookout Mountain at 4 am early Saturday while most people were still having dreams of coffee and cartoons. The yard and porch and kitchen were filled with yawns, puffy eyes and sleepy smiles.

Simple backpacks wouldn't do for this trip. Full packs were in order with all the variety of eating and sleeping gear. Sleeping on the forest floor is one thing. Sleeping on hard rock is a different thing.

By 5 am all was ready. Light breakfasts were finished. Backpacks, boots, helmets and torches were fitted and ready.

Hillary took the lead. Elka, Ava and Brad filled the gap. Tinsel brought up the rear. For a short span Frizzely, with her eyes glowing in the dark, and a few of her kits followed along, curious to see what this fuss breaking up the nighttime was.

"Guard your packs everyone. Frizzely is an honest thief who will rob you of your food if you let her," warned Hillary.

Frizzely frowned.

The Eastern Lava Tube was the most promising, and sometimes the only, route to their fantastical destination in the Deep. Marching in the dark always created a peculiar feeling. But soon the darkness would completely envelope them for more than a week.

Nervous looks of excitement and anticipation crossed the faces of the spelunkers as they looked around at the last dawning light they would see. One last huddle and they all lit torches and ducked through the viney thicket.

****

The air was thick and damp and smelled like mushrooms. A shiny world of glistening and dripping walls began to appear as their eyes adjusted.

The day was fresh and the spelunkers were charged with energy. Maybe too much energy.

"All right spelunkers," said Hillary, "we've got a good plan, but go slow. I know we're super excited, but watch each step and watch out for each other. There are some pretty dangerous obstacles ahead."

"If all goes as planned," added Tinsel, "we should make the shores of the Crystal Placid Lake by nightfall. Well you can't really call it nightfall down here, but you know what I mean. It's the most peaceful and serene place you've ever seen in your life."

"Finally! We'll get to see the Echo Chambers where we never got our picnic lunch," said Brad.

"Oh you'll get to see much more than that Bradsicle," teased Tinsel. "We've got at least ten major dangerous, treacherous, life-threatening, death defying and horrible obstacles before we reach the Dome of the Deep and we only have three days to make it."

Brad was speechless and his eyes were as big as silver dollars.

"Tinsel!" snapped Hillary. "Be nice."

"Just kidding," said Tinsel, sounding like she was dragging her voice through the mud.

"This Corkscrew Drop is much easier the second time," exclaimed Brad.

"Don't get too cocky Bradley or I'll make you go the hard way," joked Tinsel.

"Oh yeah, what's that?"

"By rope straight down the center."

"I dare you. I would beat you by half an hour and have my second breakfast finished by the time you even got there."

"Well maybe I just push you off and you can beat us by a whole hour. Of course you'll have a bit of a problem eating your lunch after that," joked Tinsel.

"Tinsel!" said Hillary.

"I knew that was coming," laughed Tinsel, "but it was worth it."

"Ok everyone let's get a move on," said Hillary. "By the end of the day we need to conquer the Corkscrew Drop, both the First and Second Echo Chambers, the Rock Face, the Death Wedge Drop and finally arrive at the Crystal Placid Lake. That is four miles of rugged and challenging spelunking."

"What about Sparks?" asked Ava. "I'm worried he might fall off the Corkscrew ledge."

"Sparks is twice as nimble as we are," answered Tinsel. "Four legs are better than two and he has the climbing ability of a mountain goat. His animal night vision sees things before we do. Just stand back if he goes into Sparks Circles. He's not so careful about not knocking you off the ledge."

"Um...I don't like that," said Ava.

"Tinsel!" said Hillary. "She's kidding again."

****

Four hours in and the spelunkers had passed the Second Echo Chamber and eaten peanut butter and jelly sandwiches and were approaching the Rock Face.

"Has anyone every hung three thousand feet in the air from a steep cliff?" asked Hillary.

"I don't think anyone should ever hang three thousand feet in the air. It's not natural," replied Ava.

"Well, being seven miles below the surface of the Earth doesn't seem to be too natural either, but that's where we're going, so get ready. We're coming up on the Rock Face and it's a three thousand foot vertical drop that we are going to rope and rappel down."

"Is it too late to go back?" asked Ava.

"Hey," said Tinsel, "Brad should really like this Rock Face."

"Why is that?" asked Elka.

"Because his face looks like a rock!" laughed Tinsel.

Brad pretended a frown but made a grin and almost laughed. Tinsel was starting to grow on him.

"Well, at least I have a rock for a face and not for a brain," joked Brad.

"Good comeback Bradley," laughed Hillary as she thought *Brad has finally learned the way to deal with Tinsel.*

All the spelunkers roped and tied off according to Hillary and Tinsel's instruction and training back at the Lookout House, Hillary moved them close to the drop-off edge of the Rock Face.

"Listen here," said Hillary as she dropped a sedimentary rock chunk the size of a bowling ball down the edge.

In the dark silence you could have heard a mouse whisper. Second after second went by with no report from the rock. After a full minute of complete silence, still nothing. Eerie or creepy is the feeling they got when at last Hillary spoke when no sound ever came back.

"After three thousand feet the sound is so small it can't make it all the way back up here. I love the giant dropness of it all."

"Dropness is not a word," winked Brad.

"It is now," smiled Hillary.

"There are ledges about every one or two hundred feet or so for us to rest and gather rope. Slow and steady and follow what we taught you," said Tinsel as she zipped Sparks snugly into her front doggy pack.

It took two hours, one bowl of dog kibble, five more peanut butter and jelly sandwiches, four beef jerky sticks and one coconut jerky stick (Ava was trying to become a vegetarian), five chocolate peanut butter cups and five and a half pints of water (a half pint was for Sparks) to get to the Rock Face floor.

There on the smooth tunnel floor, smashed into a zillion pieces, was sedimentary rock chunk dust. You could almost still hear the smashing explosion if you imagined closely enough.

"We'll rest here a half hour," announced Hillary. "Nap, read, talk, think, whatever you want to gather your strength. You'll need it. We have about three hours spelunking to go yet."

Sparks was squirming to get out of Tinsel's harness. Beagles don't spend much energy rappelling when they are carried in a pouch. As soon as his feet hit the ground, he tore across to the nearest wall and did the biggest, loudest Bark Flip of his doggy life. All the spelunkers stared at him and he looked a little embarrassed as he really couldn't explain why he did that.

"Hillary, when you said we would rest a half hour, I honestly didn't think that would be long enough," said Brad. "It was so exhausting rappelling three thousand feet, I thought I might be done for the day. But I feel great now. I feel like I could climb all the way back up and do a dance at the top!"

"We are already two miles deep into the Earth Brad. Do you know what is happening?"

"Now that you mention it, I have this strange feeling of being connected to the tunnel…to the rock…to an energy deep…"

"Tell me what it is Brad."

"…It's the…Regeneration?"

"Are you asking me or telling me?"

"It *IS* the regeneration."

Hillary smiled.

"Um…Hillary…" said Elka.

"Yes?"

"I think I have to pee. It's been six hours down in here now and I'm starting to have to go bad."

"Find a corner and some privacy and take care of your number one," said Hillary, so calmly it was like she was talking about making cookies.

Hillary's voice was so calm and permissive, Elka felt no shame in doing something that was so natural.

"Hillary?" blushed Brad. "What if we have to go number two?"

Hillary knew that was hard for Brad to say.

"You won't have to."

"What? How do you know that?"

"Things are changing as we go deeper. Soon you won't even need to eat. Or do anything else like that. Have you noticed a change?"

"I already noticed how much energy I feel. Now that you mention it I don't even feel very hungry after the rest of that descent."

Hillary smiled with secret knowledge, "Trust me, you will experience more changes than you know."

****

Two hours more and the troupe arrived at the Death Wedge Drop.

"Why does it have such a nasty scary name?" asked Ava.

Tinsel replied, "It's three words. Drop. Wedge. Death. If you drop…into the wedge…it will be death. It is a nice shortcut though if you want to try it."

Tinsel! thought Hillary.

What?! She asked, thought Tinsel.

You didn't have to answer like that, thought Hillary.

I gotta have some fun with them don't I?

I don't know Tins. Do you? Do you really have to?

Tinsel felt kind of bad now. She didn't really *need to*. She *wanted to*. Those are two very different things.

Having fun to make someone tense is having fun at their expense. To joke may be fun, don't make it a pun, to frighten or embarrass when they have no defense.

"All joking aside, why do you call it a shortcut?" asked Ava.

"Because it drops straight down," answered Tinsel. "Well, jagged straight down. Down five miles. That's over twenty something thousand feet. It bounces and jags and tunnels right down to the core just next to the Dome of the Deep where we are going…where we were *born*. If you did fall down there you wouldn't stop until you splashed into the magma five miles below. And it would take you about a half hour of bouncing and bumping before you got there. Death. Sorry."

Tinsel! thought Hillary.

Don't worry I'll be nice, thought Tinsel.

"I feel a little dizzy and sick," said Ava.

"Ava," said Hillary, "sometimes Tinsel is a little blunt, but what she is saying is true. Not to worry. We will very safely all make it across this drop. The drop is fifty feet across and the tunnel is high enough here to swing across. Years ago Mama and Papa built a scaffold to reach the ceiling and install piton eyes in the ceiling. All we have to do is get our ropes though them."

"Unless you have wings I don't see how you can do that," said Ava.

"Use your torch and see the eyehooks up above? Can you see the drawstrings we leave through them? We can't leave ropes hanging. They will get old and worn or damaged by water or mildew. So we use the pull strings for threading new ropes each time," explained Hillary.

"Here, watch," said Tinsel.

Tinsel whipped a rope out into the open space over the drop and pulled back in the drawstrings, tied her fresh rope onto one lead and used the other to pull her fresh spelunking rope up and through the metal loop in the ceiling and pulled it all the way back down. Tying the two ends together now they had a complete and safe loop to tie into and swing across.

A few special knots later, a fast sprint toward the edge, a huge leap and an echoing whoop of delight, and Tinsel was sailing out over the chasm twenty thousand feet over the magma. No carnival ride was scarier or more fun. Landing on the other side safely, the spelunker's torches could just make out Tinsel's ear to ear grin and bright glowing eyes.

"Next!" she hollered as she flung the ropes back towards the nervously awaiting troupe.

Nervous waiting, terror-filled swinging and sighs of relief and terrible fun and all the spelunking troupe were across.

"I want to do it again," said Brad.

"No," replied Hillary. "Wait for the trip home."

"Meany," said Brad.

Hillary smiled and winked.

****

As the spelunkers grew closer and closer to the depths, it grew warmer and their feet became lighter. Surefooted jumps from rock to boulder that would have twisted or broken ankles on the surface in the forest now came as easy jumps and pounces.

Except for one jump.

Even with the best of strength and skill, care has to be taken. For just one moment, Hillary didn't take care. A long leap, overshooting the rock she was aiming at, her foot went too far and too deep. In an instant she found the threat of her left leg crumpling and her head coming down toward a heavy rock.

Because their legs were moving faster now, their eyes were moving faster too. Brad's eyes moved quickly. His eyes saw Hillary begin to fall almost before she fell. And his actions were lightning. Planting feet firmly and lashing his right hand out to clasp Hillary's left hand, he held like an anchor. Hillary clutched his hand as a lifeline. Instead of planting her face on a rock, she stopped short of falling and hung there tentatively in the air. Brad let her slowly to the ground where Hillary safely stepped.

Hillary breathed out a close call sigh of relief and felt a rush of thankfulness.

Brad held onto her hand.

Hillary held onto his hand.

They smiled, turned and walked and didn't let go.

Tinsel saw everything from behind and smiled. Her eyes grew misty. Her twin star was growing up.

****

An easy hour long spelunking walk and the group had arrived at their destination for the first day. The Crystal Placid Lake.

"Why did you name it that?" asked Elka.

"Mama named it. Almost a thousand years ago. On their first long trip down where they found us," answered Hillary. "Look around and you'll answer your own question. Tell me if you think Mama named it well."

The new Initiates lined up at the water's edge to take a long hard look. There was too much to see at once. Eyes had to adjust. SilicaSuns began to glow. Light began to increase. In the water, out of the water. From the walls, from the ceiling, from the floor depths of the lake. The combined Regeneration power of all five spelunkers added together to excite the SilicaSuns to daylight.

"The lake is three thousand feet deep in the middle and a half mile across. It is filled year round by crystal clear filtered water percolating down through the earth from above," explained Tinsel. "You can drink it and swim it. There aren't any fish. Maybe a sea monster or two though."

By Hillary's eye roll, the others figured out Tinsel's tall tale as just that.

Ava removed her boots and socks and dipped her toe in the crystal amber glowing water.

"It's warm!" she exclaimed. "I expected it to be cold for some reason."

"That's from the thermal geysers of steam working their way up out of the ground," explained Hillary. "The lake is naturally heated year round."

"The lake only looks ten feet deep to me," said Ava.

"That's an optical illusion Ava, caused by crystal clear magnification of the water. The boulders you are seeing are thirty and fifty and a hundred feet down and they are the size of houses. You can dive in without the slightest chance of hitting them. And they're illuminated now down to thousands of feet by our being here and the SilicaSuns," said Hillary.

Brad, Elka and Ava's excitement grew moment by moment as they fell in love with the glowing, glistening, warm, crystal depths of the lake. Warming light came from every direction and they didn't need their torches anymore. Hillary and Tinsel exchanged glances of joy welling up inside them as the connection was growing in the Initiates.

The spelunkers all pitched in and set up camp. It wasn't work, it wasn't a chore, it was delightful. Fuel camping stoves, warm soup, biscuits and 'smores around an underground illuminated lake. There were hours of swimming and playing and laughing at silly jokes. They felt like they could go on forever without stopping or sleep. Hillary and Tinsel knew they were not deep enough yet to go completely without sleep, so bedtime was finally called against the protests of the Initiates.

Daylight dreams and nighttime sings, shores of joy and kindness rings. Wondering if asleep or wake, floating peaceful on the lake. Waking dream, dreaming wake, never again friendship forsake.

Brad had camped and slept on rocks before. And he had woken with a stiff neck and sore back. This morning as he woke, he felt like he had slept in the best King's bed ever. All the spelunkers slept like never before. They sprang to their feet immediately and fully awake and feeling like they could climb a mountain or fight a lion.

"We can leave the food and water behind now," said Hillary.

"What?! What will we eat and drink for the next 8 days?" asked Elka.

"Are you hungry or thirsty now after sleeping nine hours?" asked Hillary.

All the spelunkers realized there were no thirsts or grumblings in the tummy. And their eyes and ears heard things in ways they hadn't before. Sharp. Exact. Defined. True. Clarity.

"We are deep enough. I felt it last night. The Power of the Regeneration is feeding us now. Nutrients you have no knowledge of from the Earth, and water you don't know the source of are absorbing in through you," said Hillary. "I told you before you would be changed."

The Initiates could feel it was true.

"Instead of three days, we will only need two," announced Tinsel.

"For what?" asked Brad.

"We will sleep on the shores of the Mantle River in the Dome of the Deep tonight."

"Where did the extra day you planned go?"

"We are much stronger now than Hillary and I thought we would be at this point. We will easily go twice as far today as we did yesterday. Maybe even with time to spare."

They could begin to see the slightest low blue hum in each other's eyes and bodies. Within fifteen minutes they were packed and marching around the lake at an incredible pace.

****

The SlideAway Slope which usually took a couple hours of hammering and roping and rappelling and sliding, took only an hour as the spelunkers slid down huge curves and roped up when the drop-off became too steep. The layers of slickrock and sandstone gave both grip and slip. Courage and strength and speed were high in the five spelunkers. They worked together as a team, like a well-oiled machine constructed to drive and smash and dive without error. A precise machine that didn't slip or worry. Their movements were accurate and without fail. Without words one took rope, another took lead, another belayed.

The Shifting Shelves dropped another half mile. The spelunkers dove and jumped and rappelled from one wall across to the other, jumping gaps of five feet or more.

Ledge to ledge, down and down they went bouncing from wall to wall without a word.

The Switchbacks ran like rock zigzags, one way for a mile, then a thirty foot drop, and back another half mile. Zigging and Zagging. Running and leaping boulders. They were like burrowing animals in their own lairs moving effortlessly without error or trip or fall or bump. Even Sparks was flying from boulder to boulder like a leaping leopard. Skillful and precise. Not even any barking.

Now the Bubble Drops. Huge cavernous round hollows like bubbles where lava burps and belches created a stack of hollow balls connected in the center where they touched. Like falling through an hourglass. Only the falling was quick roping and swinging from level down to level. Their movement was fast and accurate. Too fast if you were a normal spelunker watching. You might have panicked watching. They were trained acrobats. Walking tightropes and dropping through their bubble trapezes effortlessly like they had practiced a thousand times.

They arrived at The Staircase. A gentle walk from the Bubble Drops to the Dome of the Deep. A reward of a walk. Like walking out on to stage after a death defying performance to take a bow. Relaxed and strolling into the grand cavern that was first home to the stars.

After eons and ten years, the stars were home.

CHAPTER TWENTY – Discovery

Five spelunkers strolled with quiet and awe and wide eyed respect into the grandest space that a world could make. It is hard to believe that this space is natural and not some fantastic architectural design. No person could design something like this.

To say the Dome of the Deep is huge is not large enough. It is a mountain within a mountain. It is as if the biggest, most beautiful mountain range and the widest blue sky had changed places. Mountain is now hollow and the sky is now rock.

Down in the Deep, only a mile from the molten core mantle, the Power of the Regeneration lives strongly. And the spelunkers lived within it. Enormous fields of geodes and shale and sediment and igneous. Stalagmites and stalactites and boulders and sand. SilicaSuns embedded in every wall and floor and ceiling. There is no one source of light. The light comes from everywhere.

And the Mantle River. Miles of flowing river. Not a river of water. A river of light. Molten magma. Lava. Pure and golden and turbulent. Bright orange and yellow and red. A thousand beautiful fiery glowing sunsets wrapped into a river.

The Stone Arch in the middle of the Dome of the Deep rises. A thick, strong column of rock beginning on one side and bending its way across the molten river, landing fifty feet across, touching down on the other side. Rising and spanning thirty feet high like a watch tower over the life of the river. The Arch focusing the Regenerative Power like a magnifying glass focuses light.

Lighting up the Growing Gallery below to make the twin stars birth and growth and Visions.

At the foot of the Stone Arch on the far side of the river, the Growing Gallery. The home where the Macro Geodes, the twin stars, lay since the beginning of the Earth's life, waiting. Waiting for Mama and Papa. Hillary and Tinsel born through the Macro Geodes. Nestled amongst the shale and small nesting geodes. Warming. Waiting. Nesting. Growing. Incubating. Waiting for Mama and Papa.

The spelunkers stood in the Stairway Arch taking in the beginning of the stars' life.

To his left, Brad noticed golden tears flowing from Hillary's eyes. To his right were the flaming tears of Tinsel.

We will go to the Growing Gallery, thought Hillary.

What will we do there? thought Brad.

You will each learn why you were chosen to receive the Regeneration, thought Tinsel.

Is that why you brought us here? thought Elka.

Yes. Only you can discover the Vision of Regeneration, or your individual calling. Neither Tinsel nor I can tell you that, thought Hillary.

With strength and agility no ordinary human could have, including Sparks, the spelunkers climbed the Stone Arch without fear or misplaced step and landed on the far side at the Growing Gallery under the Arch.

The Blue Refractory was now a thick, impenetrable shell around each of the spelunkers and Sparks. No hand holding. No thought. No effort. It was just there. Permanent in the Gallery.

Hillary and Tinsel sat. They removed their boots and socks and rolled up their pant legs to the knees. They stood. They held hands and instinctively walked to the glaring Mantle River shoreline.

Hillary knew that she was a Gatherer.

Tinsel knew that she was a Marauder.

They both knew they were home. At home.

They looked back over their shoulders at Elka, Brad and Ava and thought, *we were made for this*.

Turning to the glowing, they fearlessly waded forward into the slippery glowing molten rock Mantle River. Toe deep. Ankle deep. Shin deep. Calf deep. Refractory Blue hummed and pulsed. Blue lightning sizzle shot from their Refractory Blue to the Stone Arch and back.

Hillary and Tinsel turned and faced the others. Later on, Brad would say he saw the face of Unknown Initiates. Elka would say she saw a Promise of a Future. Ava saw Wisdom and Counsel. They began to walk toward the twin stars.

Stop! warned Hillary. *You cannot come in. We must come out.*

Hillary joyously kicked a hard slapping leg into the surface of the river and sent a volcano splash spewing into the air. Magma burst into thousands of sparks like molten fireworks raining down upon them all in a spectacular hot light show. The Dome of the Deep cavern lit like the day for a moment until the sparks died out on the ground.

Just because, laughed Hillary.

Roaring laughter from five spelunkers filled and echoed along miles of cavern walls. Sparks barks were the exclamation point at the end of the sentence.

Before you can enter, you must know your Vision. Your calling, thought Tinsel.

Mama and Papa are Protectors, thought Hillary. *They have taken care of us for the last thousand years. They conducted us safely in their image into this world through the Growing Gallery and Dome of the Deep. Theirs' is a long story.*

I am a Gatherer, continued Hillary. *Those who are found, I see them, and comfort them, and bring them together with us.*

And I am a Marauder, thought Tinsel. *I fix and I fight. I roam and spy.*

Now it is time for your Visions, your callings, your names, thought Tinsel.

Elka, you are first, thought Hillary. *Stand in the center of the Growing Gallery. Everyone stand at the edges and circle around her. Everyone stretch hands towards each other.*

The Blue Refractory lit between their fingertips and surrounded them all in a bubble.

Elka, close your eyes. Everyone help her. Breath slow. See slow. What do you see?

Elka's cavern world began to vanish, to fade away along with her spelunker troupe.

She envisioned herself lying on a bed asleep. Streaks of light flew to and from the stars and her forehead. Her brain. Her thoughts. Whispers and secrets and tells. Secrets of the past and present and future that no one else knew or could know. She saw connection and growing and truth. She saw difficulty and frustration and obstacles.

The vision faded and she saw herself awake in a chair with Hillary, Tinsel, Mama, Papa and other spelunkers, many others, sitting on the ground around her. Their eyes were opened widely with the truth she was telling them. And they believed her. They trusted her.

Now she was alone in the forest. Secrets told to the spelunkers were happening like she said they would. She could see them happening as if projected on a screen. Days, weeks, years. All the events she told were truly happening. Some took a long time. Others happened quickly.

She saw Kai'ed.

Elka roused from her vision and found herself lying on the ground, Hillary and Tinsel kneeling beside her.

We saw your vision, thought Hillary.

You are a Sayer. A teller of things to come, thought Tinsel. *You are changed. You are no longer an Initiate. You are a Regenerate.*

Ava, step into the Growing Gallery, thought Tinsel. *Find your calling.*

Ava stood as Elka had. The spelunkers, now with the increased help of Elka, lit the circle with Regenerative Power.

Ava's sight fell away, and was replaced with peaceful sights of knowing. Knowing how to help, how to tell, how to advise.

People gathered around her waiting. One by one they presented her with their joys, their sorrows, their fears. Her words gave them new wisdom to take away pain and worry.

She saw Elka approach with uncertainty about helping others with gifts of knowledge of the future. There was worry that she would tell too much. Ava helped Elka learn what to tell and how much to tell others about the future. Elka learned through Ava how to help people better.

Ava woke from her vision with a gentle shoulder shake from Hillary.

We saw your vision, thought Hillary.

You are a Counselor, thought Tinsel. *You will help people decide in difficulty. You won't give answers. You will ask questions to guide them. You are changed. You are no longer an Initiate. You are a Regenerate.*

You have added to Elka's gift and to ours, thought Hillary.

Brad, you are last. Step into the Growing Gallery. Find your Vision, thought Tinsel.

Brad, with slow hesitating steps, moved into the circle.

Why do you move slowly? thought Hillary.

I am afraid, thought Brad. *What if I don't have a Vision? What if I am a failure and not like the rest of you?*

That can't happen Brad, thought Hillary. *You would not have made it this far with us. Have you already forgotten what happened to your blood in the Eastern Lava Tube? This is the just the final step in finding your Vision. Don't be afraid. Trust. We have faith enough to support you.*

Faith and trust all alone, weak and lonely and struggles unknown. Faith as friends, by love it must, like water and sun, grows in trust.

A surge of trust did move through Brad. Hillary and Tinsel could see it break out shining on his face, as confidence in his fellow spelunkers flooded him.

The moment the spelunkers raised hands, darkness slammed shut on Brad's sight. A pitch black soup that not even the best torch could cut through and make any shape he could recognize.

Brad cried out in fear, *Something has gone horribly wrong!*

He felt trapped and suffocating.

His feelings and visions of black were projected as onto a canvas screen beneath the Stone Arch and the other spelunkers could see and feel his terror. Elka and Ava were afraid and began to cry out to help Brad.

Quiet! said Hillary. *Be patient. There will be times of darkness and fear in life. Wait.*

It seemed like hours, but was only minutes. A swirling white mist, a dust devil of light, began to appear. Twisting and forming, disappearing, reappearing. Now looking like a forest, now looking like a crowd. Colors came in that formed cities, horses, cars, trains, travel. Going out to people and places.

Brad began to recognize faces of people he did not know. Places he had never been. People calling to him. People refusing him. Some would say yes. Some would say no. Some could see, some could not. Some said yes when he offered the path to the Regeneration. Others would not.

The vision faded to black. This time he did not panic or feel alone. He knew now this was a waiting period he needed to learn to be comfortable with.

His vision gently faded back to the Growth Gallery and he recognized the Dome of the Deep Cavern. He recognized the Stone Arch. He knew he had his vision and he was Regenerate.

You are a Seeker Brad, thought Hillary. *You will go out. You will find others like us. As in your Vision, there will be dark times. There will be challenges against you and you will have to wait and be strong in those times. But you will find many and bring them back here.*

And there they were. Seven. And a dog.

Mama and Papa, Protectors.

Hillary, Gatherer.

Tinsel, Marauder.

Elka, Sayer.

Ava, Counselor.

Brad, Seeker.

Sparks, Troublemaker and Guard.

At that moment, they all grew a little older… and maybe even a little taller.

"In our comings and goings, in our quests and adventures, we will always return here," said Hillary, her voice sounding strange and musical now in the Dome Chamber.

Tinsel reached for hands. All hands. Five sets of hands clasping and one full set of paws following.

We will test the waters and the blood, thought Tinsel.

Five plus one walked to the River's edge. All shoes off. Pants rolled up.

One foot after another wading into the Earth's Blood.

Connecting with their blood.

Blue hum. Regeneration. Blue Refractory. An electric sparking field jumping from their glowing bodies to the flowing stream and the Stone Arch. Breaking hands now and wading deeper. In different directions, but all together.

Up to waists, up to chests. Shared knowing smiles and excitement. Laughing. Ringing out and musically echoing off miles of chamber walls.

Now plunging beneath the current. Breaststroke, sidestroke, butterfly stroke. Splashing and spraying. All were swimming and smiling. The new power and connection came naturally, all of them born for this.

Even Sparks took naturally to a fiery dogpaddle as he chased from one spelunker to the next, trying to herd them together. Blue sparks shooting from the tip of his wagging tail. Sparks' sparks.

Taking turns climbing the thirty foot Stone Arch and launching into swan, forward, backward, reverse, cannonball and every kind of twisting dive imaginable.

Splashing liquid rock in waves and showers of sparks rolling, showering, melting back in, only to be shot up again and again by frothing, flailing excited arms. Handfuls of liquid magma tossed about like a water fight in a swimming pool.

One day we will swim from here to other parts of the Earth, thought Hillary.

The spelunkers were immersed in their new world.